THE LAST PROPHET

By
Frank G. Davis

ISBN: 978-1-954253-53-7
10 9 8 7 6 5 4 3 2 1

Editing, Cover, & Layout by: solfire@phoenix-farm.com

The Last Prophet is a fast-moving fictional book that couples futuristic technologies with grounded biblical directions. The book grabs the reader with incredible developments that could easily be a prediction of future events. The biblical base and accurate references make the reader contemplate how this writing might be more than just fiction. Once started, the book is impossible to put down.

Looking at a short hundred years in the future, social and technologic advances are based on concepts envisioned today. The characters in the story line make the reader feel that they are with them experiencing God's intervention in the biblical based journeys and conflicts with Satan and his demons. Although demons are not stressed in the New Testament, the writing revels how they are ever present in today's world. Every page leaves the reader wanting more.

David S. Davis (Not Related to the author)

I had the opportunity to read the manuscript three times and was intrigued by the story. I liked the novel being set in the early twenty second century with its many increases in technology such as maglev trains and commercial sub-orbital spacecraft. For the most part, the story is fast paced with several action/adventure scenes throughout the book. I believe those with a religious background will enjoy the read.

Gene Carr

The Last Prophet is a powerful story about the end times, Frank Davis is a creative and entertaining story teller. Hang-on, this futuristic fictional tale will take you for an enlightening ride of what will happen just before The Great Tribulation. Wars, earthquakes, angels, demons and biblical prophecies will captivate you and take you on a wild ride of future events. The three main characters (Dr. Isaac Silberman, Lt. Colonel Greg Stone and Master Sergeant Priscilla Wright) were all very likable characters, witty, comical and resourceful, each with their own handicap and unique perspective. The twenty second century weapons and future technologies adds a unique sci-fi twist and made this a very entertaining novel.

Vinny DiTore, Arizona Community Church

The Last Prophet is a surprising, spiritual warfare fiction filled with twists that keep the pages turning.

Brandon Hilgemann,
Associate Pastor, Arizona Community Church

DEDICATION

This novel is dedicated to the ministers, pastors and
missionaries who preach the word of salvation.
We are saved by Grace Alone through
Faith Alone in Christ Alone
As taught by the Bible Alone
Amen and Amen

PREFACE

The Last Prophet is a Christian science fiction novel dealing with end times. It is set in the early 22nd century, a year before the seven year Tribulation is to begin. It's based on several books of the Bible, using Ryrie New American Standard Study Bible and the English Standard Version Study Bible as references.

The following books of the Bible, either quoted or referred to, are:

- from the Old Testament; Genesis, Exodus, Isaiah, Daniel and Ezekiel.
- from the New Testament; The Gospel of Matthew, The Gospel of John, The Acts of the Apostles and The Revelation of Jesus Christ as recorded by the Apostle John.

The topics presented are the following: creation, the law, angels, demons, descriptions of Disciples, Prophets and Apostles and events leading up to the end times.

This is a work of fiction based on my understanding of the Bible. I attempt to justify things that seem unlikely by quoting scripture. If the reader takes exception to something I describe, please remember everything takes place in the future, a future I created. I think of it as a possible truth, not an absolute truth.

I hope you enjoy this novel.

Frank G. Davis, August 1, 2023

CHAPTER 1

THE DECEASED

"Code Blue, Code Blue, Code Blue," repeated the synthetic female voice. It was a soft voice with a hint of concern. "Sensors show cardiac arrest in the chaplain's quarters." There was a brief pause as incoming data was processed before the voice continued. "Crash cart en route, medical doctor required stat."

Dr. Goodman was on call for the late shift and rolled out of one of the clinic's cots fully dressed. The robotic crash cart passed the clinic door with its blue light blinking in sync with its beeping alarm. He fell in behind the cart and began running. He was joined by a tech and two nurses. When they arrived at the chaplain's door it slid back automatically revealing a man slumped over in his power recliner chair. A voice from the chair was informing the med team of all the man's critical life signs.

"Defib now!" the doctor said in as calm a voice as he could manage. The chaplain was well known by both staff and residents at the Angel of Mercy Assisted Living Complex. Even though he was approaching 100, he still delighted in life and knew just the right things to say to relieve some of the depression that was abundant at most care facilities like this. Ultimately, these were places where people came to die.

The power chair quickly flattened into a bed and the nurses opened the chaplain's shirt as the voice reported, "Patient is flatlining." The defibrillator paddles extended from the cart and onto the chest of the chaplain. The voice said, "Clear!" There was a loud *whomp* sound as the patient was hit with a minimum charge causing the muscles in his body to momentarily contract. "No response. Increasing charge ... Clear." A louder *whomp* this time with a stronger contraction. The third time the setting was at maximum, but the results were the same.

The doctor checked the large clock on the crash cart to see how long the patient's heart had not been beating. He shook his head and ordered, "Inject maximum dosage of Epinephrine into the heart immediately."

The metallic arm on the cart holding the syringe placed it over the patient's chest, pushed the needle into the heart and injected the drug. Then they waited, then waited some more. After five minutes passed, one of the nurses looked at the doctor with a questioning expression. Reluctantly, he nodded his head and said, "Call it."

The nurse replied, "Time of death, 2:47 A.M. April 11, 2101."

The crash cart made its way back to the clinic lab and underwent a thorough sterilization of all the surgical equipment. The tech supervised the cleaning. The two nurses returned to the clinic sleeping area and tried to get a few more hours of sleep. Only the doctor remained. He pulled up a chair and sat next to the body. He spoke to the chaplain as if he were still alive. "I'm so sorry I couldn't prolong your life, old friend. I think you would have enjoyed your hundredth birthday celebration. You missed it by only a few weeks. I'm really going to miss listening to your sermons and the time you spent easing the fear of those about to pass on. You had such a way with calming people. You were the most compassionate man I have ever known. I'll never forget your favorite saying to those who were so close to death. 'To be absent from the body is to be forever with the Lord.' I pray you are with him now, old friend. Good-bye."

Goodman stood, wiped the tears from his eyes, and slowly walked back to the clinic. After he left, the clinic's medical examiner had the body moved to the temporary morgue. His body was then stripped of all remaining clothes and laid on a stainless steel slab, facing upward so any next of kin could identify the body. His body was covered by a clean white sheet, then the metal tray was slid into one of the several cells in a large refrigerated holding chamber until funeral arrangements could be made. Typically a body would stay a few days in the refrigerated lockers.

Two days later, a man in his early forties arrived at the Angel of Mercy administration office. He was a tall man in good physical condition, dressed in a dark gray business suit, freshly starched white shirt, and a matching gray tie. His hair was cut high and tight as worn by former military men. The expression on his rugged face was somber.

"How can I help you, sir?" asked the woman behind the counter.

"I'm here to make funeral arrangements for your chaplain," he answered in a deep baritone voice that quivered slightly as he spoke.

"Could I get your name, sir?"

"I'm Greg Stone, retired major in the Marine Corps. Your funeral director is expecting me. And your name, miss?"

She blushed slightly, no one had ever asked her name before. "I'm Priscilla Wright, but everybody calls me Pris." She took him to the funeral director's office and knocked once on the door.

"Come," was the response.

Pris opened the door and announced, "Major Stone to see you sir," then closed the door behind her after the major had walked in.

George Bronson stood, extended his hand and said, "I'm so sorry for your loss, Major Stone. Our chaplain was a very precious person to all of us here at Angel of Mercy."

"It's not major any longer, I retired from the Corps almost five years ago. Just call me Greg."

The funeral director gestured to the chair next to his desk and both men sat down. Before Bronson could say more, Stone said, "I want to apologize for taking so long in getting to your facility. The day before the pastor passed away, he sent me on a mission to New Orleans to help out with the relief efforts from the flooding. All the com systems were down and I didn't get the news of his passing until they finally opened the airport. I was on the return flight when a flight attendant gave me the news. As soon as we landed I changed clothes and called you for this appointment."

"I'm so glad you called when you did," said Bronson. "The state of Arizona has a relatively new law that if a body isn't identified within five days, it has to be cremated. Of course there can be extenuating circumstances, but you never know. Let me ask you a few questions, if I may?" asked the director relaxing back into his chair. "I'm fairly new at the position of funeral director at this facility but I remember seeing you a few times visiting the chaplain in the chapel. I'm remembering correctly?"

"Yes sir. He chose me to be his acolyte just after I retired my commission. It was about the same time he moved into your facility."

Bronson looked somewhat puzzled and asked, "I've heard the term 'acolyte' before and I know it has religious significance, but could you tell me how it applies to you and the chaplain?"

"Certainly," replied Stone. "It can be a bit confusing because it can have several meanings. In my case, I was chosen by Pastor Isaac to become his helper. Whatever he needed me to do, I did. I guess you could think of me as his assistant or maybe his servant."

"So you knew him well?"

"Yes sir, I knew the pastor very well. Before I accepted his offer to make me his acolyte, I did an extensive background check. He was considered a wonderful pastor as well as a world class theologian by his peers. He earned PhDs from several seminaries worldwide. He knew the Bible from front to back and could recite any chapter and verse without having to look it up. But his strength laid in the way he presented the meaning of those thirty thousand verses so that even a jarhead like myself could understand it."

"Well, thank you for sharing with me Mr. Stone. Perhaps we should discuss the funeral procedures and, if you would like, you can have some time alone with him before you leave."

"Thank you, I look forward to seeing him once more in private."

The funeral director opened a document on his iPad and scanned it, then said, "I'd like to confirm some of the legal details. If you don't mind, I will also be recording our session as well."

Stone nodded in consent and Bronson asked, "You are listed as the sole person having the medical power of attorney for the chaplain and he has no other heirs besides yourself. Is that correct?"

Stone nodded again and added, "Your chaplain, I think of him as my pastor. For the record, his full name is Pastor Isaac Silberman. You should have the medical power of attorney document in you records."

"Yes, Mr. Stone, I confirm we have the document. I also confirm the pastor has no heirs except for you. So you will be making the identification of the pastor's body?"

"Yes," replied Stone, his voice somber as he gave the funeral director a brief family history. "Again for the record, the pastor had been married for almost 50 years, but his wife, Rhoda, passed away a little over 20 years ago. They had two children, both deceased. Their son, Jacob, was killed in Egypt during the war and the daughter, Sarah, died of cancer at a fairly young age. He was a world traveler for most of his life. However, he spent the last 25 years living here in South Gilbert, Arizona. The last five, as you know, at Angel of Mercy Assisted Living Complex."

"Just a couple of more confirmations," added Bronson. "He indicated he wished to be buried next to his wife in our cemetery. Is that your understanding?"

Stone nodded again.

"Lastly, all funeral expenses will be covered by his estate."

The two men stood and shook hands. Director Bronson gave Stone a packet of information to take back to his church. He had Pris escort him down the hall to the temporary morgue (The Angel of Mercy preferred to call it The Holding Area of the Deceased).

As they walked down the hallway, Pris slowed, then stopped saying, "I know you! It just dawned on me who you are. I mean besides being the chaplain's acolyte. You're the man who invented the Voice of God weapon, aren't you?"

Stone stopped and turned toward Pris. He hadn't paid much attention to the young woman. His focus had been on taking care of his pastor for the last time. Now he glanced at her and saw an attractive well-dressed woman with an athletic build in her late twenties. She was wearing the facility's uniform with her light brown hair pulled back into a pony tail. Her eyes were blue and she had a soft sympathetic smile.

"Yes, that's me," he answered. "However, I would prefer we discuss it at a later time. Are you okay with that?"

Pris nodded and they continued walking down the hall. They stopped outside the entry door and Pris said, "I'm not allowed to go inside. Once you enter just say the chaplain's name and his tray will slide out for you to see him. A sheet will cover the body, just pull the sheet down to view him. When you're done with your visit, please cover him with the sheet before you leave. The chaplain's tray will automatically return to the refrigerated area after the entry door is closed."

She paused, then added, "We are so sorry for your loss. Everyone at Angel of Mercy loved the man. We'll all miss him." Stone noticed her eyes beginning to tear up as she turned and walked back toward her station.

Stone followed Pris's instructions. He walked inside and said out loud, "Chaplain Isaac Silberman."

A door opened in the wall of the refrigerated area and a metal tray slid out and hovered three feet above the floor next to a chair.

Stone walked to the chair and sat down. He was within an arm's length of the tray, but waited a moment to compose himself. Finally, he leaned forward and pulled the sheet down exposing his mentor's face and shoulders. Stone stood and looked closely at the corpse. Pastor Silberman looked different somehow, younger than Stone remembered, but the long white hair and beard looked the same. He decided it must be due to the very cold refrigerated storage area where the body had spent the last three days. Of course, the pastor's eyes were closed, but he looked angelic to Stone, serene, as if death had no hold on him.

Stone sat back down in the chair, closed his eyes and began a prayer. Isaac had said it was a waste of time to pray for the dead. Their fate was sealed, but Stone prayed anyway.

In the middle of his prayer, Stone heard a slight sound, like the ruffling of a sheet. He opened his eyes and saw the pastor looking back at him.

Stone attempted to stand but his legs buckled and he collapsed back into the chair.

Then the deceased man spoke to him.

"It's so good to see you my son. It's really cold in here. Can you get me a blanket, maybe something to eat? I'm starving."

Isaac sat up on the tray, angled his legs over the side and stood up on the cold tiled floor. "I cannot believe how cold it is in here. Is it my imagination or is it really freezing?" He turned his head to look at Stone who was staring at him, eyes wide, mouth open and drooling.

"I know this comes as a surprise to you, but if you don't find me some warm clothes and socks, I might die again. This time from hypothermia. If you're still my acolyte you better get moving or get someone else to help."

Stone jumped out of his chair as if hit by a cattle prod. He bolted out the door to the morgue and spied a service cart moving slowly down the hall. A maid was coming out of an empty room and he yelled at her, "I need two heavy blankets, socks and slippers, right now!"

The maid was startled and stepped back into the room, closing and locking the door. Stone grabbed the handle on the cart and pushed it back to the morgue. His pastor was sitting on the chair with his feet on the lowest rung to avoid touching the floor, the tray was nowhere to be seen.

Stone took a handful of blankets and quickly wrapped the man up in a cocoon of heavy wool cloth. One by one he put on slipper socks followed by heavy-weight real slippers.

When he stood, Isaac said, "Thanks, now I need food. Lots of food… and coffee." He paused, then added, "Just bring a food cart with as much food as it can hold." As Stone ran for the door, Isaac yelled, "I feel like I've been fasting for weeks. I hate fasting!"

Stone ran to the cafeteria. He saw Pris standing at her counter watching him with a look of surprise. Before she could ask why he was in such a hurry, he yelled at her as he ran by, "He's alive, Pris. The chaplain is alive. Get the doctor, stat!"

As he rounded the corner, Pris's co-worker said to her in an annoyed voice, "What's got him all lathered up?"

"A miracle, I hope," she answered as she called the doctor.

* * *

Dr. Goodman and the entire medical staff were gathered around just outside of the room watching the pastor eat. The doctor started talking first. "I want you to tell me exactly what he said as best you can remember. I gave him a quick exam before he began devouring all the food you gave him. He was so busy eating, I really couldn't make out what he was saying."

Stone nodded, then said, "I pulled down the sheet exposing his head and shoulders. His eyes were closed but he looked younger to me. I closed my eyes to say a prayer. I heard the sheet moving and I opened my eyes. He was staring at me."

"That's fine, but I really want to know what he said," the doctor replied.

"He said he was very cold, freezing—"

"Did he just say 'freezing' or did he speak in complete sentences?" the doctor interrupted.

"Why is that important?" Stone asked in an annoyed tone.

"Because I want to determine if he had any brain damage. If he could only speak a few words he might have brain damage."

Stone shrugged. "Okay, good to know. He spoke in complete sentences. He said it was very cold, freezing and if he didn't get some clothes he may die from hypothermia. Once I got him covered up, he demanded food. He thanked me for the blankets and slippers and said I should run to the cafeteria and get a food cart full of food and coffee. On my way to the cafeteria, I told Pris to tell you he was alive. That's it."

There was a pregnant pause before one of the other doctors spoke. "You're making all that up, aren't you? What you just told us is impossible. People don't come back from the dead after they've been dead for three days. Somehow you did away with the body and substitu—"

Stone stood abruptly and took a menacing step towards the doctor, "You're calling me a liar?" He took another step until he was nose to nose with his accuser. "I'm sure if you bothered to take a look at the recording your surveillance cameras made of my visit to the dead chaplain, you will see I was telling the truth. In which case you'd better be apologizing to me or maybe you'd like to spend some time on one of those trays?"

The doctor took one step back, then shouted at Stone, "You can't threaten me like that. I'll have you know I'm the senior doctor at Angel of Mercy. I'm going to call security and have you—"

"Gentlemen," Dr. Goodman interrupted in a calming voice. "Can you both take a step back and relax a little? Why don't we wait and see the surveillance video before we start making threats."

After they watched the surveillance footage, the doctor grudgingly apologized, but added, "There's no record of anyone ever coming back to life after being dead for three days. It's just not possible. There is no scientific basis…"

"You're wrong again," Stone said. "There are two recorded cases, one was dead for four days and the second for three."

The doctor looked skeptical until Stone added, "One was named Lazarus, the other Jesus of Nazareth."

The doctor's expression changed to one of contempt. "That's Biblical mythology. There's no scientific eviden—"

Stone interrupted for a third time. "You're right, doctor, up until now there hasn't been any scientific evidence to support what happened here. However, once the fingerprints, the DNA and the retinal scan of the living man matches those of the dead man, what feeble excuse will you try to use to justify your scientific beliefs? Just remember, the Bible says God's ways are not the ways of man. Too many people choose to follow the scientific ways of man rather than the ways of God who created the universe and everything in it." Stone turned abruptly and left the room. The team of doctors looked at one another. Some were smiling, some frowning and a few had deadpan expressions.

Dr. Goodman glanced at the doctor who had challenged Stone and said, "Well, looks like you lost the first round, Lawrence."

Dr. Lawrence glared back at Goodman and said, "It's not over yet. I want to see all the ID data first."

* * *

Once Isaac had finished eating everything on the food cart and washed it down with a pot of coffee, he took a shower and shampooed his hair and beard. It was hard to believe a man who was almost a hundred years old had so much hair. Pris had gone to the chaplain's room and brought him some of his clothes to wear. Once he was dressed she helped him comb his hair. The clothes looked odd on him and that was substantiated when they measured his height and weight; he was two inches taller yet twenty pounds lighter.

The Angel of Mercy Assisted Living Group Inc. brought in a team of specialists to perform every conceivable test possible. Once they were done probing and prodding, the lead specialist presented their test results. The presentation was made to a limited number of people who had to sign a non-disclosure document which required them to not reveal the results of the examinations under penalty of a huge monetary fine and time in prison. The room used for the presentation was swept for bugs and jammers to insure no one, with the exception of the invited guests, would ever be privy to the presented information.

That limited group included Isaac Silberman, Greg Stone, Priscilla Wright and the doctors who had previously treated the chaplain prior to his demise along with the medical staff who had attended him during his heart attack.

Dr. Gerald Johnson stood and addressed the audience. "Ladies and gentlemen what I'm about to share with you is startling. In the entire history of modern medicine, no one has ever died, remained dead for three days, then returned to life as a fully functioning human being. Searching the history of this type of event has revealed the longest any one has been dead and then successfully reanimated is only a few hours. There have been numerous fraudulent claims of people returning to life after dying for as much as a week. In those cases, many were done for financial gain. That is not the case here.

"To verify Isaac Silberman is the same Isaac Silberman who died and remained dead for three days before returning to life, an extensive battery of tests was run. The most revealing were fingerprints, DNA and retinal scans of both eyes. The probability of a match before death and after revival from death were all 99.9 percent. Other examinations matched up such things as dental records, all matching, and medical records which revealed both had their gall bladders removed. And finally, they both shared the presence of two small tattoos, one on each shoulder. The one on the left shoulder was a Star of David with a few small Hebrew characters. On the right, was a crucifixion cross with a date written underneath. All this data leads us to the conclusion that the man who died of a heart attack and was revived three days later are one and the same.

"Now something really surprising. It began with the tattoos. Tattoos fade over time. When Isaac Silberman passed away his tattoos were faded and blurred which indicated they were very old tattoos. After his revival the colors of his tattoos were bright and the edges were sharp as if the tattoos were new. That led to another battery of tests which were performed by a second team of doctors. The second team had no idea who the patient was and the tests were constructed to estimate the age of the patient. Their estimates ranged from 48 to 53. As unbelievable as it sounds, not only did our patient manage to return to life after being dead for three days, he returned 50 years younger."

Dr. Goodman glanced at Dr. Lawrence. The man was literally biting his tongue. He was not accepting what had been said by the group of doctors who had examined the chaplain, even though the scientific test results proved otherwise and even a blind testing resulted in the same conclusions.

"One last thing," said Dr. Johnson. "It's highly recommended we refer to the resurrected Chaplain Silberman as Isaac Silberman II or Silberman Junior. The public at large is not ready to accept our findings at the present time, maybe not ever."

With that final comment, the meeting adjourned with another reminder of secrecy.

However, they weren't done with the chaplain. A renown psychiatrist was asked to find out what the chaplain was thinking about before his death and after his revival. Greg was invited to attend the session.

The psychiatrist introduced himself. "I'm Dr. Christopher Suan, but you can call me Chris. Can I call you Isaac?"

"You can call me anything you like, young man."

"That's interesting. You refer to me as a young man and yet I'm older than you."

"Not really, but I do feel younger than I did a few weeks ago. Let me ask you a question before we begin the official session if that's okay with you."

"Certainly," Chris responded.

"Are you a Christian as your first name implies?" Isaac asked.

That seemed to surprise Chris and he hesitated for a moment before answering. "I attended a Christian church with my parents when I was a child. I was fifteen when my parents divorced and I… drifted away from church. When I was older, I married a Christian woman and I accompanied her to church while we were married. That's about the extent of my Christian background."

"Thank you, Chris. It's your turn to ask me questions."

"First question," he began. "What were you thinking about when you realized you might be dying."

"I was listening to the Gospel of John on my audio Bible. I was almost blind at the time and could no longer read the text. John is my favorite gospel. I was listening to the eighth chapter which focuses on the divinity of Jesus. All of a sudden, I felt a sharp, throbbing pain in my left arm. I hadn't been feeling well almost all afternoon and most of the evening. However, I had similar experiences and the pain usually dissipated before my alert bracelet signaled I was having a problem. The pain increased quickly and I realized this was going to be a serious heart attack."

"What were you thinking at that precise moment?" asked Chris.

"Two things," Isaac answered. "First the pain. It had spread to my heart and I was having a difficult time breathing. Secondly, I remembered a verse from the Apostle Paul. I would often read this passage to those who were close to death, 'To be absent from the body is to be forever with our

Lord.' I said it several times while I waited for the crash cart. I remember hearing the crash cart voice saying I was flat lining. At that moment, I heard a voice in my mind. It said to me, 'Fear not, Isaac. You will die but I have a plan for you. You will be my last prophet. In the fullness of time you will die again, but you will rise and spend eternity with me.' And then I saw him, it was Jesus in all his glory reaching out to me. My last thought before I died was finding out Jesus didn't have long straight hair. It was much shorter than the paintings and very curly. Then everything went black."

The acolyte sat spellbound at what Isaac revealed during his last moments of life. Chris leaned forward and asked, "I assume you're aware many people have had near-death experiences with visions of Jesus welcoming them to Heaven?"

"Yes, but my experience was different. Mine was not near-death, it was real death and when I was waking up from my death, with my eyes closed, Jesus spoke to me again and gave me instructions. He asked me not to share this information right now with anyone, except for one exception which applies to you."

Isaac stood and Greg followed. They shook Chris's hand and Isaac said, "Thank you for your time doctor and for your comments."

As they turned to leave, Chris asked, "What was the exception Jesus said to share with me?"

Isaac smiled broadly and said, "He told me you'll meet another Christian woman next week who will become your soul mate for the rest of your life. Her name is Esther. Good-bye, Chris. We'll speak again soon."

Isaac returned to the Angel of Mercy Complex and headed for the administration office. His acolyte accompanied him as they approached Pris standing behind the counter. "Good afternoon, Priscilla," said Isaac. "I need to speak to someone regarding canceling my stay here. I no longer need any assistance and will be leaving the country in a month or so. Greg will be accompanying me."

Pris looked surprised. She glanced at Greg and noticed he also looked surprised. She quickly scanned her monitor and said, "Your account shows your residence fee is debited monthly from your estate. If you tell me the date you want to close out your account, I can do it from my computer anytime you wish."

Isaac thought for a moment then said, "Let's make it six weeks from today. That will give us plenty of time to tie up any loose ends. What do you think, Greg? Would it give you enough time to get your things in order?"

"It depends on where we're going," he answered. He looked a little confused and added, "Will we be traveling out of country? If so, I'll need to get my passport renewed."

"We'll be going to Israel, Jerusalem to be exact," he replied.

Pris looked shocked by his reply. "Isn't there a war going on in Israel? I heard it was especially bad in Jerusalem. That could be really dangerous. Why would you want to go there?"

"Don't worry Pris, Major Stone will be my protector. He's a decorated combat Marine. Besides, the war will be over four weeks from now."

Pris opened her mouth in surprise, then closed it, not knowing what to say.

Stone said it for her. "How could you possibly know when the war will end? It's been going on for several years with no indication it will end soon."

Isaac sighed, then said in a hushed voice so only Stone and Pris could hear, "Ever since I recovered from my death, I'm a different person. Actually, I'm still the same person, but my relationship with God has been… upgraded. I see visions now I never saw before, glimpses of the future and a voice which tells me things no human would know. It seems to me it's the voice of the Holy Spirit guiding me."

He stopped to see their reaction. Pris was the first to speak. "That's the most amazing thing I've ever heard!" She turned to Greg and said in a barely audible voice, "Was he like this before he died?"

"No," he answered. "Nothing like this. I mean, he was the most knowledgeable person I've ever known when it came to the Bible and the current history of the Holy Land, but never visions, at least that I know of." Stone looked at his mentor and added, "If Isaac says he has instructions from the Holy Spirit, I believe him. Everything that has happened during the last few days makes me think of how Jesus told his disciples to wait for the Holy Spirit. He came during the feast of Pentecost and turned the disciples into apostles who could heal people, raise the dead and receive instructions from him."

Isaac smiled at them both. "My case was a little different. I was raised from the dead by God. However, I received a renewed mind and body in the process. All of the apostles with the exception of John, died violent deaths. They all aged during their time on Earth. So far, I haven't healed anyone or restored any dead to life. Several of the apostles raised the dead and healed the sick. That may not be my calling. Yes, I see visions of the future. However, I've only been renewed for a few weeks. I know I have to go to Jerusalem soon and the war will end two weeks before I arrive. At the present time, I have no idea what I'm supposed to do when I get there. I was told my acolyte was to join me, again I don't know why, at least, not yet. He's supposed to move into my spare bedroom until we leave for Jerusalem. Is that okay with you Greg?"

Stone nodded and added, "I'm still your acolyte. Whatever you say goes."

"In the meantime, I have seen a vision that I will return to my old church as a guest pastor. For four weeks I will preach sermons regarding creation, sin and salvation. I was led to believe I didn't have to prepare for these sermons. I would be in Christ and Christ would be in me. He would speak through me the truth of his word."

They headed back to their apartment. Halfway there Isaac stopped abruptly. Greg continued to walk a couple of steps before he realized the chaplain wasn't next to him. "Are you all right?" Greg asked with a look of concern.

"I'm fine," Isaac replied with a slight smile. "Give me a minute."

Thirty seconds passed as the chaplain closed his eyes. A few people passed by the two of them and one orderly whispered "catatonic" as she walked by which brought a slight smile to Isaac's face. Greg was becoming more concerned and he was about to say something, when Isaac opened his eyes.

Isaac blinked his eyes a few times and said to Greg, "Sorry for the delay, I had an incoming vision. You're supposed to have lunch with Pris in the cafeteria now. I'm going back to our apartment and will snack on whatever leftovers we have. Enjoy your lunch." He resumed walking, leaving Greg standing in the hall for a few moments, scratching his head. Then the acolyte turned and headed back to the cafeteria.

Pris was sitting at one of the cafeteria tables by herself as Greg walked in. He waved at her and noticed she already had her lunch tray. "Can I join you for lunch?" Greg asked.

She nodded and said, "Go get your lunch. I'll wait and eat with you."

They made small talk as they ate, but Greg could tell Pris had something on her mind she wanted to discuss. "Where's Isaac?" she finally asked. "I thought you two were inseparable."

"You're going to think this is crazy, but we were walking back to our apartment when he stopped in the hallway and had a vision. He said God told him I was supposed to have lunch with you."

Pris's eyes opened wide and she said, "You're kidding, right?"

"Nope, scout's honor," Greg answered. "So what do you want to talk about with me? No, don't tell me. Let me guess. You want to pick my brain about the Voice of God weapon."

Her eyes opened even wider. "Did Isaac tell you that was in this vision too?"

"No, I just figured you'd want to know about the VOG since you mentioned it when I first met you."

"Good for you. And you're right. I'd really like to find out about the secret weapon that turned the tide in our favor at the battle of Rome."

"You were there?" Greg asked. It was his turn to be surprised.

"Yup. First Ranger platoon on site at the Vatican. I was a squad leader. We were the first squad to the get the VOGs. They saved our butts, that's for sure."

"I'm impressed," said Greg. "Rangers are the Army's elite soldiers. What would you like to know about the weapon?"

"Pretty much everything," answered Pris. "For starters, how did it get the name of the Voice of God?"

"That's an easy one. Two reasons, really. The first is the sound the weapon makes when you pull the trigger. It sounds like a man screaming in anger. Second, the first place the weapon was deployed was in Vatican City. Several of the clergy said the scream reminded them of verses in the book of Revelation where God used his voice like a two edged sword to vanquish the wicked. Hence, the Voice of God."

"Next question," Pris asked. "How does it work?"

"The weapon is a super-sonic pulse weapon that fires a brief narrow-beam pulse of sonic energy at Mach 5. The frequency of the sonic energy is classified, however it's optimized so that the pulse disintegrates whatever it comes in contact with and goes no further. That includes tanks, buildings or enemy soldiers. It's range is limited to a hundred yards at which point the beam begins to spread and the energy quickly dissipates. However, it makes for a terrific close quarter weapon. As you must be aware, the VOG is about the size of the traditional assault rifle. It's power comes from power magazines which are good for about a hundred firings. Each weapon comes with six power mags."

"Don't forget the ear muffs," added Pris. "One of my squad members lost her muffs, but continued to fire on the enemy. She was stone deaf for almost a month, but she had the highest kill rate in the squad."

"Anything else?" Greg asked.

"Yeah. How did you come up with the idea for the VOG?"

Greg leaned back for a moment to gather his thoughts, then said, "In my senior year at the Naval Academy in Annapolis, I was working on a research paper. It needed to be completed by the end of the semester. One night, I was watching a science fiction vid where there was a gun battle with lots of ray guns being used. One of the bad aliens came in with a large reflector dish using it to send sound waves at the good guys. Of course the good guys won, but I got to thinking about an acoustic weapon. So the last day of the semester, I turned in a proof of concept paper to my professor. After graduation, I was supposed to ship out to

Africa. I had the option of joining the Navy or the Marines. I picked the Marines and was ready to ship out when I was ordered to report to my professor. My first thought was the committee that reviewed the research papers was not happy with my science fiction report. I was wondering if they were going to bust me back to cadet when several high ranking officers told me I was to report to a top secret multiservice research lab to continue the development of a superior weapon.

"For the next ten years, my team and I worked our butts off to get a superior weapon our enemy couldn't defend against. Once we developed what we thought was the ultimate weapon, a squad of brave Marines took prototype VOGs into combat to determine how to optimize the weapon. I was their squad leader. The first time I shot one of the enemy, I was devastated by the results. It wasn't like when a person is shot with one or more bullets. There was no blood, no screaming in anguish of the bullet wounds they received. They just disintegrated into a pile of human dust. In most cases, their weapon and armor disintegrated right along with them. There was no screaming, just the visual echo of a life ending.

"I received many promotions during my tour of duty. Twenty years after I was given the gold bars of a second lieutenant I respectfully resigned my commission as a major. I was done with war."

He looked away from Pris then added, "I remember a famous quote by an Indian warrior chief. I think his name was Tecumseh, but I could be wrong. Maybe it was Chief Joseph. One of them said, 'I will fight no more forever.' That's my new mantra."

Pris reached across the table and took Greg's hand and squeezed it gently. He looked back at her and noticed the tears in her eyes. She did a quick glance at her smart watch and grimaced. "Thank you so much for sharing with me. I'm

running late, but I want to tell you about my war experiences."
She stood up. "Maybe another time?" she asked.

Greg nodded and she turned and hurried back to work.

The auto-drive Uber/Lyft e-car pulled into the parking lot of Grace Community Church. Like all things changing with time, the two competing companies had merged into one service a few decades ago, at the same time all their human drivers were replaced with the auto-drive technology.

Isaac and Greg stepped out of the cab and watched it silently drive away. Greg began to walk toward the entrance, but Isaac put a restraining hand on his arm. "Give me a minute, please. I want to take this all in," he said to his acolyte. "I want to compare my memories of my church with the current church. You know, I was present at the ground breaking ceremonies more than 75 years ago. I was a junior pastor then, barely out of seminary."

He stopped and scanned the buildings that made up the current church complex from one side of the property to the other. "It's much larger than the original. The sanctuary for the first church could only accommodate a congregation of 450. Plenty big enough when it was built. We had only one service then and the church was big enough to seat the entire membership, except on Christmas and Easter when we added folding chairs for those who only attended on those special occasions."

They began walking to the entrance of the church complex. They followed a paved pathway as wide as a city street adorned with shrubs, trees and a variety of colorful flower beds. They strolled along looking at the relatively new buildings with names in large letters displayed above the entrances. There was the Youth Building that catered to the smallest babies up to teens about to graduate from high school, followed by the Adult Learning Center used for Bible studies three nights a week and also before and after the regular weekend services. The Administration Building housed offices for each of the many pastors and the support staff who handled the business issues of the church.

There was also a gymnasium, a maintenance building, a library and tucked into the back was the original sanctuary which was used for church services in a variety of foreign languages. Isaac walked up to take a look inside, but all the doors were locked. He looked disappointed.

In the center of the complex was a new multi-storied sanctuary which had been designed by a world renowned architect. In front of the steps leading to the entry was a directory that said there were two services on Saturday and three on Sunday.

They walked up the steps and entered the sanctuary lobby through one of the six double doors. It was early, the first service wouldn't begin for another hour. As they walked down one of the aisles toward the pulpit, Isaac stopped, turned slowly around taking in as much detail as possible. He estimated the new sanctuary could accommodate at least a thousand people in the main floor, the balconies, the choir loft and the orchestra pit.

They stood in silence for a moment before Greg said, "I had no idea how extravagant this complex was. It must have cost a fortune, probably several fortunes."

"A waste of money, if you ask me," replied Isaac. "Unfortunately, nobody asked me. It reminds me of a comment made several hundred years ago about a Spanish cathedral, 'It's not only a place of worship, this cathedral *is* worshipped.'" He shook his head and sighed, then added, "What fools we mortals be."

He turned and walked to the stage with his acolyte following. They climbed the four carpeted steps and stopped to check out the five high-back leather arm chairs where four of the church elders would sit. The middle chair was normally reserved for the senior pastor who would present the sermon. Since the pastor was on vacation, Isaac would be sitting in that chair. He motioned for Greg to take a seat on one the four seats for the elders. He walked to the pulpit and looked at all the empty pews, then turned and studied the choir loft that could house at least fifty members of the choir. He turned back and looked down at the orchestra pit filled with various instruments too large and heavy to tote around the church. He had no idea how many musicians would be present.

As he looked up he saw a man walking rather quickly toward the stage. He wore navy blue slacks, a white dress shirt, a clip-on tie and a head set with a boom microphone. He had thinning hair and was a bit over weight. He took the stairs two at a time and stopped in front of Isaac. He extended his hand and said, "Hello, you must be our guest pastor. I'm the sermon director, you can call me Bud." He pumped Isaac's right hand. "I need your sermon script and I assume you left your suit in the dressing room off stage. We're going live in an hour and I'd like to do a rehearsal before the choir and musicians arrive."

Bud glanced over and saw Greg sitting in one of the elder's chairs. "Oh my goodness! You can't sit there. Those seats are reserved for the elders. Please get—"

Isaac cut him off. "The man in the elder's chair is my acolyte. One of your elders will not be coming today and my acolyte will be taking his place."

"Does he have a suit?" the director said looking at the casual clothes Greg was wearing.

"No he doesn't and neither do I. During the next four weeks, while the senior pastor is on vacation, things will be different. Please pay close attention to my instructions. When the doors to the sanctuary are opened and the congregation is walking in, the orchestra will be playing a hymn of your choosing. When the hymn is completed the doors to the sanctuary will be closed and no one else will enter. No smart phones will operate during the service."

Greg was looking closely at Bud while Isaac was speaking. Bud looked as if he was in a trance, but at the same time he was very focused on what the pastor was saying.

"Once everyone is seated, the choir will sing two songs accompanied by the musicians. I'd like you to pick which hymns you think best. One will be sung by only the choir. For the second, the congregation will stand and join the choir in singing the last hymn. Do you agree, Bud?"

"Yes Pastor Isaac, it will be as you say. Thanks for letting me choose the hymns." Greg thought Bud's voice sounded strangely normal.

"After the hymns, have one of the elders read off the most important announcements. That should take no more than five minutes. Less would be better." Bud nodded and waited quietly for further instructions. "After the announcements, have another elder give an opening prayer. After the prayer, I will begin my sermon. I promise I will end at the scheduled closing time. Does your congregation sing the doxology after the sermon?"

Bud answered, "Sometimes, but not always. They usually skip it when they run over on time."

"If I promise you I'll finish my sermon with enough time to sing the doxology, what would you recommend?" asked Isaac.

"I have always liked the doxology. I think we should do it."

"Thanks, Bud. I agree. Do you have any questions for me?"

He nodded then said, "What would be the title of your sermon?"

"How about, What Does It Take To Get Into Heaven. How does that sound to you?"

"Great title. I look forward to hearing your sermon."

The beginning of the first service went as planned by Isaac and Bud. The eight automatic doors to the sanctuary opened exactly on time just as the orchestra began playing the first hymn. When the hymn ended, the doors automatically closed. Those who were late to the service were forced to sit or stand in the extensive lobby area.

There was a short pause before the next hymn. The music director turned to the choir loft signaling the choir to stand, then turned back to the orchestra and the hymn began.

It seemed to most of the congregation the orchestra played flawlessly and the voices of the choir blended together in a way never heard before as if they were a host of angels instead of mere humans. The congregation rose for the second hymn and joined the choir in the singing. The music director marveled as the combined singing filled the sanctuary with a beauty never heard before. Even the voices of those in the congregation who were singing impaired seemed to be on key. It was inspiring!

An elder stood and read a very short list of announcements, followed by the opening prayer by a second elder. As Isaac predicted, one of the elders was not at the service and no one seemed to notice his acolyte's casual attire. The third elder stood and gave a very brief introduction of the guest pastor.

Isaac stood from the middle chair and walked to the podium and said, "It's so good to be back at Grace Community Church. My name is Isaac Silberman. As I toured your campus earlier today, I noticed that original sanctuary built seventy-five years ago still remains an important part of the current complex. While touring the campus I couldn't help noticing the grandeur of it all. To my eyes it rivals the temple in Jerusalem built by Solomon so many thousands of years ago."

He paused and looked at all the people who nearly filled the seats of the sanctuary. He smiled and said, "But I'm not here to speak of beautiful churches. Today I have a few questions to ask of you before I begin my sermon. If you believe there is a Heaven, please stand up. If you can't stand, just raise your hand."

Almost everyone stood, some reluctantly. A few remained seated with their hands in their laps.

"Thank you. You may be seated. Second question, if you are absolutely sure you are going to Heaven, stand up or raise your hand."

This time there were considerably less people who stood or raised their hands.

Isaac nodded his head a few times then said, "I'd have to say a substantial part of the congregation isn't sure of their salvation for some reason. We'll address that reason in a few minutes. Let's continue with my survey. How many of you believe there is a Hell, either a place of eternal damnation or a place of pain and annihilation?"

This time only about half of the congregation stood or raised their hand.

"Last question; it has two parts. The first part: How many people believe Jesus is God in human form?"

As best as the pastor could tell, the entire congregation believed in Jesus in this way.

"The second part of the question: How many people believe a former angel named Satan really exists?"

More than half the congregation took a seat or lowered their hands.

"Hmmm. That's very interesting. It appears that most of you believe in a Heaven, some of you aren't so sure you will be chosen to go to Heaven, but less than half of you believe there is a Hell. How strange. Even more disturbing is less than half of you believe there is a fallen angel named Satan. He has many names and titles. One I would like to add is The Father of Sin."

That brought a few chuckles from the audience. He waited a moment for the people to calm down before he said, "Let me tell you of one important fact. If you don't go to Heaven you are destined to go to Hell." He paused again and took notice many of the congregation were no longer smiling. Others had expressions of concern and a few even looks of fear. Several looked angry.

"Let me ask a question of those of you who aren't sure you're going to Heaven. What do you think would be keeping you out of Heaven? Is it sin? Sin that you cannot control? Temptations that seem to sneak up on you after days, weeks, possibly months of resisting those very same temptations?"

People began to stand, some raised their hands. Others who said they were sure they were going to Heaven were also standing until more than half the congregation were on their feet or raising their hands. A man in the front row had tears streaming down his cheeks, his body wracked with sobbing. Isaac stepped down from the pulpit and approached the man. Bud was right behind him with a microphone.

"Why are you crying?" Isaac asked the man in a soothing tone. "Please tell me what you are feeling right now."

Bud went to a knee and aimed the mike at the man. After a moment the man was composed enough to speak, "I'm crying because I'm weak. I can't... control myself... I know I shouldn't..." He collapsed back onto the pew and began crying even harder.

Isaac looked around and saw so many sad and crying faces. He sat next to the crying man and said to him in a gentle voice, "You're not weak my friend, you're just human. The Apostle Paul made it plain in his letter to the Romans, 'No one is righteous, not even one.' In another place Paul said 'the things I do, I don't want to do and the things I want to do I do not do.' Even Paul was a sinner, all human kind are sinners. We are born sinners and will be sinners until the day we die."

Isaac stood and turned to face the others who were still standing, many still crying. "But our God is a gracious God. In John's Gospel he says, 'For God so loved the world, he gave his one and only son that whoever believes in him shall not perish, but have everlasting life.' When you believe that God's one and only son, Jesus of Nazareth, who was the only man to live a sinless life, died as a sacrifice to God for all of our sins, past, present and future, **you are saved!** You are saved and will remain saved for the rest of your life on Earth. Yes, you will continue to sin, but you are still saved."

Isaac stood and gestured for Greg to come sit with the man while he returned to the pulpit. "Ladies and gentlemen," he continued in his soothing, deep baritone voice, "there are three very important features I must share with you about sin. The first is this. When you believe, truly believe, Jesus is the son of God you are saved. That means you accept Jesus is God in human form. As a result of that belief, you have been saved from the penalty of sin. As I mentioned before, we remain sinners, but our sins will not be counted against us. As Paul said, 'The wages of sin is death.' God the father requires those who sin to die an eternal death. But Father God accepts the death of his son, Jesus the Christ, to cover the sins of all mankind as long as they believe. We don't have to do anything except to believe Jesus and God are one. We are saved by the grace of God, a gift from God, through Faith in Jesus Christ.

"Once we are saved from the penalty of sin doesn't mean we can do every despicable sin we can think of and as often as we want and still think God is happy with us. Let me give you an example. The Apostle Paul received a letter from the church in Corinth early in the history of the church. It seems there was a church member who openly had sexual relations with his father's wife. When the church found out about this flagrant sin, the young man's defense was he believed that Jesus was God so he was saved and could sin as much as he wanted. When Paul read the letter, he sent a letter back telling the Corinthians to kick the man out of the church and to not have anything to do with him unless he repented. Sometime later the man did repent and he was allowed back into the church. What does it mean to repent? It means you confess your sin to God and you do your very best not to repeat that sin.

"Let me repeat that. As true Christians we need to do our very best not to sin. We don't need to agonize over our sins, but we should not revel in them. Bit by bit, day by day, we should strive to diminish our sins. This is a very important feature of sanctification. We should strive to be more Christ-like. When we give in to temptation, we should confess our sins and pray for God's forgiveness. Then we should do our best to not repeat our sin. This is an ongoing process as we are being saved from the power of sin.

"One more comment on this: don't flirt with sin. As an example, don't say to yourself, 'Wow, it's been over a year since I've done that sin. I don't think it would matter if I kind of did something like a sin, just a little sin, just this once.' That's Satan, the great tempter, working on you. Be like Jesus after he was baptized by John the Baptist and had spent 40 days and 40 nights fasting. When Satan came to tempt Him, Jesus shut him down. Do your best to be like Jesus.

"So you can see, sin is tenacious. That's because Satan and his demons are relentless. There's an invisible war going on all around us that will finally come to an end. That will be on Judgment Day, when Satan and his minions are thrown into the lake of fire. On that day we will be saved from the presence of sin."

There was a short question and answer period before the closing prayer. One of the elders asked Greg if he would like to say the prayer and to Isaac's surprise, Greg answered with a yes. His prayer was short and yet in some ways very powerful.

They closed the service with the singing of the doxology.

Praise God, from whom all blessings flow;
Praise him, all creatures here below;
Praise him above, ye heavenly host;
Praise Father, Son, and Holy Ghost.
Amen.

After five services in two days, Greg Stone was exhausted. His exhaustion was both physical and emotional. Listening to so many people unsure of their salvation was painful to hear. Their feelings of failure were heartbreaking. However, by the end of each sermon, tears turned to expressions of hope. They accepted they were sinners, after all they were only human. They also embraced the gift of salvation with open arms. They were saved!!!

There were still doubters. Some services had more doubters than others. Several completely denied the gift of grace. Their mantra was, "It can't be that easy!"

While Greg Stone was exhausted, Pastor Isaac was a bundle of energy. After the third service on Sunday afternoon, Greg fell asleep on the drive back to their apartment. He managed to make it to his temporary bedroom, but didn't bother to take off his clothes. He was snoring with his shoes on as soon as his head hit the pillow.

While Greg was sleeping, the pastor decided to get back to work as the chaplain at Angel of Mercy. He held a regular service in the chapel then made rounds to comfort those who were unable to make it to the chapel service. He noticed several of the staff attended the service, including Pris and Dr. Goodman.

That would become the pastor's routine between the five weekend services at Grace. By the middle of the first week, Greg became revitalized and joined the pastor. He was amazed at how alive he felt after several days of sleeping 12 hours.

The second weekend they arrived at the entrance of Grace Community Church an hour before the first Saturday service, or as Pastor Isaac called it, the Sabbath Day. They strolled along the tree lined walkway to the steps of the sanctuary where they were greeted by Bud.

"Good morning, Pastor. It's so nice to see you and your Acolyte this morning," beamed Bud. He glanced at their casual dress, but said nothing.

"And a good Sabbath to you, Bud," Isaac replied. Greg nodded and Bud returned the nod.

"What are your instructions for this weekend?" Bud asked.

"I was thinking about staying with the same program we used last week. It seems to me it went well. What do you think?" asked Isaac.

"I think it went really well, Pastor. In fact I heard numerous comments of praise for your sermon."

"That's nice to hear, Bud. So let's stay with the same program. I'd like you to choose all three hymns for this weekend's services. I really enjoyed the music you selected last time."

Bud beamed even brighter. "Thank you, Pastor, I already have them picked out for your approval."

"You don't need my approval, Bud. I trust your choices."

The pastor turned to Greg and asked, "What did you think about last week's music?"

"I also thought it was great," answered Greg. "Great choices Bud. I don't think I've ever heard better worship music."

Bud's smile had reached its limit. It couldn't get any bigger, but then it changed. "Pastor, I almost forgot. Elder Grant won't be joining us this weekend, he's come down with a serious cold. He asked that Acolyte Greg give the opening prayer. Is that okay with you Pastor? The Elder mentioned he was very impressed with his closing prayer last week, very well done."

The pastor looked at Greg. "Is that okay with you?"

"Absolutely, Pastor," Greg answered.

"One last thing," added Bud. "Several of the staff from Angel of Mercy are in the lobby. They told me they watched one of your sermons from last week on YouTube3. They wanted to say hello."

As Bud left to take care of the music selection, Isaac and Greg walked up the steps to the lobby entrance. Before Greg opened the door, Isaac said, "I believe there are four people waiting for us. They are Pris, Dr. Goodman, Dr. Suan and his soon-to-be fiancé, Esther."

"How could you possi…" Greg began but faded out. The pastor had already opened the door and stepped into the lobby. They chatted for a bit and Dr. Suan introduced Esther. Isaac gave the good doctor a knowing wink.

Just as they did last week, the doors to the sanctuary opened automatically as the orchestra began playing another beautiful hymn. The congregation filed in through the doors on the first floor and the balcony. Everyone chose a pew and took their seats. Bud made sure the four friends had seats in the front row. They seemed very excited as if they were going to experience something very special. The service followed the same pattern as the first week with the orchestra and choir. Again it was breathtaking. When the worship music ended, an elder read a short list of announcements projected on numerous large screen monitors tastefully positioned on the walls of the sanctuary.

When the elder was finished he turned and introduced Greg. "Acolyte Greg Stone will now lead us in our opening prayer, all rise please."

Those who could stand, stood up, the remainder sat with heads bowed as Greg walked to the pulpit. His voice was strong yet humble. He praised God for his blessings, he asked for mercy for those who were troubled, he asked for an end to the war in the Holy Land and closed with the Lord's Prayer.

The pastor watched the front row as Greg prayed and noticed Pris, her head partially bowed but her eyes focused on Greg's face for the entire prayer. Isaac gave her a slight nod indicating his approval.

When Greg finished and walked to the chair on the stage, the pastor strode to the pulpit and said to the congregation, "Good Sabbath, my friends. For those of you who are new to me and the rest of the congregation, my name is Isaac Silberman. I'm going to be your guest pastor for the next few weeks. Just in case you missed my not-too-subtle hint, I'm Jewish."

He paused as a ripple of amusement passed through the sanctuary. When it subsided, he continued, "I don't want you to worry, I was a Jew by birth, but am Christian by faith.

More laughter.

"I was born again here in America and have been a Christian since my rebirth. It seems like it was only yesterday.

"Today, I will begin with various theories of creation. However, I also want to cover angels and demons if time permits."

He paused briefly, eyes closed as if he were saying a prayer, then began. "There have been numerous theories of creation. Let's start with the scientific theories. The first theory I'm aware of is the Steady State Theory. It goes like this. The universe was never created. It has existed for billions, trillions or maybe quadrillions of Earth years. It has no beginning and it has no end.

"I'm not sure how long that theory persisted, but eventually, some astronomers theorized the universe was expanding and would continue to expand. They claimed they had the data to prove their point. It was called the Expansion Theory.

"Next came the Big Bang Theory in which other astronomers claimed space has always existed, filled with uncountable small atomic particles that eventually agglomerated together by gravitational attraction which in turn led to a cataclysmic nuclear explosion producing stars, planets and life in all forms over a period of innumerable years. That's a very long time as well as a very long sentence.

"That theory still exists as the dominant belief today amongst astronomers and cosmologists." He stopped for a moment and smiled. "This was very confusing to me. I grew up speaking Hebrew and by the time I had learned some English, I had heard the word cosmologists and understood what it meant, or I thought I did. I couldn't understand how someone who applied makeup to women's faces could know anything about our universe. But I digress."

There was more laughter.

"Research by the more elitist cosmologists discovered data they claimed proved the expansion of the universe had limits. It was slowing down and in time, lots and lots of time, the universe would stop expanding and collapse in upon itself. This would ultimately lead to another universe-forming nuclear explosion. They claimed this cycle would continue *ad infinitum.* So there you have the evolutionary theories of creation by scientists, astronomers and cosmologists along with a few cosmetologists. Who knows what they will come up with in the future?"

He took a sip of water and waited for the laughter to subsided before continuing. "Let's look at what the Bible says about creation. Let me preface that with my own opinion regarding the validity of the Bible. After numerous years of study, I have come to the conclusion that the Newly Revised American Standard Bible is a 99.9 percent accurate translation of the ancient Hebrew and Greek texts. When I read in the book of Genesis which says God created the universe and everything in it in six days, I believe it. There are a number of good Christians who don't. They would like to believe that during creation, when the Bible speaks of a day, it's not a 24 hour day. They quote the Bible text from second Peter about a day is like a thousand years to the Lord and a thousand years is like a day. They incorrectly interpret this to mean every day of creation was a thousand years long. What it really means is every 24 hour day is like a thousand years to God."

He stopped for a moment as if to gather his thoughts, then said, "I want to insert some supporting scripture. My favorite book of the Bible is the Gospel of John. It's emphasis is on the divinity of Jesus. My favorite part of that Gospel is in the first few verses: 'In the beginning was the Word, and the Word was with God, and the Word *was* God. He was with God in the beginning. All things came into being through Him, and apart from Him nothing came into being.' I have to admit, when I first read those three verses I was very confused. I thought Word was a very unusual name and how could he be with God and be God at the same time and what does 'the beginning' refer to? I consulted my Christian Rabbi who told me the word 'Word' really meant Jesus and when the Apostle John says Jesus was with God and he was God means Jesus was God in human form. He went on to say the beginning referred to the beginning of creation.

"That cleared up some of my confusion, but it took a considerable amount of time before I came to realize why John referred to Jesus as the Word. It wasn't just a nickname, it meant Jesus was the Word of God and the Word of God is the Bible, the whole Bible. When we read the Bible we're listening to Jesus. And most importantly, Jesus and God are one.

"Now let's look at what was meant by 'the beginning.' The easy answer is the beginning is creation. However, we need to take a more detailed look. First of all, what existed before creation began? The answer is, only God existed. There was no matter, no energy, no space, no time and no life. There was only God. As John said, 'All things came into being through him.' Why did God decide to create the universe? I have no idea. I believe only God knows.

"This leads us to another question. When did God create the angels? The best answer I came up with is he created them when he felt like it. The Bible gives us very little information about angels, especially regarding their creation. I personally believe they were created before the creation of the universe. That would include Earth and everything on it. I think Revelations 12, verses 7 through 12 supports my belief. Those verses speak of a war in Heaven between the archangel Michael and Satan. It doesn't explain why there was a war; however Satan, and the angels that followed him, lost the war and they were thrown down to Earth. The Bible doesn't reveal exactly when they were exiled to Earth. It can be assumed it occurred shortly after creation was completed because when we first we hear of Satan it is in the Book of Genesis when Adam and Eve were in the Garden of Eden. If he hadn't tempted Eve to eat the fruit from the tree of the knowledge of good and evil, perhaps there would be no sin in the world today... or maybe it was only a matter of time.

"Satan shows up in the book of Job and throughout both the Old and New Testament books. He's the center of attention in the Book of Revelation. I mean that in the worst sort of way. The NRASB lists eighteen different names and titles for Satan. He hates God in all three of his persons. Satan sees human suffering as a way to get back at God for banishing him. He does that in a variety of ways. As an example of his evilness, let me tell you four of his titles: Murderer, Liar, Accuser and Tempter.

"One last comment before I get back on the topic of creation. I believe Satan and his demon angels were banished from Heaven during the first day of creation. They were thrown down to the total darkness of a barren rock called Earth. They remained there until creation was completed and they will continue on Earth until Judgment Day. Michael and the angels who were loyal to God remained in Heaven, but occasionally they return to Earth to carry out whatever assignments God gives them. An example of this would be the angel Gabriel coming to Earth to tell the virgin Mary she was going to be the mother of a son named Jesus."

He stopped for a quick drink of water, then said, "Getting back to creation, has anyone ever heard about the Gap Theory?"

Several hands were raised. Isaac shook his head. "That's a shame," he said. "There is no Biblical support for that theory. You should just forget about it, but in the interest of completeness about covering goofy theories, let me say a few words. It is the belief there is a gap in creation between the first day and the second. This gap covers an indeterminate period of time, however during the gap angels were created. God created Lucifer, also known as Satan or the Devil, to be the most important of the angels. However, Satan became jealous of Jesus and God banished him to Earth. Enough said. In my opinion, more than enough. Let's move on."

He reached into his pocket and pulled out an egg. He extended his hand above his head and waved the egg back and forth for all to see. "What do I hold in my hand?"

"An egg!" exclaimed many in the congregation.

"Excellent," he shouted back. "Which came first, the chicken or the egg?" He waited for someone in the congregation to answer. Nobody raised a hand. "Okay, let's take a vote. How many think it was the chicken?" A quarter of the them raised a hand.

"How many think it was the egg?" Even fewer hands went up.

"So I guess the rest of you either aren't sure or you just don't care. Let me tell you why this is important. The Bible tells us from creation until the birth of Jesus is about 4,000 years. Since Jesus was born, a little over 2,100 years have passed. That means the Earth is almost 6,100 years old. Almost all of the scientific community and many religious leaders believe that is impossible. One of their key data points has to do with the stars. Numerous astronomers have measured the light from distant galaxies which are over a million light years away. That is a scientific fact and I believe it is true. In fact, the farthest galaxy from Earth we know of at this time is JADES-GS-z13-0. It is 320 million light years away from us. That means it takes a beam of light from there 320 million years to be seen on our Earth. If the Earth is only 6,100 years old, we would only be able to see stars that are 6,100 light years away which would mean there would be only a handful of stars visible in our night sky. That's pretty strong evidence that our Earth is much older than 6,100 years.

"If that's true, the validity of the Bible is in question. If we can't believe in the Bible, maybe the scientists are right after all. Maybe human beings were not created, maybe they're the result of hundreds of millions of years of evolution… That's a pretty scary thought, isn't it? Even worse, maybe there's no God after all."

The congregation sat stunned. The pastor stood in silence, his face expressionless. From the pulpit he looked at their shocked expressions, even on the faces of the four guests in the front row. After a long moment, Isaac started to smile and said, "Don't worry, none of that is going to happen. I guarantee it. You can start breathing again."

He moved to one side of the pulpit, pulled the egg from his pocket and said, "This is not the correct answer. The correct answer is the chicken. In fact when you read the Bible closely, every day of creation results in some form of maturity. When he wanted plant life, God spoke and mature trees, bushes and all species of plants appeared. They weren't saplings or shoots or seeds, they were fully mature plants. When he wanted fish and other sea animals, he spoke and the waters were teaming with every kind of fully grown sea creature imaginable. They didn't arrive as fish eggs or minnows. When he wanted birds, he spoke." The pastor pulled the egg out of his pocket again, pointed at it and said, "Is this what he got?"

There was a resounding No! from the congregation.

"You're right, he got fully feathered birds of every breed, including chickens. If he only created eggs none of them would have hatched. Who would have sat on them to keep them warm? The same goes for animals. God spoke and mature, fully grown animals came into existence.

"On the sixth day, the last day of God's creation, he created man. Man was created in the image of God. He also created a mature woman. Neither were created as babies. Babies wouldn't have survived without mature parents to nurture them."

He stopped for a moment to take another drink of water, looked out at the congregation and said, "Preaching makes a man thirsty." He took another sip then placed the glass back on the pulpit.

"I need to clarify one point. When the Bible says man was created in God's image, it doesn't mean we have any of God's powers or abilities. Man is not Godlike. People are not even like the angels. In Hebrews 2, verse 7, the Bible tells us God made man 'a little lower than the angels.'

"What does that mean? If the angels are immortal, are spirits who can take the appearance of human beings and can travel from Heaven to Earth in an instant, how could we be considered 'a little lower than the angels?' To me, it would seem like a huge gap, like comparing an amoeba with a horse. If that's the case, just think how much less is man than the creator of the universe.

"A side note, both Adam and Eve were created with belly buttons." That caused some surprised looks and a few raised eyebrows.

"I believe you can see the trend developing here. When God rested on the seventh day, The Sabbath Day, of creation he said what he had created as very, very good. It was a mature world. Nothing was missing, at least not on the surface.

"However, what about the interior of the Earth? Enter Phillip Gosse and his book, written in 1857. It was titled *Omphalos*, which is Greek for belly button. He believed creation involved only mature things like forests and grasslands, fruit trees and vegetables for harvest, all sorts of creatures and as such they all had belly buttons or their equivalent. Hence my comment that Adam and Eve were created with belly buttons. To substantiate his beliefs, he pointed out that after Adam and Eve were created, they were immediately placed in the Garden of Eden. That garden supplied them with all the fruits and vegetables they needed to survive. They were permitted to eat from every fruit tree except one, the tree with the fruit of the knowledge of good and evil. We all know how that turned out after Satan arrived. But even when they were kicked out of the garden, God showed them how to survive by harvesting grains and vegetables along with weeds and thistles. It was difficult, but they survived.

"So the surface of the Earth prospered and life went on, just as God had planned. But what about the interior of the Earth? God had a plan for that too. I call it the AS IF plan. Grosse suggested that the fossils of ancient plants and animals discovered by archeologists were not proof of evolution. They were not created millions of years ago. Instead he surmised God created the evidence of fossils AS IF they had evolved millions of years ago. As you might expect, the scientific community totally rejected his theory. Most Christian scientists were also skeptical. Why would a loving God try to confuse mankind? It made no sense to them.

"It makes no sense to me either, but a lot of things that God has done I don't understand. For example, why didn't he create a world without Satan, without sin? Why would he permit the atrocities that men do to themselves? Why would he destroy God-fearing people in wars or natural disasters like plagues, earthquakes and floods? My answer is, I have no idea why God does these things. What he does and why he does it is beyond me. The only thing I can say is summed up in Isaiah 55 verses 8 and 9, 'For *MY* thoughts are *NOT* your thoughts, neither are your *WAYS MY WAYS*, declares the LORD. As the Heavens are *HIGHER THAN* the earth, so are *MY WAYS*.' Let me close with the JADES galaxy, 320 million light years from Earth. I believe the universe was created mature, AS IF it were created all those millions of years ago. Maybe God did it so mankind could look up into the star-filled night sky and marvel at his awesome creation.

Early Monday morning, the pastor began his usual routine. The first thing after finishing his trip to the restroom was to say his prayers. Ever since his acolyte had moved into his quarters at Angel of Mercy, Greg joined the pastor in praying. There was a patio adjacent to the living room that looked out onto a beautiful view of a park.

It was springtime and the flowers which lined the walkways of the park were in full bloom and their fragrance was an added pleasantry. In the background, the sounds of a variety of song birds filled the air as the two men kneeled and began their prayers.

The pastor always began with the same scripture verse: "This is the day the Lord has made. Let us rejoice and be glad in it." He said this prayer aloud in English and Greg would join him. When finished with the verse, Isaac would pray aloud in Hebrew. Greg didn't speak Hebrew, so he didn't understand, but the sounds of the pastor as he prayed were comforting. He had no idea if Isaac was repeating the same prayer every day, but he doubted it. It didn't seem so much like a prayer. Instead it was more like he was having a personal conversation with Jesus. The pastor would speak a sentence or two then pause while he appeared to be listening. After listening to the pastor's prayers for a while, Greg would pray his own silent prayer in English. The prayers would go on for no more than fifteen minutes. When they were finished, they would both bow until their foreheads touched the floor for a few moments then rise and go about the activities of the day.

Most days they would eat their breakfast in the cafeteria; occasionally Pris would join them. After breakfast, Pris would go back to work while Isaac and Greg would begin making their rounds. The two of them would first visit those who were confined to their rooms, spending as much time as each person needed. Obviously, there wouldn't be enough time to see them all in one day.

Pris was a huge help in selecting who they would visit first by determining who was having the most problems, either physically or spiritually. She also told Isaac how grateful most of the people they visited were after he had returned to the living. However, during the two weeks after Isaac passed away and was born again, busy with all sorts of medical people, one elderly lady complained that the pastor shouldn't have gotten so old he couldn't keep up with his responsibilities.

In addition to the individual visits, they held a half-hour group service in the chapel every afternoon during the week. Pris was almost always in attendance and Dr. Goodman would also show up when he wasn't on call. They never saw Dr. Lawrence at any of the services.

As busy as they were, they managed to have some alone-time almost every day. Actually, it wasn't alone time, Greg seldom left Isaac alone. The acolyte decided he would be more than just a servant, he would provide security for the pastor any time they were out in public.

Many Christians were enthralled by the way he taught the Bible. However, not everyone loved him or the sermons he taught. Apparently, the two sermons he'd presented at Grace Community Church had been recorded on a number of YouTube derivatives. They had gone viral overnight with very mixed reviews. He received an increasing amount of positive comments from Christian clergy as well as from common folks all over the world. Unfortunately, there was also an increasing amount of hate emails and social media posts with every new sermon. Some of it even included death threats. Fortunately, nothing was said about him dying and being revived three days later, that seemed to be a secret that for some reason was being kept by medical staff.

Greg asked Isaac to wear body armor whenever he went out in public. Isaac laughed and shook his head. "I appreciate your concern, but don't worry about me. God brought me back to life once. He will protect me much better than body armor until I have finished my mission."

Greg asked, "What is your mission and when will it be over?"

Isaac smiled warmly and answered, "Only God knows. He hasn't told me yet, but he told me we are going to Jerusalem after the last two sermons at Grace Community Church. I should be safe for at least four weeks before we travel to the Holy Land."

In spite of Isaac's assurances, Greg decided to suggest Angel of Mercy hire additional security personnel to patrol the building inside and out. He ran it by Pris first.

"I think it's a great idea, Greg. I'm glad I thought of it," she said with a smile.

"Wait a minute," he protested. "I'm the one who thought of it, not you."

"Nope," she said with a shake of her head. "Once you told me about the death threat messages, I went straight to management and told them we needed more security and I didn't mean overweight ex cops."

"Really? I'm very impressed. I guess great minds think alike. So how many—"

Before he could finish, Pris said, "Beginning this afternoon we will have teams of four security personnel on duty 24/7. They will all be armed with non-lethal weapons."

"What type of non-lethal weapons?" Greg asked curiously.

"They're the latest version of the wireless Taser-12s. They're equipped with high velocity tracking darts. Their magazines hold twelve of the darts. Are you familiar with them?" Pris asked.

"No, not really," Greg replied. "Once I became an acolyte, I haven't kept up with any type of weapons, but I'm curious how the Taser-12 works."

"The latest version is really incredible. It mostly involves the tracking feature of the darts. The pistol version has a maximum range of a hundred yards so it's limited to close quarter use. The velocity of the darts is varied, but I requested the supersonic version. Now here's the really exciting feature. You can use it as a point-and-shoot weapon or a tracker. In tracker mode, you pull the trigger half way and it locks on to the target. You get a beep and a light flash indicates you are locked on to your target. You finish the trigger pull and the dart is fired and follows the target wherever it goes. Once you're used to the weapon, it takes about a second to lock-on and shoot.

"The charge on the dart is the same as the wire version. It will put your target down for at least fifteen minutes with no permanent damage unless you hit them in the eye."

She watched Greg's thoughtful expression and knew what he was going to ask. Before he spoke, she said, "Yes, they're very pricey. Yes, I ordered one for you and one for me as well. We have an appointment at the Taser Inc. shooting range tomorrow at 0900 hours."

Greg's eyes opened wide in surprise, then he smiled and said, "Have you've been having visions like Isaac, or did you just read my mind?"

"Neither, I'm psychic or maybe I just thought you'd like to be well prepared to guard the pastor. Isn't that what a good acolyte should do?"

"Roger that!" he said with a smile. "Looking forward to shooting with you tomorrow, and by the way, let's not tell Isaac about the tasers. He's kind of touchy about weapons."

* * *

The following weekend the third sermon was presented. Pastor Isaac turned over most of the details to Bud. Everything went according to plan with Greg Stone's name listed on the church bulletin as Assistant Elder Stone. Isaac continued to wear casual attire, but his acolyte wore a three-button suit coat to cover a set of body armor. Isaac figured the body armor was to keep Greg alive when he took a bullet; similar to what the Secret Service vowed to do to save the president. The pastor was unaware of Greg's new weapon which he carried each time he went out in public.

After the announcements and opening prayer led by Greg, Isaac stood, walked to the pulpit and said, "The topic of today's sermon is The Law. It says so in your church bulletin so I guess I should tell you about the law."

He paused briefly to see if anyone laughed at his comment. There were a lot of smiling faces but few laughs. "So this is going to be a tough group today. However, the law should never be a laughing matter. Today, I want to tell you how and why the law came about, the history of the punishment for violating the law and I will also cover the validity of the law today.

"The law, God's law, first showed up about 3,600 years ago at Mount Sinai. I assume all of you have read how God chose Moses to lead the Israelites from over 400 years of slavery in Egypt to the Promised Land. If you haven't, I strongly recommend you take your study Bibles and read the second book of the Old Testament. It's titled Exodus and the first half of the book tells all about how Moses introduces the law to nearly two million Israelite slaves. I can't think of a better way to spend the Sabbath day in worship. We pick up the story after Moses comes down from the mountain carrying two stone tablets with ten laws written on them. They are better known as the Ten Commandments written by the finger of God. Eventually there were a total of 613 laws, but we found out later the Ten Commandments are forever, the others not so much, for various reasons. The laws were divided into three categories: moral laws, civil laws and ceremonial laws. The moral laws are presented first, beginning with Exodus 20. These are the Ten Commandments, written in stone by the finger of God. The first four laws deal with how man is to interact with God. The remaining six laws define how the Israelites are to interact with each other.

"The civil laws could be likened to our current civil laws. They dealt with how the Israelites were to conduct business with each other. These laws were not recorded in stone. Instead they were written of materials like papyrus or parchment.

"The ceremonial laws defined how worship was to be conducted. They defined special holidays referred to as feast days. Passover and Pentecost are examples. They also encompassed how animal and grain sacrifices were to be made to God. The Day of Atonement is an example. It was carried out one specific day each year when the high priest was to sacrifice animals to rid the Israelites from the burden of sin. The ceremonial laws were also written on papyrus or parchment.

"We will focus on the moral laws for several reasons. First, these ten laws are considered the most important. They are written in stone by God, a material that could last forever, where the other two categories of law are written by men on animal skins or reed mats. The Ten Commandments were presented first in the book of Exodus. The other two categories appeared last in the book of Leviticus. Most important, the Christian Church believes the ceremonial laws were done away with the day Christ Jesus was crucified by the Romans at the request of the Jews.

"It's time to look at the Ten Commandments which have not changed since their inception 3,600 years ago."

The pastor nodded at Bud who projected the first four commandments onto the large monitors throughout the sanctuary.

"Let's read these together out loud.

1. <u>You shall have no other gods before Me.</u>
2. <u>You shall not make for yourself an idol.</u>
3. <u>You shall not take the name of the LORD your God in vain.</u>
4. <u>Remember the Sabbath day, to keep it holy.</u>

"Wow!!!" exclaimed the pastor. "What a rush to hear you all read the laws of God. It sent chills down my spine. Let me add a little content to each of the first four commandments. Don't worry, I'm not going to change the words, just expand on them a bit. If you go to Exodus 20, you'll notice there is a more detailed version of the commandments. I would suggest after this service is over, take your Bible and read exactly what the Bible says."

The pastor took a laser pointer and highlighted the first commandment. "God will not tolerate any other gods. In actual fact, there are no other gods, only God. The Lord's concern is that people might begin to worship other objects as if they were a god. It could be a mythical being like Baal, or it could be a golden calf or any number of other things. So there is only one real God."

Isaac used his pointer to move to the second commandment. "This has a close resemblance to the first, but the difference here is God saying you should not make any type of idol. It could be a wooden carving or a statue of a huge creature or maybe money or anything that you worship in place of the true God."

He moved the laser to the third commandment and said, "This is also very explicit. Don't use the name of God as a curse or a swear word. It defames the name of God. It is disrespectful and God will not tolerate it."

Pointing at the fourth commandment, he paused for a moment before saying, "This commandment is perhaps the most controversial of the first four. It says we should cease from all work and instead worship God on the Sabbath. The Sabbath is the seventh day, which in English is Saturday. I strongly believe we should be worshipping on the Sabbath, because that's what the Ten Commandments require. Most Christian churches worship on Sunday because they honor the resurrection of Jesus. However, that's not what the fourth commandment requires. I'll have more to say about the Sabbath later, Let's move on to the remaining six commandments."

The monitors changed to display the last six commandments. The pastor used his pointer to highlight the first of the six.

"Again, please read them out loud with me

1. <u>Honor your father and your mother.</u>
2. <u>You shall not murder.</u>
3. <u>You shall not commit adultery.</u>
4. <u>You shall not steal.</u>
5. <u>You shall not bear false witness.</u>
6. <u>You shall not covet.</u>

"The expanded version of commandment five reads as follows: 'Honor your father and your mother, that your days may be prolonged in the land which the Lord your God gives you.' I find it interesting that God placed this commandment first in the laws that dealt with how humans interact with each other. The law against murder is second.

"Moving on, what were the penalties for violating any one of the Ten Commandments?"

There was a short pause, followed by a man's voice, "Death by stoning," he said in a deep voice.

"Very good," replied the pastor. "And where did the stoning take place?"

Another man's voice spoke up, "They took the guilty person outside their camp."

"And who were the people who stoned the guilty person?" asked the pastor.

A woman shouted out, "Anyone with a rock!"

Many in the congregation laughed at the woman's reply, as the pastor stared at her for a long moment, shook his head and said, "I believe that's the most enthusiastic answer to that question I have ever heard, and it's absolutely correct." That brought on even more laughter.

"A few more questions. How many witnesses did it take to convict a person of breaking one of the commandments?"

"Only two," answered an older woman.

"That's also correct. It took only two witnesses to convict any Israeli adult man or woman or any Gentile who was residing with them. That is the reason for the ninth commandment. Any false witness to a crime would also be stoned to death."

"A few more questions and we'll move on. To whom did the Ten Commandments apply?"

"Just to the Israelites," another man answered.

"It warms my heart to preach to a congregation who really knows their Bible," he said to the whole congregation with a warm smile. "Another correct answer. Gentiles, who were anyone other than an Israelite, were not expected to honor the commandments. But it also permitted the Israelites to murder and steal from the Gentiles without being stoned.

"Let me give you an example of what happened to an Israelite who broke his promise to follow God's laws. The first one mentioned in the Bible has to do with the fourth commandment. It's recorded in the book of Numbers, chapter 15, verses 32 to 36. 'Now while the children of Israel were in the wilderness, they found a man gathering sticks on the Sabbath day. And those who found him gathering sticks brought him to Moses and Aaron, and to all the congregation.

They put him under guard, because it had not been explained what should be done to him. Then the Lord said to Moses, 'The man must surely be put to death; all the congregation shall stone him with stones outside the camp.' So, as the Lord commanded Moses, all the congregation brought him outside the camp and stoned him with stones, and he died.

"Another question. When was the penalty by stoning done away with?"

The pastor waited for a response from the congregation. When no one volunteered he said, "This was kind of a trick question. The answer is, when the Roman Empire annexed most of the middle east, the Jews came under the control of a Roman governor. The Roman emperors prohibited the people of captive countries from executing anyone. They could present their case to a Roman governor and if he decided the person deserved to be executed, the Roman soldiers would be the ones to carry out the order. That's why our savior, Jesus Christ, was crucified by the Romans and not killed by the Jewish Sanhedrin. However, the Jewish leaders were the ones who insisted Jesus had to die.

"Some may wonder why the Sanhedrin wanted Jesus dead. There are so many reasons, I could preach for months to cover them all, but one main reason comes to mind. Most of the pharisees and scribes could not accept Jesus was the Messiah. Even though there were numerous prophesies about Jesus, about where he was born, which tribe he was in, the miracles he would perform, they denied him. They were afraid Jesus would become powerful like King David. They couldn't accept this hick from Nazareth was ever going to replace the Romans. If anyone could, it was going to be them. Jesus had to die."

Before the pastor could continue, one man shouted out, "How about Steven? The Jews stoned him to death after Jesus was crucified. How did they get away with that?"

"What an excellent question," replied the pastor. "To the best of my knowledge the Bible doesn't tell us how the Jews were able to stone Steven and get away with it. I think his stoning was caused by spontaneous rage when Steven said the Jews were responsible for the death of the Messiah. If the Romans ever found out, they would have crucified those who took part in the stoning.

"Just a few more questions. Does anyone know what happened to the two stone tablets? Does The Ark of the Covenant ring any bells for you? In the latter part of the book of Exodus, Moses was given instructions by God on how to build a special place to store not only the stone tablets with the Ten Commandments inscribed on them, but also Aaron's rod and a jar of manna. That special place was the Ark of the Covenant and was carried by Levites everywhere they traveled. When King Solomon built his temple in Jerusalem, the ark was placed in a special room, called the Holy of Holies. That room was separated from the rest of the temple by a curtain only visited once a year by the High Priest. That day is known as The Day of Atonement, in Hebrew it's called Yon Kippur. On that day, all the sins of the Israelites were supposed to be forgiven.

"That tradition was continued until 586 BC when the Babylonians captured Judea and the city of Jerusalem, It is believed that the Ark of the Covenant and all its contents were hidden away from the Babylonians. Solomon's Temple was totally destroyed, but the ark was never found. No one knows for sure where it might be.

"What was the main purpose for the commandments? It was to define sin. The common belief was if you kept the commandants you wouldn't be guilty of sin, you would be right with God, a righteous person. If you are not guilty of sin you will go to Heaven or so the Jews believed. Then Jesus comes along and in the fifth chapter of Matthew he teaches that just thinking about violating the law is a sin. There's an old expression, 'the thought is taken as the deed.' For example, how many of us have gotten so angry at someone you wished they were dead? If you did, that's murder in the eyes of God. Or perhaps you came across a wallet lying on the sidewalk, you open it up and find lots of cash. You know you should try to find the owner and return the wallet along with the cash, but you really want to keep the money. That's stealing in God's eyes.

"So who are the righteous? In his letter to the Romans, the Apostle Paul says 'No one is righteous, no not one. For we all fall short of the glory of God.' Since we are all sinners, what will happen to us on Judgment Day. Again, Paul has the answer, 'The wages of sin is death.' Then what good are the Ten Commandments if we're all going to die?" He gripped the sides of the pulpit and took a moment to look at the congregation to be sure he had their complete attention, before continuing. "The Commandments are goals we can never attain. We need a savior. His name is Jesus. The only sinless man ever to walk on Earth is Jesus Christ, the Son of Man and the Son of God. He was crucified on a Roman cross so that we may have life. He paid the price for all the sins of mankind and all he asked in return is that you believe in him. Believe he is God in human form and your sins are washed away. You just have to believe."

He stopped to take a sip of water. He wanted everyone to take a moment to consider what he had just said. "So what about the Ten Commandments? Some say they served their purpose, but have no meaning in the life of believers nowadays."

He paused again and shook his head, then said, "That is utterly ridiculous. Apparently, the supposed believers haven't been reading their Bibles. Let me give you one more Bible quote for this Sabbath Day. In Romans 2, verses 14 and 15, Paul says, 'For when Gentiles, who do not have the law, BY NATURE do what the law requires, they are a law to themselves, even though they do not have the law. They show that the work of the law is written on their hearts.' The law on the stone tablets may be lost forever, but for you, believers in Jesus, the law is written on your hearts and it will be with us until we shed our body and join our Lord in Heaven.

"I'd like to close with what Jesus said about the Ten Commandments. Please look at your monitors and read along with me. In chapter 5 of Matthew, verses 17 through 19 Jesus says:

'Do not think that I came to abolish the Law or the Prophets, I did not come to abolish but to fulfill. For truly I say to you, **until Heaven and earth pass away**, not the smallest letter or stroke shall pass from the Law until all is accomplished. **Whoever then annuls one of the least of these commandments, and teaches others to do the same, shall be called least in the kingdom of Heaven; but whoever keeps and teaches them, he shall be called great in the kingdom of Heaven.'**

"I believe this proves without a doubt the Ten Commandments of God are forever, and not for just the Jews. It includes all who believe in God. Not just God the father but God the Son and God the Holy Spirit as well, the entire trinity."

He paused to look over the congregation, then said, "Let me share one last, very important verse from scripture. In the Gospel of John, chapter 14, verse 15, Jesus said, **'If you love Me, keep my commandments.'**

"Elder Stone, please close us in prayer."

After prayers on Monday morning, the pastor and his acolyte headed to the cafeteria for breakfast. They took their trays loaded with food and drink back to a table that Greg chose. It was next to a wall and far from the entrance. He insisted they both sit on the same side with their backs to the wall. They sat as Isaac turned his head and asked his acolyte, "Don't you think this is a bit too much?"

Greg took a sip of hot coffee, then answered, "Not at all. I feel it's a reasonable precaution."

As the pastor began to eat his lox and bagel, Greg continued speaking between bites of fluffy scrambled eggs. "Pris told me that during the last three weeks there have been an increasing number of requests to visit Angel of Mercy. Almost none of them have family or friends living here. Pris says most of them are media people looking for an interview." Greg stopped talking to take a bite of bacon, followed by toast and jelly, then added, "She said they're turning away most of those people, and they have hired four additional security people to screen all visitors."

The pastor took a long sip of coffee, added more sugar and a little cream and took another sip and nodded in approval. "Don't you think I would get a vision to warn me of any danger between now and when we leave for Jerusalem?"

Greg laid down his fork to give the pastor a thoughtful glance. "Doesn't the Bible say, God helps those who help themselves?"

Isaac smiled and answered, "That quote is not from the Bible. The scripture I would consider appropriate is, Trust in the Lord."

They finished their breakfast and returned to their apartment. While Isaac began visits to those confined to their quarters, Greg started reviewing yesterday's social media for hate posts and death threats that might seem credible. After an hour, he was depressed due to finding a substantial increase in haters. He decided to take a break and workout at the gym/physical therapy facility. But first he contacted the pastor to make sure everything was all right.

He had been running on one of the tread mills for about ten minutes when Pris jumped on an adjacent one. She laughed at Greg's look of surprise and shouted, "Race you to the finish line!"

They both upped their speed settings to maximum and took off sprinting. "You're never going to beat me," shouted Greg good naturedly.

"Oh yeah?" she laughed and shouted in return. "Let's see who lasts the longest!"

After ten minutes, their T-shirts and sweatpants were soaked with sweat and the treadmill displays showed their heart rates were far above the recommended maximum. Pris reached up with her left hand to wipe sweat from her eye, lost her balance, twisted as she fell onto her back, and was catapulted off the fast moving belt.

She crashed into a heap onto the concrete floor skidding at least fifteen feet before stopping when her head banged into the steel frame of a massage table.

Greg was beside her in a flash, quickly followed by two of the physical therapists.

She was unconscious and Greg thought she might be dead; however, the two therapists were quick to get her vitals and confirmed she had a concussion. Greg could already see the goose egg forming on her forehead, close to her right temple.

A few minutes later one of the therapist made a preliminary diagnosis. "She has a pretty severe concussion, it looks like she may have a hairline fracture on the ulna of her right forearm and left patella, maybe on her tailbone as well.

Both of her protheses are pretty badly damaged and may have to be replaced."

That last comment shocked Greg. "What protheses?"

The two therapists looked at each other. Then the woman shrugged and the man said, "I'm not sure I should be telling you this. Pris lost her right leg and left shoulder during the battle of Vatican City. She almost died. Actually she did die, twice in fact. However, they were able to save her. When she was well enough they replaced the damaged organic parts with state of the art protheses. It must have cost the army a small fortune, but hey, she deserved it after being awarded two Purple Hearts, a Silver Star and the Medal of Honor. She didn't tell you about that?"

Greg was stunned. "No, she hadn't gotten around to it," he said, his voice almost a whisper.

He could hear the sound of the approaching ambulance that would take Pris to the emergency room of nearby Mercy Hospital. He found Isaac and described what happened to Pris. The pastor didn't seem surprised, it was as if he knew it was going to happen. However, he and Greg both said prayers for Pris's recovery.

* * *

They both checked in on Pris at the hospital daily during the week and also early on the Sabbath morning before they headed to Grace Community Church for the two services. Greg was very subdued, but was glad to see Pris was recovering. With the pastor's permission Greg spent all Friday morning with her. Pris told him the protheses would not have to be replaced, only repaired and everything else was healing nicely. "I won't be able to attend church this weekend. I was really looking forward to seeing you and the pastor at church one more time. I should be released from the hospital by the middle of next week, so we can spend some time together before you leave for Jerusalem. I mean, if you want to."

"Of course I want to," was Greg's reply. "Only on one condition, no more treadmill races!"

She laughed, gave him a hug and a warm first kiss then waved good-bye.

The pastor and his acolyte arrived at the church complex two hours early. The pastor checked the church bulletin and discovered there was an early service at the original sanctuary. "Would you mind accompanying me?" asked Isaac. "I'd really like to see what they've done with the place."

Greg looked at the bulletin from last week, then back at Isaac. He said, "It says here the service is in Mandarin Chinese. Do you speak Mandarin?"

"Not that I know of," replied the pastor.

When they reached the original sanctuary, the front doors were wide open and the sound of organ music drifted out onto the plaza. They walked up the steps and a Chinese couple handed them a bulletin written in Chinese characters. They both looked mildly surprised, but the man began speaking to them in broken English, "So sorry. No much English. Maybe you other church?"

Isaac smiled warmly at them and said in Mandarin, *"There is no need for you to be sorry. It is I who should apologize to you and your wife for showing up unannounced."*

The wife's mouth dropped open in surprise, so did Greg's. The woman quickly covered her mouth with her hand as her husband replied, *"You speak Chinese better than any person I know. Perhaps better than I. Did you spend many years in the Middle Kingdom?"*

"Unfortunately, I have not had the pleasure. However, if our Lord permits, I would love to immerse myself in your culture. I understand you are the pastor of the Chinese mission. How many years have you shepherded your flock?"

For the next ten minutes the two pastors conversed in Chinese like they were life-long friends. When the service began, Pastor Liu and Mrs. Liu introduced Isaac and Greg to a congregation of almost three hundred worshipers.

After the introduction, Pastor Liu asked Pastor Isaac to speak to the Chinese congregation. For the next fifteen minutes, Isaac spoke not a word that Greg understood. As the two of them walked to the new sanctuary, Greg asked him what he had said to the Chinese congregation.

"I'm not really sure. I think it was God speaking through me. To me it seemed as if I was speaking English but it sounded completely different. Whatever I said, they seemed to like it."

He stopped for a moment and seemed to be lost in thought, then said, "It reminds me of how the disciples spoke in different languages after the Holy Spirit descended upon them at Pentecost. Do you think that's possible?"

Greg was surprised the pastor asked him that question. After he thought about it for a few moments he replied, "I have no idea, but what you suggested seems logical. Except, ever since you returned from the dead, nothing seems logical. My only hope is you don't start speaking in tongues when you preach later today."

They walked down the tree lined walkway to the main church and met Bud standing at the bottom of the lobby steps.

"*Buenos dias Señor Bud ¿Cómo estas?*" asked Isaac.

Bud looked at the pastor for a second, then over at Greg and asked, "Why is he talking like a Mexican?"

"I hope he's just messing with us," answered Greg. "I think he'll be speaking English for his sermons, but you never know."

After the worship music, the announcements, and opening prayer by Elder Stone, Isaac walked to the pulpit. He stood quietly looking around the vast sanctuary and then began. "Ladies and gentleman I want to thank you for giving me the opportunity to preach some of my favorite sermons to this vast congregation. I will cherish the memories of the time I spent with all of you. Your senior pastor will be returning next weekend. My closing sermon will be about prophets and apostles. Let me start by describing the difference between the two. A prophet is a man who God uses to pass on information. That information could be intended for a king, a specific group of people or a whole nation. Some prophets passed on many different visions from God to a wide variety of people, others had only one vision intended for a specific person or reason. Let me give you a couple of examples.

"Around 705 BC, God gave Jonah a vision. He was to go the city of Nineveh, the capital of Assyria, and tell the people God was going to destroy them if they didn't change their ways. Instead of following God's command, Jonah attempted to escape by sailing away to a distant land. That didn't please God and he caused a great storm. Jonah was washed overboard and swallowed by a really big fish. After three days in the belly of the fish, Jonah had a change of heart. The fish vomited him up and Jonah traveled to Nineveh and spread the word of God to the entire city of 120,000 people. Because of Jonah's message, the king ordered everyone to stop their wicked ways. God accepted their changes and did not destroy them."

Before Isaac went on with the examples, he asked a question, "Does anyone wonder why Jonah tried to avoid going to Nineveh?"

A young man stood and said, "Maybe he was afraid he would be killed by the people of Nineveh?"

"Good answerer, but unfortunately incorrect," replied the pastor

A middle aged women raised a hand and the pastor called on her. "He didn't want to do what God ordered him to do because he wanted the Lord to kill all of the Assyrians.

They had already captured Israel in 722 BC and Jonah was afraid they would try to capture Judea if God let them live."

"Perfect answer, that's exactly why Jonah tried to run away from God. However, God used a big fish to help Jonah to change his mind and do what God wanted."

He walked to the left side of the pulpit, his eyes downcast as if lost in thought for a moment, then faced the congregation and asked, "Why do you think God forgave the Assyrians?"

He waited for a moment, but when none of the congregation raised a hand the pastor said, "Just a few years after Jonah visited Nineveh, the Assyrian army put Jerusalem under siege. King Hezekiah, the leader of Judea, prayed for a miracle to save his people from the ruthless Assyrian king, Sennacherib. He and his officers shouted insults to God day and night. The same God who had shown them mercy just a few years before. After many months of siege, the Assyrian army was going to storm the walls of Jerusalem. Their army was ready and willing to kill everyone inside the city. All of the soldiers went to sleep confident this would be an easy victory. However, that night Hezekiah received his miracle. That night, the angel of the Lord went out to the Assyrian camp and killed 185,000 Assyrian soldiers. Sennacherib escaped and went back to Assyria, where he was later killed in the temple of his god by his own sons. Judah never became part of the Assyrian Empire.

"Perhaps Jonah's mission to Nineveh had a purpose he could never imagine. Perhaps he wanted to give them a chance to change their evil ways, and they did, for a short time. But they went back to evil ways again. They called down the wrath of God upon themselves."

He walked to the other side of the pulpit. "The next example is the Prophet Isaiah. The Book of Isaiah is the largest of all the Bible books of prophecies. It has 66 chapters compared to Jonah which has only four chapters. Isaiah is often thought of as a condensed version of the Bible's 66 books. Some have said the first 39 chapters cover Old Testament issues while the last 27 chapters deals with the New Testament. Many of Isaiah's visions where meant to give instructions to five kings, Uzziah, Jotham, Ahaz, Hezekiah and the last one, King Manasseh, the worst king Judea ever had. It is reported when Isaiah confronted King Manasseh for not following God's instructions, he had Isaiah killed.

"This is another one of those books you should read on a Sabbath day. It would probably take several days to complete. Let me give you one particular prophecy which I find very compelling. In chapter 44, verse 28, Isaiah tells us that God says, It is I who says of Cyrus, 'He is my shepherd, and he will perform all My desire.' And he declares of Jerusalem, 'She shall be built,' and of the temple, 'Your foundation shall be laid.' That prophesy was written by Isaiah 150 years before the Persian King Cyrus was born. He was the king that authorized the Jews to return to Jerusalem.

"There are 17 books in the Bible which come under the heading of Prophets. There are even more who are mentioned in other Bible books. Some have suggested Moses should be included and I agree with that. The Muslim religion considers Jesus a prophet, however since Jesus is God in human form, we consider him much more than just a prophet. Now, let's talk about apostles. It is true there is some overlap between prophets and apostles. However, there are fewer apostles and they are a very exclusive group. To the best of my knowledge the word 'apostle' does not show up in any of the Old Testament books. The Greek word 'apostle' is translated in English to mean 'messenger.' However, before there were apostles, there were disciples, which is also a Greek word which means follower or student."

He stopped for a moment, then asked, "How many of you are new Christians?" Isaac did a quick count of the raised hands. "I estimate about 200 out of 1,000 are new to the faith.

How many of the remaining 800 are familiar with how Jesus acquired all his disciples? And just so you know, at one point Jesus had around 70 disciples." He did another quick count then said, "So, almost half of you aren't aware of how Jesus got his disciples. Therefore, I feel it's my duty as a pastor to inform you of how this went down.

"In the beginning, just after Jesus had been baptized by John the Baptist and the Holy Spirit descended onto him, Jesus selected the first disciples. As time went on, more people heard his message and observed his miracles. Eventually, Jesus acquired a huge following, but most of those who followed him were in it for the free food and the healing. Once fed or healed, they no longer followed.

"At one point, the Bible tells us Jesus sent out 72 disciples to precede him as he made his way to visit various locations. For those who would like to get more information about this event, read Luke 10. Apparently, as Jesus began to reveal more details about his mission on Earth, many of them no longer followed him. When they realized Jesus was not going to become the new king of Judea and drive the Romans out of the promised land, many more of the disciples left him. When it became clear Jesus was going to die, all but the original twelve deserted him. And one of the twelve, Judas Iscariot, betrayed him.

"Before Jesus was crucified, Judas committed suicide. After the crucifixion Judas was replaced by Matthias. The ascension of Jesus took place after Matthias was chosen. Fifty days after the crucifixion, at the Festival of Pentecost, the Holy Spirit descended upon the twelve disciples. They became imbued with the power of the Holy Spirit who remained with them for the remainder of their lives. At that moment they became apostles whose mission was to spread the message of salvation to the known world. They had the power to see visions, cast out demons, heal the sick, and some, even to raise the dead."

The pastor took a sip of water, then said, "Raise your hand if you think there were additional apostles beside the twelve ."

Many hands were raised. The pastor seemed surprised by the number. He pointed to a woman in the first row of the balcony. Bud aimed a boom mike at her and she said, "I think all the authors of the New Testament should be considered apostles."

"Interesting answer. Anyone else?"

A man in the second row, stage right, stood and said, "I think Paul should be considered an apostle because he wrote almost half of the New Testament and the Bible says he raised a dead boy who was killed when he fell out of a window. In addition he established more churches than any of the other apostles."

"Excellent reasoning," Isaac replied. "I agree, Paul should be included with the twelve. However, does the Bible say he received the Holy Spirit?"

The man seemed like he wasn't sure, then he smiled and said, "Of course. When he was Saul of Tarsus heading for Damascus to arrest Jewish Christians, Jesus appeared to him, changed his name and turned him into the Apostle Paul."

"But what about the Holy Spirit? Did the Spirit give him the powers the other twelve were given?" the pastor asked, goading, or perhaps leading, him to the truth.

The man paused and looked somewhat confused., "But aren't God the Father, Jesus and the Holy Spirit all God?"

"Yes!!! Give that man a Kupe doll. That's called the Trinity and each branch had the power to establish an apostle. I have to admit, my two favorite apostles are John and Paul, in that order. John wrote five books in the New Testament, the Gospel of John, John 1, 2 and 3, and the last book of the Bible: The Revelation of Jesus Christ. His writings on the divinity of Jesus is are monumental. Paul, formerly Saul of Tarsus, wrote 13 books of the new testament to churches he had founded and individuals whom needed his help. Both apostles have written extensively on End Times. Paul in 1st and 2nd Thessalonians and John in Revelation.

"Don't forget that Daniel in the Old Testament also had some pretty important visions about End Times, but he's considered a prophet, not an apostle. Granted, Revelation takes a lot of study to figure out what John is saying, whether it is literal or allegory. Theologians are divided on the exact meaning. However, they all agree, ultimately the universe will come to an end to be replaced by a new Heaven and a new Earth, Satan and his demons will no longer interact with humans, there will be no sin and all those who believe Jesus is God will be given immortal bodies. That sounds like a win-win to me.

"How about James and Jude, Jesus' half-brothers? They both wrote books in the Bible. Then there's Luke and Mark. They also wrote books in the Bible as well as joined Paul on his missions. Or Barnabas and Silas, they both accompanied Paul on his missions to Asia. Should any of them be considered apostles?"

He looked at the large clock on the wall below the balcony, shook his head and said, "I'm running out of time. Let me close with this. Most theologians believe Paul was also an apostle. Many also consider that Jesus' half-brother, James, should be known as an apostle, but many more disagree. None of the other candidates made the cut."

"One last question then Elder Stone will close us in prayer and we'll sing the doxology. Who was the last apostle to pass away and about when did he die?"

A vast majority of the congregation stood and said almost in unison, "The Apostle John." A smaller group said in a garbled voice, "The end of the first century."

After the closing prayer by Elder Stone and the singing of the doxology, many began filing out into the lobby area.

However, a large crowd made their way down to the front of the pulpit to shake hands with the pastor and wish him well.

Elder Stone also received well wishes and one young lady asked for his autograph which surprised the girl's mother and embarrassed Greg.

Twenty minutes later, the sanctuary was empty and a cleanup crew quickly began to prepare for the next service. Bud joined Isaac and Greg on the left side of the first row of pews and they began discussing how they felt the first service went and any changes which might be needed for the second one.

Greg noticed two men dressed in dark-blue workmen's overalls walking down the right aisle. The man in front was tall, well over six feet with an athletic build and black hair, cut high and tight. The second man was shorter but more muscular with light brown hair, also cut high and tight, military style. He was carrying a small metal case. They climbed the steps to the stage and headed for the pulpit. Greg stood and asked Bud in a low voice, "Do you recognize those men?"

Bud glanced up, looked at the two men, shook his head and turned back to Isaac.

Greg walked up to the front of the stage and smiled as he asked, "Hi guys, what are you up to?"

The man with the case was kneeling down and doing something under the pulpit. The other man was standing behind the pulpit with an annoyed expression as he answered Greg, "There's a problem with the sound system; we'll have it fixed in a minute."

That got Bud's attention, he stood and said, "The sound system's fine, I checked it myself this morning…" He looked at the taller man and said in a challenging voice, "Who are you people?"

As soon as Bud said that, Greg moved to the right side of the pulpit with his Wireless Taser-12 held hidden behind his leg. He quietly turned the safety off while Tall Man was listening to Bud. Before Tall Man could say anything, Short Man shouted from under the pulpit, "Shoot them now!!!"

Everything seemed to slow down for Greg. He saw Tall Man raising his hand from under the pulpit holding a very large pistol, a .44 Auto Mag. He was just about to shoot Bud when Greg fired his Taser-12. His dart hit Tall Man in the chest with a very loud *ZAPP*. The gun fell from his hand as his body convulsed as he collapsed almost on top of Short Man still kneeling under the pulpit. Short Man wasn't sure where Greg was so he took a quick peek around the side of the pulpit. Bad mistake. The pulpit wasn't wide enough to cover his entire body. Still on his knees, he peaked around the wrong side of the pulpit exposing his backside to Greg who fired a second dart into his bottom with the same result: *ZAPP*, convulsive shaking, quietness.

Bud was frozen in shock while Greg did a quick scan of the entire sanctuary. He spotted a third shooter in the balcony, his assault rifle to his shoulder, his finger almost on the trigger. Greg yelled very loudly, "**GUN! get down,**" just as Third Shooter pulled the trigger. The bullet hit Bud in the back driving him forward onto his face. He began screaming in pain before he lost consciousness.

As Third Shooter was making his shot, Greg fired the Taser-12 on tracker mode. Third Shooter made a quick move away from the dart, smiling as he quickly prepared to shoot Greg, but the dart moved with him and hit him in the shoulder. There was a slight scream just before the *ZAAP*, followed by convulsions as Third Shooter fell over the balcony rail onto a first floor pew.

Now that he was pretty sure there were no more shooters, Greg's attention shifted to Isaac, watching him check on Bud. Apparently, when Bud approached the two strangers, the pastor contacted the police, fire department and EMTs.

Greg jumped up onto the stage and checked on what Short Man had put under the pulpit. It was a ticking bomb, counting down in red numbers with a little less than a minute before it would detonate!

Greg jumped from the stage, helped Isaac pick up Bud and they moved as fast as they could to get out of the sanctuary. They barely made it to the lobby before the bomb went off.

There were several people still left in the lobby. However, when the gunfire began, many of them decided to exit the building. Apparently, some of the congregation weren't convinced it was gunshots and curiosity had them beginning to move close to the sanctuary doors that remained open. A couple of the greeters took a quick look around the corner of one of the entry doors just as the bomb detonated. The concussion of the explosion knocked both of them to the ground as the shockwave tore the doors off their hinges and blew out the floor-to-ceiling windows of the lobby. The people in the lobby screamed as they were knocked off their feet and tables and chairs became dangerous projectiles. Isaac, Greg and Bud literally came flying through the mangled doorway and crashed onto the carpeted lobby floor, unconscious.

By the time Greg and Isaac regained consciousness, the sanctuary was engulfed in flames and the lobby was a chaotic mass of firemen and EMTs. Greg was the first one who managed to crawl to his feet and heard the sound of numerous sirens, probably from the local police to secure the crime scene. He struggled as he helped Isaac up. They had no idea how long they were out, but Bud wasn't moving and Greg couldn't find a pulse. One of the EMTs pushed Greg gently aside and searched for a pulse. She quickly began CPR on Bud. After a few minutes, she checked his pulse again. She turned to look at Greg and Isaac and shook her head. "Sorry for your loss," she said sadly and moved on to her next patient.

Greg stood stunned. It had been almost a decade since he had been in combat and the memories began flooding into his brain. The fear, the panic, began to overwhelm him until Isaac placed his hand on Greg's shoulder and said in a calm, compassionate voice, "Don't worry, Greg. Everything will be all right. No one will die here today, except for the shooters."

Before Greg could reply to the comments of his pastor, Isaac reached out and grabbed the EMT as she walked by. "He's alive, please check him again."

The EMT started to protest, but before she realized what she was doing, she checked Bud's pulse again. Her head snapped toward Isaac, a look of amazement on her face. "You're right!!! He *is* alive. How could I have missed it?"

"Don't blame yourself," said Isaac, his voice still calm and soothing. "He probably had a very weak pulse, difficult to find. What's important is that you found his pulse, perhaps you should send him to a hospital as soon as possible."

The woman nodded in agreement, then turned and called for a gurney. In less than a minute Bud was in an ambulance heading for the closest hospital with sirens and flashing lights.

Greg hadn't said a word since Isaac had spoken to him so calmly. He watched everything that happened in total disbelief. As the ambulance took Bud away, Greg turned toward Isaac. His voice was choked and barely audible. "You did this, didn't you? You brought Bud back to life!"

Isaac shook his head and said, "No, not me. God told me it wasn't Bud's time. God started his heart beating again. Praise God from whom all blessings flow."

Greg noticed the pastor wasn't too steady on his feet. The acolyte reached out and took Isaac's arm to steady him and guided him to the steps that led to the lobby. They both sat down and waited for their strength to return and watched the bedlam from the large patio area. Apparently, many of the attendees at the first service had stopped to chat with their friends. Adding to them were those who arrived a bit early for the second service and were present when the bomb went off.

Greg estimated there could have been as many as 500 people who were injured from the blast. Most of the injuries were superficial, but they would still be in pain and have trauma from this horrible event. Others had more serious damage. Fortunately, none of the congregation was killed, but several were taken away in ambulances and would have to spend some time in the hospital.

They had no idea how long they sat there; it was quite awhile before Isaac could stand and walk down the lobby steps toward the temporary medical tent in the church's plaza. Before anyone who was caught in the explosion was released, they underwent a complete emergency examination. While they were being examined, a uniformed police officer came up to Greg. "You're Greg Stone, aren't you?"

Greg nodded and answered, "Yes officer, that's me. How can I help you?"

The officer answered, "The surveillance camera inside the sanctuary showed how you took out the three shooters. That was some righteous shooting, Major. However, procedure dictates you need to surrender your weapon until we can verify you fired in self-defense."

Greg pulled the Taser-12 from his waistband and handed it to the officer butt first. "Why did you call me major?" he asked as the officer took the weapon.

"Are you kidding? You're famous. I served in the Marines at the Battle of Rome. If it weren't for you, I'd have been a long time dead. Your Voice of God weapon saved my life as well as about a hundred grunts like me."

As he spoke to Greg, the officer checked out the Taser-12. "This is one of those non-lethal weapons isn't it? That's pretty gutsy going up against live ammo. I'm sure you'll get your weapon back by the time you're done with your physical exam. Anytime a non-lethal weapon is used in a shoot-out against live ammo it's almost always ruled a righteous shoot. Can I shake your hand?"

"Sure," answered Greg, a little embarrassed by the request and shook the officer's hand.

As the officer walked away, Isaac looked at Greg and said, "You didn't tell me you had the gun."

"No, I didn't tell you," Greg replied. "I figured if God wanted you to know, he'd have given you a vision.

"Oh really? Well, I have to admit you did an excellent job of protecting all of us. I hope and pray you won't have to do that ever again, but it seems like being prepared is a good idea."

"Do you have any insight as to who the three men who attacked us were?" asked Greg changing the subject.

"Not sure they were attacking us," answered Isaac. "Maybe they wanted to destroy the church. The bomb was set to explode between the services when there would be a minimum number of people in the sanctuary."

"So you haven't received any visions about this?"

"Not so far," Isaac replied.

The doctor approached and told them they were cleared to leave. "Just take it easy for a few days. No more gun battles if you can avoid them," she added with a smile.

They stopped by the police tent on their way out and Greg was able to pick up his Taser-12. He slipped it into the waistband of his pants and covered the gun with his sport coat. The coat was ripped and torn and covered in dust from the explosion. Isaac also looked the worse for wear.

As they walked toward the parking lot, Isaac turned to look back at the church once more. He stood there transfixed for a few moments, then turned to Greg. "What a shame to lose such a place of worship. I suppose they'll have to use the old church until they can build a new one. By the way, the men who caused this tragedy weren't in control of themselves. Demons were controlling them. We are going to have to rid ourselves of these creatures before we can leave for Jerusalem."

The two men hobbled across the parking lot. Both paused for a moment to catch their breath while the maximum strength Tylenol began to kick in. Isaac said to Greg, "Let's stop at the hospital before we return to Angel of Mercy. Both Bud and Pris are at the same hospital and I'd like to see them for a little while. Is that okay with you?"

"Yes, sure. I would really like to visit them both. Do you already know their room numbers?"

Isaac just smiled as they headed out to the transit waiting for them in the parking lot.

They arrived at the hospital fifteen minutes later. Isaac went to the information desk to find out Bud's status. The elderly woman behind the desk asked, "Are you related to Mr. Clark?"

"I'm his pastor. He was admitted a few hours ago. Probably one of the first from the Grace Community Church explosion," answered Isaac.

"Oh my goodness! What a tragedy that must have been," she said as she scanned her iPad9 for information on Bud Clark. "Here it is. Will you look at this," she exclaimed. "We have eight patients from the Grace explosion here at Mercy. That includes Mr. Clark. It says here Mr. Clark was admitted to the ER, but he was transferred to an intensive care unit just a few minutes ago. If you'll give me your smart com I'll download the directions so you can find his room. Please register at the nurses' station when you get to his pod. It's a security requirement," she added apologetically.

They followed the path to Bud's room and stopped at the nurses' station. A male nurse who looked more like a pro linebacker asked for their identification. He did a double take looking at their cuts, bruises and bandages. "What happened to you two?" he asked. "It looks like you should be admitted along with your friend."

Greg gave him a faint smile and replied, "It's all superficial, nothing major. I hear you may have more patients from the Grace explosion. Are any of them here?"

"Not in this pod," the nurse answered. "This is the Intensive Care Unit Pod, we restrict visitors to family members only with the permission of the attending doctor. I see on your pass that you are pastors from the church. Is that right?"

Before Greg could answered, Isaac replied, "Yes, I'm the pastor and Greg is a church elder. We have several more visits to make, could you tell us the room number for Bud Clark please?"

"Sure, Pastor. Mr. Clark is in 1207 on the left side of the hall just behind the nurses' station."

When they entered Bud's room, there were two doctors standing at the end of the bed. They looked up at the pastor and his acolyte with expressions of confusion on their faces. "We aren't permitting any visitors at this time," the shorter of the two said.

"I'm Pastor Isaac Silberman and this is Greg Stone, my acolyte. And who might you be?" asked Isaac, ignoring the doctor's not so subtle suggestion they should leave.

The two doctors looked surprised. "I'm Dr. George Stanley," the taller one replied. "I'm the heart surgeon who removed a bullet from this man's back thirty minutes ago."

The other doctor said, "I'm Dr. Srinavasan, the staff cardiologist. Do you know this man?"

"We're the two men who carried Bud out of the church sanctuary after he'd been shot in the back and just before he was hit by the force of a bomb blast," answered Greg.

Both doctors took a half step back, shocked by Greg's frank description of the attack. Dr. Stanley said, "Your friend should be dead."

"No he shouldn't," replied Isaac in an indignant voice. "That's not a very nice thing to say about Bud."

"What?" The doctor was confused and then realized what he had literally said. "Sorry, I didn't mean he *deserved* to die. His wound was so severe we thought there was no way he could recover from the shooting, let alone the damage done by the explosion."

Dr. Srinavasan added, "It was a miraculous recovery." He paused then added, "Could you tell us exactly what happened? We've been so busy, we haven't had time to find out what happened at the church."

Greg gave them a step by step description of the shootings as if it were an after-action-report. There was a stunned silence for a moment then Dr. Stanley said, "My God! What you just told us reminds me of an old fashioned shoot-out like you see on the vids. Let me tell you what happened to Mr. Clark. By measuring the entry wound we believe a standard 5.56mm NATO round was used. It appeared the bullet hit the right shoulder blade and fragmented with at least a small shard grazing his heart. Except we have several very big problems. There were no exit wounds and we can't find any bullet fragments inside his body. It's like the bullet just dissolved. However, metal bullets don't dissolve."

Dr. Srinavasan added, "There was some evidence of internal bleeding of the heart where it was grazed by the bullet fragment, but a follow up showed the wound had healed over. That never happens, especially not that quickly."

"Then maybe your first impression was correct. It truly was a miracle," said the pastor.

"I'm not a big believer in miracles," said Dr. Stanley. "However, this time it seems like the only believable answer."

Before they left Bud's room, Dr. Stanley informed them Bud would be sedated for at least a few days and they would have someone from the hospital contact them when he was allowed to have visitors.

They left the ICU pod and headed to Pris's room, which turned out to be a twenty minute walk and two elevator rides.

When Greg knocked on the open door, Pris let out with a squeal. "I'm so happy to see you both! I've been worried you were…injured in the shoot-out or in the explosion or both. With all the cuts and bruises I guess you were right in the middle of the battle. Sit down and tell me all about it."

Isaac took Pris's hand and gave it a gentle squeeze, then said, "Let Greg tell the story, he's really the hero. Without him and his secret dart gun we would have all been killed." He sat in a chair next to the bed and gestured for Greg to begin.

He laid it all out, emphasizing how important the Taser-12 was in protecting himself and Isaac. "If you hadn't ordered the weapon for me, none of us would have survived. Unfortunately, the shooter in the balcony shot Bud just before I could get a shot off. Isaac was tending to Bud's wound while I discovered the bomb. We grabbed Bud and carried him up the aisle toward the lobby, but we were a few steps too slow. The bomb blew us through the doorway and onto the lobby floor."

He paused for a moment and glanced at Isaac who turned his head away. "We didn't think Bud would make it, but he managed to survive. We just came from his room in the ICU. The doctors said he was going to be okay. It was going to take a while, but he would be all right. So how are the protheses repairs coming along?" Greg asked.

"They finished those repairs a couple of days ago," Pris answered. "Now they're working on interface issues between my body and the protheses. They are having some problems getting my right arm working correctly. The tech thinks they will have it fixed in a day or two. The leg interface is working fine. I'm still having some issues with the concussion. I get some bad headaches almost every day. They had me on oxy the first couple of days, but they're trying to wean me off them. They don't want me to get addicted. They're want to do another brain scan later today. I just feel tired and dizzy most of the time."

Isaac stood up and moved close to Pris's bed and asked, "How are you feeling right now?"

"Not so hot," Pris replied. "What do you have in mind?"

"Will you permit me to touch your head for a few minutes. I promise not to hurt you."

"I trust you completely, Chaplain" Pris said.

Her head was lying back on the pillow and Isaac leaned forward and placed both hands on her forehead, one on each temple. "Oh, your hands feel so cool," she said in a dreamy voice. "So pleasant. I didn't realize how tight my muscles were. I feel like I'm relaxing now. It feels so good…getting tired now…no pain…sleep now…"

Her eyes fluttered closed as she drifted off to sleep.

Isaac removed his hands from her forehead and turned to Greg. "I think we should let her sleep. We have some other things to deal with back at our apartment. She will be much better tomorrow morning, so will Bud."

They took an Uber/Lyft back to the apartment and entered through the back to avoid any media that might be lurking around the complex's front door. Once inside, the pastor was all business.

"We need to determine who was behind the attack on us and the church and what were their objectives," said Isaac.

"I don't think they were after us," replied Greg. "I think their target was the church. We just happened to be at the wrong place at the wrong time. I mean, we did five services every weekend. That means we had three intermissions between sessions each week. When you count the intermission today that comes to a total of ten intermissions. How many times did we remain in the sanctuary between services?"

"I think today was only once. No, wait. It was twice," replied the pastor.

"You're right it was twice," said Greg. "At the beginning of intermission, the cleaning crews freshen up the sanctuary, but that takes 10 to 15 minutes which leaves 15 to 20 minutes with an empty sanctuary. If we hadn't questioned them it would have taken them less than 10 minutes to plant the bomb under the pulpit. That would have given them plenty of time to exit the sanctuary. And I'm pretty sure the bomb would have gone off while the sanctuary was empty."

"So they weren't trying to kill anyone? The church was the target? That's an excellent working theory, Major Stone," said Isaac. "An alternate theory could be they were going to detonate the bomb during the second service, but because Bud challenged them they set the timer to a minute. The man under the pulpit told his assistant to shoot us. If you hadn't intervened, they would have killed us all and still managed to escape the sanctuary. By the way, how did you know there was a bomb in the case?"

"I got a quick look at the metal case as the two men came down the aisle. I thought the case looked familiar. When I saw the opened case under the pulpit, I recognized it immediately. It's a military grade suitcase bomb. While I was on active duty in the Marines we used a lot of them to blow up enemy structures. A relatively new version of the plastic explosive named Semtex is used in the bomb. It's about twice as strong as C-4 and even stronger then newer C-6. The detonator is solid state and once activated it can't be shut down. I've never heard of any of these bombs being available outside of the services. Maybe the autopsies of the three bombers can shed some light on who they were affiliated with and why they wanted to blow up the church."

"Perhaps the funeral director at Angel of Mercy could help us locate the medical examiner who will be performing the autopsies," suggested Isaac. "Or maybe the police officer you spoke with at the church after the bombing can give you a point of contact. You know, the one who was so chatty about your dart gun."

"I think I have a better idea," replied Greg, ignoring Isaac's jibe about the Taser-12. "I got to know a NCIS ME pretty well during my tour of active duty with the VOG testing. If he's still on active duty, I'm pretty sure he could help." Greg paused, he was a little uncomfortable broaching his next question to Isaac.

Before he could ask, Isaac said, "You want to ask me about my comment regarding our attackers being possessed by Satan's demons, don't you?"

Greg gave him an embarrassed shrug and said, "Yeah, I was wondering if your vision revealed the identity of the bombers and their reason for the attack."

"I apologize for not speaking to you about this sooner," said Isaac. "With the shootings, bombing, taking care of Bud and calling on Pris, I got distracted. The answer to your unspoken question is 'not yet.' When Bud got up to challenge the men, I immediately recognized them as being possessed by demons. Sometime soon I will give you more details on demonic possession, but for now let me tell you what my vision revealed. The demons were in control of the men. No matter how much they resisted, the demons forced the men to act as if they were bombers who wanted to destroy the church and possibly the entire congregation of the second Sabbath service. The three men were in the Marines Reserves. They were spending their annual two weeks of active duty at a local armory. Two of them were demolition experts and the third was a sniper. I assume they had access to the bomb, but we should check it out to make sure."

Greg just stared at Isaac for a long moment. "How could you possibly get all that information on the three men in no more than a minute. Do your special talents include mind reading? Or did you get a burst transmission from God for you to read later?"

"Actually, I received a regular vision while you were telling Pris about what happened at the church," he answered. "I waited to share it with you until now."

"I was joking!" yelled Greg. "It seems like you're getting a lot of visions lately."

The pastor shrugged his shoulders and replied, "When God talks, I listen."

Greg decided to changed topics and asked, "So why would Satan and his demons want to blow up Grace Church?"

"Really! you're going to ask me that question?" asked Isaac with an expression of disbelief. "Because he's Satan! For Heaven's sake, that's the kind of thing Satan and his demons do."

"I know that," retorted Greg. "But why did he choose that particular service to bomb the church?"

There was a long pregnant pause, while Isaac considered Greg's comments. He finally said, "An excellent question, my son. The obvious answer is it was just random chance, but I doubt it. I have a few ideas as to why he picked that day and time for the bombing, but I want to consider my options. As soon as I'm pretty certain, I'll get back to you."

* * *

The local Gilbert police knew that one of the federal alphabet agencies was going to end up working the case. The question was, which one. The Gilbert chief of police was prepared to turn over all the crime scene information, which included a set of badly mangled and charred dog tags. All the military services still issue dog tags to their service men and women, and each service's tags had a distinct look. It took a while to clean up the set of tags; eventually, they were able to identify them as Marine tags. Once that was determined, NCIS got involved immediately.

The director of the NCIS Washington DC office wasted no time in sending out a team to begin their investigation. The working theory was that three men who attempted to blow up the church in Gilbert were members of the Marine Reserves. As reservists they were required to spend two weeks a year on active duty. A Special Agent in Charge and two NCIS special agents along with Greg's ME friend were on a NCIS Gulfstream en route to Phoenix, Sky Harbor Airport within an hour.

Gilbert police detectives met the NCIS agents at Sky Harbor as they deplaned at the executive terminal. As they drove to Gilbert Police HQ, the NCIS agents were given a high-level overview of the attack. They were also told they had two interrogation rooms and three offices made available to them for the duration of their investigation.

Bright and early the next morning, the three agents went over the interrogation list. Marine Major Greg Stone was at the top of the list. They chose the major to be the first interview since he had been involved in the shooting. He was ordered to bring his weapon with him. The pastor was also on the list and both turned up at the temporary NCIS HQ.

Greg was ushered in first while Isaac sat quietly in a chair outside the interview room. Once inside, he turned in this Taser-12 to one of the investigators who in turn handed it off to a weapons expert. He was asked to tell them his side of what happened at the church. He had told his story so often he could pretty much recite it verbatim. The investigators sat quietly until he was through. Then they began their questions.

"Major Stone, one of the EMTs on site at the church said she thought Bud Clark had died from the gunshot wound in his back. She reported she performed CPR on Mr. Clark for several minutes, but was never able to detect a pulse. When your colleague, Pastor Silberman, asked her to recheck his vitals a few minutes later, she found a pulse. Don't you think that's strange?"

"No, not really," answered Greg, then asked, "Special Agent Glenn, have you ever been in combat?"

"Just answer my question, please," Glenn said stiffly.

"I did answer your question. It's your turn to answer mine," repeated Stone, his voice calm. "If you'd ever been in combat with people fighting for their lives you'd see the occasional wounded trooper who you'd swear was dead. They would not be moving, their eyes would be opened, glazed over with a fixed stare. At first the corpsman wouldn't be able to find a pulse, but thank God for their perseverance. They would stay with the wounded Marine until they were absolutely sure they were dead, and even then, they would circle back and check them a few minutes later. Once in a great while, a miracle would happen and they would save the apparently dead Marine. Bud Clark had just been shot in the back by an assault rifle. According to the doctors, they said the bullet grazed his heart. Then, in addition to the gunshot wound, he was hit by the shock wave of the explosion. What he went through was exactly what Marines go through in combat situations. The EMT did her very best, but she was not combat trained. Bud lived because we asked her to check his pulse just one more time."

The room was quiet for a moment, Stone was tired of waiting so asked, "What have you found out about the attack on the church? Why did three Marines destroy a multimillion dollar building, a place of worship? Were they under orders or stoned on drugs or did they just hated churches? Also, how did they get a top secret weapon out of the armory undetected. If you can't answer my questions, I respectfully request a meeting with the Special Agent in Charge. I don't want this type of attack to ever happen again."

Greg was escorted to the SAC's office by Special Agent Glenn who said, "Please take a seat, Major Stone. The SAC will be with you shortly."

True to his word, five minutes later, Special Agent in Charge Ken Blakely stepped into his temporary office. Stone stood and shook the man's hand. He was a little confused by the SAC's demeanor. He expected some push back from the SAC for chewing out his special agents, but that wasn't the case. The SAC had a big grin on his face. "Have a seat please, Colonel. Sorry to keep you waiting."

Greg was even more confused. He didn't want to start off their conversation correcting the SAC. However, he thought it best to make sure he set the record straight. "I'm sorry, but I'm not and never have been a colonel. In fact, I'm no longer a Marine. I resigned my commission as a major over five years ago."

The SAC kept on grinning as he said, "I beg your pardon, looking at your orders, I did make a mistake. I should have addressed you as Lieutenant Colonel Gregory Stone. You may have thought you resigned your commission; however it appears you are still a Marine, previously on inactive reserve duty. A two-star at Quantico gave you a promotion to Lieutenant Colonel and placed you on active duty. You are ordered to be my adjunct Special Agent in Charge and will be charged with leading the investigation of the crimes committed at Grace Community Church in Gilbert, Arizona." The SAC paused to see the new Lieutenant Colonel's reaction. Stone just sat staring at him in stunned silence. The SAC continued, "Your assignment begins immediately. I've been ordered back to the NCIS HQ in DC. The two special agents and the ME will report to you and you will provide me with daily sit reps."

The SAC stood, picked up his go-bag, reached out and shook Stone's hand. "Good luck, Lieutenant Colonel Stone, and remember, once a Marine, always a Marine."

He watched as the SAC closed the door on his way out. Greg stumbled as he moved behind the desk and fell back into the high-back, leather chair. He thought to himself, *Me and my big mouth. What have I gotten myself into this time!?*

CHAPTER 12

BACK IN THE SADDLE, AGAIN

The first thing the new Lieutenant Colonel did was to have special agent Glenn bring Isaac to his office. Greg had the pastor take a seat and he told him all that had happened. The pastor sat quietly, nodding occasionally, his features calm.

When Greg had finished, the pastor asked, "What are you going to do first?"

"Say a prayer I don't mess this up."

Isaac smiled and said, "And then what?"

He waited for a moment then asked, "How can I protect you when I can't be with you all the time?"

"You are, and will remain, my acolyte. However, I don't need your protection. I never did."

"How can you say that?!!" asked Greg, his voice agitated. "If I hadn't saved you in the church, you'd be dead now. So would Bud."

"No, I wouldn't have died," his voice was still calm and soothing. "God is my protector, not you. He promised me I would go to Israel to fulfill whatever he has in store for me. I accept that as God's truth. He would have found some way to ensure I would not have been killed. Don't think for a moment I don't love you. I care about you more than you can possibly know or understand, but we have different tasks ahead of us. For the next couple of weeks, you will lead the investigation and you will discover the answers to all our questions. I will continue to be the chaplain at the Angel of Mercy Assisted Living Complex, having services every afternoon. In addition, I will call on those who are preparing to join our Lord. I plan on visiting Pris and Bud at the hospital until they are released. I will also check on the hospitalized members of Grace Church. Perhaps when you find the time we can get together and share how things are going. So what will be the first thing you will do as the adjunct SAC?"

Greg didn't respond for a moment; he was trying to process everything the pastor said. Then things seemed to snap into place. He looked up at his mentor and said, "First, I'm going to assign my two special agents to visit the armory and speak with the people in charge. They need to get background on the three attackers and anything that might indicate they were planning the attack and why. The next thing would be for them to question the people in charge of the suitcase bombs. When was the last shipment and how was it handled? While they're busy at the armory, I'm going to call on the ME to see the results of the autopsies."

"It sounds like you've got a good plan. I'll leave you to it while I head over to the hospital to visit with Bud and Pris. Perhaps we can compare notes in the evening, assuming you have time. If not, maybe tomorrow." The pastor stood and added, "I look forward to you briefing me sometime soon. And oh, by the way, there's been a halt to the fighting in Israel. A truce has been signed between all parties, just like my vision prophesized."

After the pastor left and Greg recovered from the fact the Israeli war was over, he briefed the two special agents on what he wanted them to find out at the armory. After they left, he headed to the basement of Gilbert Police HQ where the MEs did their work. He looked forward to seeing an old friend again. More important, he really wanted to find out what the autopsies revealed.

"Well, hello there, temporary SAC. Long time no see. Or should I call you Lieutenant Colonel Stone?"

"Just Greg will be fine, Josh," he answered as he grabbed the man in a strong bear hug. "How do you like being an ME for NCIS?"

"It sure beats being a corpsman during the war, although I have to say once your VOG weapon came on line, I didn't have to patch up many of the enemy. I just swept them up in a dust pan. Unfortunately, we didn't kill all of them."

Josh stepped back and got serious. "If it hadn't been for you, I'd never have made it out alive. Even to this day, I still can't believe how you scooped me up and put me over your shoulder while I was bleeding and screaming, then ran all the way to cover. All the while blasting the enemy into dust bunnies as you went. You were a hero to all the grunts that day."

Greg was embarrassed by his friend's praise. "Josh, what I did was reflex. You're the real hero. I just laid down suppressing fire while you patched up half a dozen troops with bullets flying all around you. You were shot three times, three fricking times! You were screaming at me to let you continue to treat our squad. The men you treated wouldn't be alive today without you patching them up. So three purple hearts and a silver star certifies you were the hero."

They both stood quietly for a moment, letting the memories of the atrocities of war fade before Greg asked, "So how did you end up being an ME?"

"I was in medical school when I was drafted by the navy. I'd spent two years in college with a pre-med major. I guess the navy thought I was a good candidate to become a corpsman. They ran me through the Navy Corpsmen Training Program and shipped me off to one of the many combat zones. During my second tour is when you saved my life. After I recovered from the wounds, I got a medical discharge. I used my VA benefits to finish med school. When I graduated, I saw there were openings for a couple of medical examiners. I signed up with NCIS."

"I lost track of you after you were discharged from the navy," said Greg. "When I heard an NCIS team was getting involved in the church bombing, I noticed your name as the ME who would be coming with the special agents. That's when I called you."

He stopped for a minute and Greg seemed hesitant, but asked his question anyway. "If you don't mind me asking, why did you chose a career as an ME instead of a surgeon?"

Josh's smile was sad, but he answered. "When I was a corpsman, every time a man or woman died while I was treating them, I felt like I'd let them down. Listening to their screams of pain just before they bled out... I don't know. It was like I was dying too. As an ME, I don't have to feel that pain anymore. My subjects are already dead."

There was another pause, then Josh said, "That's enough about me. Let me tell you about the three men you're interested in. Cause of death for the two next to the pulpit was the explosion. All that remained of them were multiple body parts. With the help of the police ME we managed to put most of the pieces back together as best we could. However, I estimated about twenty percent of the parts are still missing. They were probably vaporized by the blast or consumed by the fire caused by the explosion. The body of the shooter on the balcony was intact, but he was so charred by fire we couldn't begin to identify him. He had no fingerprints since his fingers were burned off, and no retinal scans since he had no eyes. We weren't able to find any teeth so dental records were worthless. The only thing we recovered from him were the remains of his dog tags and they were nearly illegible. It took several hours to be able to read a portion of the info on the tags. That's how we were able to determine at least one of them was a Marine. The cause of death for the balcony shooter was the fall from the balcony. His neck was broken when his head slammed the into back of one of the pews. Your Taser-12 incapacitated the two near the pulpit and they had no chance of escaping before the bomb exploded. Your non-lethal weapon didn't kill them, hence the name non-lethal. Nice shooting by the way. I'm going to have to get one of those weapons for my own protection."

"So other than the cause of death, is there anything else I should know?" asked Greg.

"Nothing I can think of," replied Josh. "There wasn't much to work with."

Stone's com unit buzzed. It was Special Agent Glenn. "Hey boss, sorry to break up your reunion, but we need to talk right now."

Greg left the morgue and headed back to the temporary SAC office where they met up with the other special agent, Jack Harris. The three of them left for the armory, stopping to pick up Isaac. The two special agents seemed annoyed at the presence of the chaplain, but said nothing. When they arrived at the armory they were joined by Chief Master Sergeant Collins and Captain Grant. They took seats in a small mess hall near the entrance to the armory.

"What have you got for me?" Greg asked. By the looks on the faces of the two special agents, he was pretty sure he wasn't going to like what they had discovered.

"There were nine men who showed up for reserve training at the armory, all from the West Coast," began Special Agent Harris. "Each one had data chips authorizing them to spend two weeks at the armory performing a variety of routine maintenance activities as well as classroom training on various weapons. Apparently, the armory was expecting the men, their sign in was routine and the chief master sergeant assigned them to quarters in the barracks attached to the armory. The lone dog tag discovered at the church matched one of the data chips. They showed up two or three at a time during the same day. That was two days before the attack on the church. All of them were dressed in fatigues and wearing dog tags. Their ranks varied from lance corporal to sergeant.

"The next day, one day before the church bombing, the armory received a shipment they weren't expecting. The chief master sergeant who signed for the crate had it placed in a fenced in holding area until they could figure out what to do with it. He expected it was a snafu shipment, intended for one of the larger armories that had better secured facilities. The shipment had been delivered late in the afternoon. Chief Master Sergeant Collins claimed he couldn't reach anyone to arrange for the crate to be returned or forwarded to the correct armory. Instead, he chose two of the new reservists, gave them assault rifles and had them stand guard over the holding area. The next morning, the morning of the church bombing, all nine of the new reservists were AWOL, including the two who were ordered to stand guard over the crate. In addition, the holding area had been breached and the crate was missing. When the inventory officer checked the paper work, he discovered the missing crate was supposed to have 120 hand grenades. In retrospect, they now believe the crate had several of the new suitcase Semtex bombs, similar to the one used in the church bombing."

"Why did they change their minds about the hand grenades?" asked Greg.

"Each of the Semtex bombs come with special packing and instructions," answered Glenn. "There was a dumpster fire a couple of blocks away from the armory. The fire department believed it was caused by one or more arsonists. While they were sorting through the ashes they came across some special type of wrapping paper that was badly charred. However, one word which could be read was Semtex. The fire department contacted Gilbert PD who in turn contacted the armory to see if they knew anything about a package with Semtex written on it. By the time the armory found out, the church bomb had already been detonated."

"Do you have any good news?" asked Greg.

"Unfortunately no," answered Glenn. "Your turn, Harris."

"The fire department estimated there was enough debris of wrapping material for at least three, maybe four bombs. It looks like there may be other bombings, maybe some time soon."

"Don't forget the nine reservists," interrupted Glenn. "All of them were seasoned combat Marines, some had done multiple tours. When the armory filed AWOL charges with Marine HQ, they bounced the charges. They said all of the nine had perfect records. Four had been awarded a variety of medals for their service. Instead of AWOL charges, HQ wanted NCIS to determine if they were victims of violent crimes. There's video coverage of the barracks showing the two armed guards entering a darkened barracks at 0100 hours. The lights were turned on and the remaining seven were dressed in overalls instead of their uniforms. The two armed men changed out of their uniforms into similar overalls, picked up their weapons and joined the others as they walked out of the barracks, turning off the light."

"Were there other Marines in the barracks beside the nine?" asked Stone.

Harris looked perplexed. "No, the rest of the barracks were empty. Additional reservists were due in the next day."

Stone asked, "Did you see the video or just read the written report?"

Harris replied, "It was the written report generated by the surveillance AI."

Isaac interrupted the flow of the back and forth with his own question. "Can we see the surveillance video of the barracks when the men were leaving?"

Both Glenn and Harris turned toward Stone. They looked annoyed. Glenn asked, "Why is he asking questions? He's not part of this investigation."

Stone glared back at the two special agents and replied, "Think of him as my confidential informant with a top secret clearance."

Glenn grudgingly nodded his head. Stone said, "Play the video."

The chief master sergeant turned a large iPad15 to face Isaac. The others moved so they could also see the screen. He fastforwarded the vid until the two armed guards entered the barracks and turned on the light. All seven of the men were sitting on their bunks at rigid attention wearing dark blue overalls. They all stood and faced the barrack's door and did not move until the two guards had changed clothes and joined the line. As they began to walk out, the audio indicated the men were arguing, not with each other, but with themselves. They also appeared to be physically resisting leaving the barracks. Eventually they all left. The last one out turned out the lights and slammed the door shut.

"What the hell did we just watch?!!! asked Captain Grant. "What was wrong with those men?"

The chief master sergeant shook his head in bewilderment and mumbled to himself, "That's the damnedest thing I've ever seen. Were they on some kind of drugs?"

After a moment of silent contemplation, the pastor stood up and said, "Thank you, Chief Master Sergeant Collins for showing us the video. It was quite informative." He turned toward the others in the mess hall and added, "Unfortunately, I'm not at liberty to share my conclusions at this time."

A day passed since they had viewed the incredible video. No new information was available. Isaac had withdrawn from his rounds at Angel of Mercy. According to him, "I need to meditate on all this."

Stone was returning to the apartment he shared with his mentor when his com beeped. It was a text from Isaac telling him to meet up at Mercy Hospital. Pris was going to be released today and Bud was finally off sedation and able to have visitors.

Greg replied to the pastor's text then wondered if Isaac had a vision and was coming to share it, or was it just a coincidence and was on the way to visit him? Greg mentally shrugged his shoulders. Either way, the acolyte was looking forward to seeing Isaac as well as Pris and Bud.

Isaac was waiting in the lobby of the hospital and suggested they have brunch in the cafeteria while they waited for visiting hours to begin. Isaac was delighted to discover the cafeteria had lox and bagels and chose a dark roast coffee to drink. Greg ordered bacon, eggs and toast with orange juice. He'd missed breakfast and his stomach was telling him it was time to eat. They carried their trays to a table facing the cafeteria entrance with their backs next to the wall.

"It's so good to see you again, Greg, I missed our times together. I know it's only been a few days since you took on the role of SAC. I see you still carry your dart gun."

"When I'm on duty, I'm required to carry a side arm. The dart gun is the lesser of the two evils," replied Greg.

"Are you on duty now?" asked the pastor.

"Technically yes; I'm still on duty. You are a witness and I'm questioning you. Can I ask you some questions regarding your visions? I'm hoping you can help me figure out who our bombers were and what their motives were for the attack. I'd also like to find out if you suspect there will be additional bombings and if the answer is yes, what would be the likely targets? We're pretty sure there could be one or two more bombs unaccounted for." Greg stopped talking and went back to finishing his brunch, waiting to hear the pastor's replies.

The pastor finished his meal and took a last sip of his coffee. He stared intently at his acolyte for a moment before he answered. "I believe I can answer most of your questions. Some of my answers will come from my visions and others from deductive reasoning."

He glanced at his wrist chrono and said, "Visiting hours have begun, would you have time to visit Pris and Bud before I brief you?"

Greg shook his head. "I may be recalled at any minute. The real SAC could be sent back to Arizona at any time. I'd really like to wrap this up as soon as possible. I want to close this out before we leave for Jerusalem."

The pastor stared at his acolyte for a moment, then closed his eyes. Another moment passed and he opened his eyes and smiled. "If I could guarantee you would solve the case before we leave for the Middle East, would you be willing to visit Pris and Bud before I brief you on what I know?"

Without hesitation, Greg answered, "Yes, absolutely yes. Finish your coffee and let's stop at Pris's room first. I'm sure she'll want to see Bud before we leave the hospital."

Pris let out a happy squeal when Isaac and Greg walked into her room. She was sitting on the edge of her bed with a large cloth bag filled with her stuff. She jumped off the bed and grabbed Greg first and gave him a strong hug. It surprised him how affectionate she was in front of the pastor. Then he was equally surprised at how strong she was. He could hardly breathe and his face started to turn red.

"Oh, whoops. I hope I didn't hurt you. They upped the power setting on my protheses. I'm not used to it yet. Did I break anything?" Pris meekly asked.

"Only his masculine pride," interjected the pastor while Greg struggled to catch his breath.

Pris blushed. "Maybe I should have them dial down the power setting on my arm prothesis."

"No way," Greg managed to say. "It might come in handy. You never know."

Pris turned toward Isaac and said, "The doctors were very surprised about how quickly I recovered from my concussion. Ever since you laid your hands on my forehead, the headaches went away and the goose egg on my temple was completely gone when I woke up in the morning. You must have healing hands, pastor. Thank you so much for my recovery."

The pastor seemed embarrassed by Pris's praise. "I'm not responsible for healing you. You were in very good physical condition at the time of the accident. It stands to reason you would recover quickly. All I did was say a prayer that all would be well with you."

Before either Pris or Greg could say more, the pastor said, "Let's go visit Bud now. He was transferred from the ICU pod last evening and I hear he is no longer sedated. We should just drop in for a short visit, then return to Angel of Mercy. Greg and I have some business to take care of once we're home."

The visit with Bud was very brief. Even though he wasn't sedated he was barely conscious. The three of them wished him well and the pastor said a prayer for healing, just as he had done for Pris.

They programmed their Uber/Lyft transport to drop Pris at her condo, just a few blocks from Angel of Mercy. She still wasn't a hundred percent and she admitted she was feeling tired. She wasn't sure if she should stay home one more day before returning to work. Both the pastor and Greg strongly suggested she stay home and get more rest.

Greg had not heard from the general so he assumed he was still the SAC. The two men sat at their apartment's small kitchen table and Isaac began to tell his acolyte what he wanted to know. "Do you remember my first sermon at Grace Community Church where I mentioned something about an invisible war?"

"I think so," Greg replied. "Isn't it about a war between the Archangel Michael and Satan? Wasn't it a war taking place in Heaven?"

"Not exactly," answered Isaac. "That war was when Satan and his demons were cast down to Earth on the first day of creation. This invisible war has existed since that day and will continue until the end of time. From Satan's perspective, he must know he will lose the war. Perhaps he thinks he can live forever if he turns human beings away from God. To accomplish his goal, he uses human beings like chips in a poker game. He wants to show God how weak his creations are, how easy it is for him and his demons to draw humans away from worshiping him. He revels in the creation of atheists who refuse to believe in God, but also in convincing humans there are no such things as angels or demons.

"In my first sermon, I asked how many people believed in Hell. These were people who thought of themselves as true believers and more than half of them didn't believe there is a Hell. Just as many didn't believe there was a fallen angel named Satan. The non-believers thought of Satan as a mythical figure who represents our weakness to give in to temptation. Over a century ago there was a standup comic named Flip Wilson whose favorite line was, 'The Devil made me do it.' He used that as an excuse in his skits when he was caught in some type of fake crime. Of course he used it as a joke. The majority of the viewers thought no sane person would ever believe Satan was a real creature. But in fact, he's real, very real. However, many believers feel they sin because they are weak. And they are, to some extent. But they don't realize Satan and his demons work tirelessly to make sin happen. From the first sins of Adam and Eve, Satan has plotted to show God how weak people really are, what failures they are to God. When given free choice, the vast majority eventually turned away from God. Satan believes he has won victory after victory over our Lord and will continue to win forever.

"Take the story of Noah as a prime example. Everyone on Earth had rejected God, with the exception of Noah, his three sons, and their wives. Everyone else no longer worshiped God or ever believed he existed, they were all evil. So God decided to kill them all and start over. It's been like this down through the ages: Sodom and Gomorrah are other examples. Even to this day, the vast majority do not worship God or even believe God exist. They can't be bothered to study the Bible, they just find scientific excuses to deny him.

"What I've just mentioned is when Satan's demons tempt people into sinning. That has to do with free choice and getting people to not choose to believe in God, or to believe in the wrong gods. A special case of demon control is demonic possession. That's when the demon takes complete control of the individual, usually against their will.

"Throughout the Bible, there are stories of men and women being controlled by demons residing inside them. In many cases, Jesus and his apostles cast out the demons from the possessed persons and they returned to normalcy. However, for the last couple of centuries very few people believe in demonic possession, including most Christians. They think of it as a myth or a fairy tale, even though the Bible clearly describes examples of demonic possession and the exorcism of those demons. For example, in the Gospel of Mark, chapter 5, verses 1 to 13, it is recorded that a man with many demons possessing him was called Legion. The man begged Jesus to rid him of the demons. Jesus exorcised all of the demons and sent them into a herd of pigs which immediately ran off a cliff and died.

"In another example, the Apostle Paul in The Acts of the Apostles, chapter 16, verses 16-34, exorcises a demon from a woman slave.

"However, it should be noted that only Jesus and his Apostles were able to remove demons. In the Acts of the Apostles, chapter 19, verses 13 to 16, a group of Jewish exorcists attempted to drive out a demon. In verse 15 and 16 the demon spoke to the Jews and said, 'I recognize Jesus, and I know about Paul, but who are you? Then the demon overpowered them and they fled from the house, naked and wounded.'

"Moving on to our situation at the church. I was distracted by my conversation with Bud when the two men approached the pulpit. As soon as Bud challenged those two men, I knew they were both possessed. I have no idea how I knew, I just knew.

"When you shot them with your dart gun, I sensed the demons left. Just before the man with the rifle shot Bud, I sensed another demon in the balcony shooter. However it seemed like time slowed down for me. I could feel the thoughts of the shooter. He was terrified. He didn't want to take the shot, but the demon overpowered him and shot Bud. When you returned fire with your dart gun, I detected two very distinct feelings. The instant the dart struck the shooter, the sense of demonic possession disappeared. At the same instance the demon left, there was a feeling of relief from the man. Unfortunately, his body was paralyzed by the dart and he fell over the balcony railing as we were carrying Bud up the aisle. If he hadn't broken his neck from the fall, the explosion and subsequent fire would have killed him."

Greg sat in stunned silence as the pastor stopped speaking. It was a lot to deal with, nothing he'd ever considered or even thought possible. Before he could even think of a question to ask, Isaac continued.

"After we watched the video of the nine reservists in the armory barracks, I'm convinced all nine of those men were demon possessed. You could see them resisting the demons but to no avail. I definitely believe those who are left will try at least one or possibly more bombings. I also believe the targets will be churches that have services on the Sabbath with a substantial number of Jewish Christians in their congregations."

"Why would you think they would retur—" Greg began, but the pastor was on a role.

"I believe shooting the possessed individuals with the dart guns will result in the demons abandoning the human bodies. The paralyzing effect of the darts renders the humans useless to the demons. I also believe I know the time and location of the next target. It will be this coming Sabbath at the Grace Church Complex. Since the bombing at the new sanctuary, they are holding services that are limited to one hour in length at my old, original sanctuary. Because of the limited seating for the smaller sanctuary, they will be doubling up on the number of services. I checked with the scheduling people of the church and requested they hold a service for Jews for Jesus, a Jewish Christian group within the congregation. I volunteered to be the pastor at that service."

"Wait a minute, you what?" exclaimed Greg. "You've got to be kidding. You're setting yourself up as a target? I can't let you take—"

"Please, Greg, let me finish," interrupted Isaac. "I'm almost done."

Greg stopped talking and the pastor began again. "I believe the demons' mission at the new sanctuary was to destroy the church and to kill everyone in it. I checked the names of the three Marines whom the demons possessed. One of them had a Jewish last name and the other two had close Jewish connections. I checked the remaining six and four of the six had Jewish connections. I wasn't able to determine the origins of the other two. I'm confident they were targeted by Satan or by one of his elite demons to hit the church. I may be wrong, but I strongly believe this was done to weaken the bonds between America and Israel. The war has just ended in Israel and America has sent many troops to support the Israeli soldiers. The bond between the two countries is stronger now than it has been in a long time. Satan is looking for a way to weaken the relationship between the US and Israel. The next attack will be a much larger event than the first to determine the effectiveness of this approach.

"I want to supply Satan with a target he can't pass up. I want it to be done in such a way that the Marines with the Jewish names won't be killed. I also wanted to insure none of the Jews for Jesus will die either. That's where you come in."

Greg jumped up and said, "What?! Oh, I see. You want me to save the church and everyone in it, including men with bombs and probably assault rifles. Have you lost your mind?!!!"

Isaac ignored Greg's outburst and said, "It has to be you. I have every confidence you will prevail just as you did the last time."

"Well thanks for nothing. It's not going to be the same. I surprised them the first time. They weren't aware I could fight back, but they will be now. I'm sure I'll be their first target. And I'll have only one lousy dart gun to defend myself."

"I was thinking about asking Pris to help out," said the pastor in a calm voice. "She has a dart gun too, doesn't she?"

Greg just stood there, shocked by the pastor's naiveté. He searched for the right words, but was at a loss. There were no right words. "Pastor," Greg began in a shaky voice, "I'm sorry, but you've never been in combat, you don't underst—"

"What makes you think I've never been in a war?" Isaac interrupted in a sad, soft voice. "In fact, I served two tours in the China War. Once as a combatant and another as a chaplain. I've killed more than my share of the enemy. Now they are considered our friends. I find that so strange."

The pastor's words left Greg speechless. He looked in awe at his mentor and watched as a tear ran down the man's cheek before he turned away.

Greg was mortified that he had challenged his pastor. He finally found his voice and said, "I'm sorry for ever doubting you, Pastor. You should choose someone more qualified to be your acolyte."

"No my son, you will always be my acolyte. I never intended to put the entire burden on you. You see, I've already discussed some of our plans with Pris. Before I finished, she volunteered to help. And one more thing, Pris was able to get me a Wireless Taser-12 and had me qualify with it. Now we have three of us armed with non-lethal weapons."

Greg sat quietly trying to process everything the pastor had said, then one very disturbing thought crossed his mind. "Isaac, how do you know Satan or one of these demons isn't listening in to our conversation?"

The pastor smiled and said, "An excellent question, Greg. I'm pretty sure I have a foolproof approach to keep the devil from finding out our plans. His name is Uriel. I contacted him before I began planning this mission. I asked for his help and he said he would construct a device that would block any mission details. He said to think of it as a thought jammer that prevents specific types of thoughts being accessed by certain types of spirits. That went into effect prior to any thoughts I might have regarding this mission. It extends to everyone who will be involved and will last until the mission ends."

It turned out, Pastor Isaac had been two steps ahead of his acolyte. The first was getting Pris on board. The second step was gathering enough Jews for Jesus volunteers with combat experience.

The current population of the greater Phoenix metropolitan area was a little over eight million people. A significant number of them were either Jewish immigrants or second generation Jews born in America. The pastor sent out requests for volunteers from the various Jews for Jesus groups in the area asking for combat ready warriors for a secret, two-hour mission against the forces of evil in the city of Gilbert.

The next day, three hundred men and women showed up at the Gilbert armory. Some thought it was a gimmick so they left immediately once they found out it was going to involve real combat. Out of the remaining group, Greg and Pris chose a little more than 200 soldiers. The armory was able to supply 150 of the Wireless Taser-12 nonlethal weapons. Training began immediately and ran for two days. It finished up the evening before the planned church service.

While the soldiers went through their training at the armory, Pris, Greg and Isaac gathered together to determine exactly how they were going to handle the demonic controlled Marines. To keep his two special agents busy, Stone assigned them to find out where the Semtex bombs were being hidden.

To help with their assignment, they were given two Semtex sniffers. Of course that wasn't the technical name, but it did describe their function. They were flown in over night from the NCIS Research Lab in DC with a warning not to damage the equipment. They were relatively new and very expensive. A technician hand-delivered them and spent two hours showing the special agents how they operated. The sniffers were about the size of a hand held weapon, but the shape was completely different.

The agents split up. Glenn was beginning his search from the armory. Harris began his search at the dumpster where the Semtex wrapper had been found. Stone told them not to try to recover the bombs, he only wanted them to locate the bomb's positions. He emphasized how much damage the bombs could do if they were inadvertently detonated. Stone told them to com him immediately if they got any leads.

Pris still had some sick leave available and spent at least half a day to keep up to date on their plans. The three of them also visited the shooting range for an hour both days. Greg was mildly surprised at how good a shooter the pastor was. Although he should have realized some combat skills stay with a person for a long time.

The three of them met together in the pastor's apartment with a floor plan of the old sanctuary spread out on the kitchen table. Since the pastor had been involved with the building of the first Grace Community Church 75 years ago, he led the others through the layout of the church details.

"At the front of the church, there are three double-door entrances. All three doors face east. The doors lead to the lobby area which is 100 feet wide by 30 feet deep. There's a women's restroom down a short hallway to the south and a men's restroom to the north. There are some closets next to the men's room where various supplies are stored such as communion elements, Bibles, collection plates for tithes and offerings and gift bags for people who are new to the church. On the other side, there's another closet for folding chairs that are placed in the lobby for overflow people for Christmas and Easter services or for special guest pastors."

He stopped for a moment, his eyes closed as if he were picturing the lobby. When he opened them, he turned toward his acolyte and asked, "Greg, what do you remember of the lobby when we went to visit the old church? I'm sure it was different than when I was a junior pastor there."

The question caught Greg by surprise. "You mean the time you did a mini sermon in Chinese?"

"What!?" exclaimed Pris. "You speak Chinese?"

"Not really," answered Isaac. "I'll explain later. It's not relevant to our current plans." The pastor turned back to Greg and asked again, "What do you remember of the lobby?"

"The thing I remember most about the lobby is the large cross on the lobby's back wall. It wasn't a fancy cross. It looked like it was made out of rough hewn logs. I imagined it was very close to the crosses used to crucify Jesus and the two prisoners. The cross was on the left side of the center doors to the sanctuary. On the right side of the doors were three flags, the American flag, the Arizona State flag and a Christian flag."

Isaac and Greg spent about ten minutes describing as much as they could remember about the church. Pris asked a few questions about the layout.

The pastor waited a moment to see if there were any more questions. There were none. "Okay, so now we have a pretty good idea of the layout of the church, how do we defend it from demonized Marines?"

Stone replied first. "I can't believe they would be dumb enough to try to repeat the approach they used at the mega church. For our service, I understand there will be six of our troops at the entrances and one at each of the emergency exits as well. They will be armed with non-lethal dart guns. No one is getting into the church who is wearing overalls and carrying a metal case."

"How about a demonized Marine dressed in church-going clothes with a Semtex bomb strapped to his body, under a sports coat?" asked Pris.

"Doubtful, but we should place some sniffers above the exterior doors," replied Greg. "No matter how the demons are dressed, or whether they are carrying metal suitcases or not, the sniffers will detect the Semtex and set off an alarm. We should place additional sniffers at the outside of the two emergency exits."

Greg noticed Pris had a pensive expression. "What's up Pris?"

"I know the explosive material in the bomb is the advanced Semtex," she replied. "But what other parts are required for a suitcase bomb?"

"Well," Greg replied, "let's start with the Semtex. Semtex is classified as a plastic explosive, as are C-2, C-4 and C-6. The term 'plastic' can be a little confusing. Think of it as a block of clay which can be formed by hand into any convenient shape desired. All of the plastics mentioned are considered stable. That means you can drop it, throw it against a wall or hit it with a hammer and it won't explode. To explode it requires a blasting cap. The blasting caps I'm familiar with look similar to the metal barrel of a fountain pin. The metal tube is pushed into one of the blocks of Semtex. There are wires that run from the blasting cap to the trigger mechanism which includes a timer. When the timer is set, a countdown begins. When the timer reaches zero, an electric pulse runs down the wires to the blasting cap. The blasting cap explodes with enough energy to detonate the Semtex."

Greg noticed the pastor was also listening intently to his explanation about Semtex. He was a little embarrassed he hadn't gone over the workings of the bombs with him before now.

Before Greg could continue, the pastor asked, "Do the makers of the plastic explosives also build the entire bomb?"

Greg shook his head and said, "Not that I'm aware of. The suitcase bombs the Marines used were made by companies contracted by the Corps. What I remember when I was on active duty developing the VOG weapon, the Marine Corps had contracts with three separate contractors. The

Marines supplied the contractors with precise designs they had to follow. Every time an order was placed and a shipment of bombs received, they would randomly select five percent of the order and take them to a test range for evaluation."

Pris asked, "Does that mean they exploded all the test bombs?"

"Yes, but before the detonations, they tested all of the components which made up each of the bombs. If any of the components failed, the whole order was scrapped without further testing. If they all passed the component testing, they would move on to detonating the bombs. They always took a ton of measurements to determine if all the test explosions made or exceeded the requirements."

"Were there ever any misfires of the suitcase bombs used in combat that you are aware of?" asked Isaac.

"None that I know of," answered Greg. "Everyone I observed were spectacularly efficient in destroying buildings and anyone who was inside."

There was a brief pause while Pris and Isaac considered Greg's tutorial on suitcase bombs.

Isaac was the first to speak. "What are we missing? Do you think we made the church too secure? Maybe once we identify them as demonized Marines, we let them into the church before the service begins, then we drive off the demons with our dart guns and neutralize the bombs."

"That sounds pretty risky to me," said Pris with a little shiver.

"I think we should visit the church and do a walk-around to get a better feel for the facility and how to position ourselves," said Greg.

"I agree," replied the pastor.

A half hour later they were at the church complex. Their Uber/Lyft dropped them off in the back parking lot close to the old church. As they walked from the lot, Isaac stopped as they approached the south side exit door close to the stage. He reached out and grabbed the handle and gave it a hard pull. The door was locked tight. He looked closely at the handle and verified there was no keyhole. It could only be opened from the inside.

They continued on to the front of the church, turned and climbed the four steps to a short landing that ran the full width of the front. The pastor grabbed the handles to one of the side doors and gave them a pull. They were locked tight. The pastor nodded his head in approval.

Greg suggested he check the emergency exit on the other side of the church while they tested the other two front doors. As Greg left, Pris pulled on the handles of the middle doors. She was surprised to find the doors unlocked and nearly lost her balance from the hard pull.

"Can I help you, Miss?" came a voice from the lobby, which startled Pris even more.

Before she could reply, Isaac said in Mandarin, *"Hello Pastor Liu. It's so good to see you again."*

Now Pris was really confused. Isaac seemed to be speaking in an Asian language. She stared at the pastor and then at the stranger in the lobby. Isaac stepped into the lobby and continued to converse with the Asian man. She noticed the man was speaking in a very polite manner, shaking Isaac's hand and smiling at him. It seemed to her that they were very close friends.

Greg came up behind her and said, "Have you met Pastor Liu yet?"

She shook her head as both Isaac and the Asian man turned towards them. Greg introduced Pris. *"Pastor Liu, this is a close friend of ours. Her name is Priscilla."*

Pastor Liu extended his hand and gave it a courteous shake along with a slight bow.

He turned back to Isaac and the two men resumed their conversation in the foreign language.

"I didn't know you two spoke… I'm not sure which Asian language? Japanese maybe?" she asked in low voice, so as not to interfere with the two pastors' conversation.

"It was Mandarin Chinese. I speak only a few phrases," Greg admitted, also in a whisper.

"What did you say to the man when you introduced me?"

"I told the pastor you were a criminal and not to be trusted."

Pris's eye's went wide and her mouth dropped open in astonishment. However, when she saw the grin on Greg's face she realized it was his attempt at teasing. She was embarrassed. "Not funny," she growled and slugged his arm.

The blow was supposed to be a love tap, but Pris had forgotten the extra power she had from her upgraded prosthesis. His knees buckled from the pain of the blow. It knocked him sideways and he began to stumble. Pris quickly reached out and pulled him back to a standing position. "I'm so sorry, Greg. I didn't mean to hit you that hard." She had pulled him close and whispered in his ear, hoping the two pastors had not seen what she had done.

She and Greg turned to look at Isaac. Pastor Liu was nowhere to be seen. Isaac just shook his head and said, "Playtime is over children, we have work to do."

Pris quickly scanned the entire lobby. "What happened to Pastor Liu?" she asked meekly.

"He was just leaving when we came in," answered Isaac. "He was preparing for a Bible study later this evening. He was placing study handouts on several of the pew seats. I asked him if it would be all right for us to familiarize ourselves with the church. I told him I was preaching a sermon two days from now. He told me it wouldn't be a problem. He gave me a key and said to lock up the central door when we leave and return the key to the office when we are through. He also told me the central door was the only one that can be unlocked from the outside. When services are being held, the other two entrance doors must be unlocked from the inside."

The three of them split up and did a very thorough inspection of the lobby and the sanctuary which included the restrooms, closets and extra rooms used for a variety of purposes.

One relatively new addition was the area at the back of the sanctuary next to the wall that separated it from the lobby. It was an elevated platform that housed all types of electronics. There were different vid cams that recorded the services for viewing on YouTube for those who couldn't attend in person. There were numerous microphones which were attached to the pulpit, drop down mics that hung above the bleachers where the choir sang and four additional microphone pickups for the sounds of the band/orchestra. Each mic was attached to a volume control board that looked like something from a recording studio. Last, but not least, there were two large vid monitors, one on each side of the sanctuary, mounted high on either side of the enormous, colorful cross. A tech would be responsible for filling the monitors with the various types of slides used for each service. The slides would include the scriptures used during the sermons as well as the words to hymns sung at the beginning of the services along with announcements.

The old church provided services in many languages so slides were made available for each language. Services were held in Chinese, Japanese, Korean, Cambodian, French, German, Spanish and Russian.

Once they finished the walk-around, Greg suggested they take another approach and determine where a suitcase-sized bomb could be hidden within the church. He went to one of the church's dumpsters and found three empty cardboard boxes about the size of the bomb's suitcase. They spent another hour searching for potential hiding spots but didn't find any reasonable locations.

By the end of the day, they were tired. However, they felt pretty comfortable they'd covered all the possible hiding places.

That night, just before each of them went to bed, the pastor said a prayer requesting a vision regarding the potential attack. Pris and Greg decided to put a note pad by their beds so if anything new occurred to them while they were sleeping they could quickly jot down a note, then go back to sleep.

Just before Greg went to bed, he contacted his two special agents using FaceTime3. "Are you two making any progress?" he asked.

Special Agent Harris went first. "I was at the dumpster this morning. It hadn't been emptied yet and pick up was later this morning. The sniffers worked great. I got really strong signals and was able to determine a path leading away from the dumpster. When the garbage truck showed up, I had them dump the contents on a large tarp I'd brought with me. The driver thought I was kidding until I showed him my creds. After he turned over the dumpster onto the tarp, I said he had to come back at the end of his shift to pick up the tarp and the debris. Three hours later I'd finished my inspection. I couldn't believe how much disgusting stuff is thrown in the trash. I went through three pairs of rubber gloves and half a dozen masks. However, it really paid off. Way at the bottom was stuff the fire hadn't reached. I found enough special Semtex wrapping paper for a total of three bombs, not four. I also found three empty boxes for timer/triggers and another empty box of blasting caps. At the very bottom, I found three badly burned boxes for small metal suit cases as well. I think they put the bombs together at the dumpster site or somewhere close. Early tomorrow, I'll continue to see if I can find where the assembled bombs are located."

It was Glenn's turn. "I followed the Semtex trail using the sniffer. It led me directly from the armory to the dumpster site.

I assisted Harris in his search and also helped him shovel the crap back into the garbage truck. I'll join him tomorrow. I feel pretty sure we're going to find the bombs before they attack again."

Stone congratulated the two special agents for what they discovered and approved their plans for continuing the search. He also reminded them to stay frosty. He didn't want them going all cowboy on this mission and end up at Boot Hill.

Greg woke to the sound of his com unit buzzing. The room was dark and he had to stumble around to find where he'd left it. He saw the dim flashing green light on his dresser, picked up the com unit and touched the receive button. "Stone here," he managed to say in a sleep-slurred voice.

"It's Harris, SAC. Glenn's with me. We've located the bombs. I'm sending you the location. It's an abandoned house. Have to go, I think they've spotted us."

Greg checked his wrist chrono, it read 0350, the middle of a moonless night. He headed for his bed but bumped into the chair next to the bed and sat down clumsily. He waited for Harris's message, hoping to get more detail on what his special agents discovered, then he waited some more. Fifteen minutes later he pushed the Last Text Loc button on his com unit. It gave him a rough location of where the text had come from.

He turned on a table lamp next to his bed, threw on some clothes, strapped on his Taser-12 and opened the bedroom door. The pastor was standing in the doorway, which really startled Greg and he took a quick step back as he automatically reached for his weapon.

"Pastor! I wasn't expecting you—"

"Where do you think you're going at this time of night?" the pastor asked, his voice stern as a father correcting a wayward son.

Greg started to explain, but Isaac cut him off again. "Did you ever stop to think this was a trap? Didn't you tell your men not to go all cowboy and think they were going to make a big arrest of six demon-possessed men with three times the fire power? I know you're still half asleep and feel responsible for your two agents, but I can't let you go out there without backup... a lot of backup."

His acolyte just stood there, without his shoes or socks, and stared blankly at his pastor. After a prolong pause, Greg managed to say, "They're not agents, they're *special* agents and they're my responsibility." He looked down at his bare feet, shook his head, turned and walked back to his bed then sat down. "How did you know I got the call?"

Isaac, dressed in his pajamas with bedroom slippers on his feet, sat down on the chair next to Greg's bed. "I had a vision," he began. "The situation has changed, but the vision was not well defined. What I do know is your men are no longer available to you."

"That's pretty vague, isn't it?

"What part of 'not well defined' do you not understand?" asked a frustrated Isaac. "The only thing I know for sure is I'm the primary target of the demons now, the church and the Jewish Christians are secondary."

"So what do we do? Maybe cancel the service and see what happens?"

"No, I'm not ready to make that decision yet. This is the most complicated vision I've had and I need to meditate on it. In the meantime, you should go back to sleep. It's 4:00 AM. Don't get up until 7:30. You're going to need the rest. Let's meet for breakfast in the cafeteria. See if Pris can join us."

Greg began to protest, but the next thing he remembered was the sound of his alarm going off. He opened his eyes and noticed the sunlight streaming between the drapes. He was still dressed in his clothes with no socks nor shoes. His Taser-12 was lying next to him on his bed in its holster. He grabbed his com unit and contacted Pris.

The three of them met in the cafeteria. Greg felt well rested as Isaac began briefing them on his vision. "I have to admit, the vision I had last night was very challenging to me. My previous visions were always very clear, very specific. This last one was somewhat vague. However, I believe certain parts of this vision were quite clear. Let me share those parts with you first."

He looked at Greg and pursed his lips together before speaking. Greg knew he wasn't going to like what the pastor was going to tell him. "Both your special agents have been compromised. The vision indicated we should not trust either of them. What's not clear is *how* they were compromised. It could mean they are now under the control of demons just like the Marines were, or perhaps the local police caught them skulking around in the middle of the night and are holding them in jail. It could be anything between those two options."

"I can find out if they're in jail as soon as we get done here," said Pris.

"I'd rather you didn't. There was kind of a warning in the vision to just stay away from them," was the pastor's apologetic response. "Let's just leave it at that and move on to the next part of the vision." Isaac searched the faces for clues as to what they were thinking.

"I don't like it, but I see your point," replied Greg. "Let's get to the next part."

The pastor gave a slight nod and said, "The main part of the vision has to do with the attack. The vision confirmed it would be on the next Sabbath at 'the house of God filled with the chosen people.' That last phrase was the exact wording."

Pris asked, "Was the vision only audio or was it a visual vision too?"

Both the pastor and his acolyte smiled at Pris's wording. She blushed and said, "Come on, you know what I mean."

Isaac said, "I'm glad you asked. I should have been more descriptive. A creature, I assumed he was an angel, spoke to me. When he said, 'the house of God filled with the chosen people,' he spread his hands and I clearly saw the original Grace Community Church with men wearing yamakas on their heads as they entered the church. He went on to say the three of us would be involved in 'a time of conflict and chaos,' and we should 'put on the armor of God and make ready the Voice of God.' When the angel said this, a breastplate of metal armor appeared on his chest and a scepter appeared in his right hand. He finished by saying, 'the holy ones will prevail, but some will fall and wailing and grief will abound.'"

When Isaac finished, the three of them sat in silence, trying to get their minds around what was to come. Greg was the first to speak. "It sounds like we are going to be in for a battle and some of the good guys may die. Since it's only some, I take that to mean the church will not be destroyed, but it could be damaged."

Pris added, "I think it means all three of us should be wearing body armor and somebody needs to be packing a VOG in addition to their non-lethal Taser-12. I volunteer to carry the VOG."

Before Greg could object, Isaac said, "Thank you Pris, I believe you would be the best qualified to handle the VOG based on your military experience. Lieutenant Colonel Stone, when we finish up here, could you escort Pris to the armory and see if Captain Grant could loan us three sets of body armor and a couple of VOGs plus whatever else you think we need."

"Yes sir, General Pastor," replied Stone.

"Very humorous, Lieutenant Colonel," said Isaac without a smile. "Let me caution you, the last piece of information the angel gave me was a warning. One of Satan's high ranking demons is leading this attack. These creatures are very ruthless. If they weren't restrained by God and all his angels, the human race would have perished thousands of years ago.

"For some reason known only to God and probably Satan, I have a mission which God has chosen me to accomplish. Satan may or may not know what my mission is, but since God chose me, Satan wants me dead, really dead this time. So I'm his main target. Anyone who stands between me and Satan is just cannon fodder. Destroying the church and killing all the Jewish Christians is just going to be icing on the cake. At the same time, Satan doesn't want this to look like some type of supernatural event. He will give his attack a look of some crazy Marine fanatics, perhaps atheists, who want to destroy Christian churches and anyone who happens to be in them at the time."

Before Greg and Pris left for the armory, Pris had two of the relatively new security staff clear the pastor's residence prior to his entering. One of the guards was placed in the hallway next to the door and the other on the patio near the patio entrance.

While they were on their way to the armory, Greg asked, "When was the last time you fired a VOG?"

"About six months ago," she answered.

Greg looked surprised.

"I'm an Army reservist," Pris added. "Once I got my prostheses functional, I was taken off medical leave and put on reserve status. I spend two weeks every summer on active duty training, just like the nine men who showed up at the armory. Last summer I was at Fort Carson in Colorado and requalified with the VOG."

"What's your rank?" he asked.

"I'm a sergeant and I was a platoon leader at the battle of Vatican City. How about you?" she asked. "When was the last time you fired a VOG?"

"About five years ago," he answered.

"Maybe we can get you requalified at the armory," she said with a smile. "I'm pretty sure that second VOG was intended for you."

They were met at the entrance of the armory by Captain Grant. Greg had put on his fatigue uniform with the silver oak leaves before leaving his apartment. At Greg's suggestion, Pris put on her own fatigue uniform with sergeant strips on the sleeves. Captain Grant came to attention and saluted Stone. The lieutenant colonel returned the salute.

"I have the two VOGs you requested, sir, along with the ear muffs and visors," the captain said. "I included two fully charged magazines. I also have the all the wireless Taser-12s you requested and five Semtex sniffers. What size of body armor to do you need?"

"One small, one large and one extra-large," Stone replied.

Pris asked, "Captain, does your shooting range accommodate the VOGs?"

"Of course, Sergeant. See Gunnery Sergeant Crow at the south end of the building."

The gunnery sergeant welcomed the two Marines to his range. He gave them a quick briefing on safety procedures then assigned them to adjacent shooting galleries. The gunnery sergeant watched them closely to make sure they followed the correct procedures. "Before you begin, I need to tell you the VOGs you have are not the secure models. You just need to place your right hand on the hand grip and hold on for 30 seconds. A blue light will flash and you need to say you name and rank. At that point your weapon is operational. We usually limit these models for training and I would appreciate it if you give them back to me when your mission is over."

They each placed their weapons on the chest-high tray, facing downrange with the power magazine removed. They set the six metal targets downrange at 25 foot intervals and put on their ear muffs. Actually they were more than sound suppressors, they included both a boom mic and audio receivers so they could speak with each other. After their radio check, they slid the clear plastic visors over their eyes.

Both of them turned to face the gunnery sergeant who was wearing his own muffs. "Insert your mags and power up your weapons," he ordered. "When you get the green light on your mag, give me a thumbs up."

Their green lights began blinking and they both turned and gave him the thumbs up sign.

"Fire at will!" he ordered and they both turned and began firing. They could still hear the muted screams of the VOGs as the target disintegrated. The next target was now 50 feet away and they fired again. They continued until the last target which was at 150 feet.

Pris had perfect scores on all six targets. It took Greg two shots to hit the last two targets. He was satisfied he was good enough, but Pris suggested he try the last two targets again. The gunnery sergeant nodded his agreement, then added, "You don't qualify if you don't hit all six targets on the first shots. If you don't qualify, I can't let you take the weapon with you. What will it be Lieutenant Colonel Stone?"

The second time around, he hit each target on the first shot.

They packed up the weapons, the muffs, the visors and the magazines then thanked Gunnery Sergeant Crow for his help. They walked back up to the armory entrance and picked up the duffels with the body armor and thanked Captain Grant. "Good luck to you both and good shooting," he said as he snapped a salute.

Stone returned the salute and said, "We hope so, Captain."

The ride back to Angel of Mercy was a quite one. Each of them seemed lost in thought about the meaning of the pastor's last vision. What did it all mean? It seemed they'd have to figure it out as they went along. They had to be ready for anything.

The Uber/Lyft dropped them off at the entrance and Pris had to quickly change out of her combat fatigues and dress in her work clothes. She made it just in time for the beginning of her shift. Greg manage to get the three duffels onto a transport cart and wheeled it down the hallway to the pastor's apartment.

The first thing he noticed was the lack of a security guard at the apartment door. Greg unlocked the door with his apartment card, pushed the door open with his Taser-12 held at the ready and quickly checked on Isaac. The pastor was lying in bed with his eyes closed. The acolyte could see the rising and falling of his chest as he breathed normally. Greg assumed he was either sleeping or meditating. Checking the door to the patio, Greg saw that it was locked, but there was no security guard on the patio either.

The lack of security really upset him. Since the pastor was the primary target, strict security needed to be in place 24/7. He went into the hall and brought the duffels into the apartment, then sat down and contacted Pris.

"Hi Pris, I need the code for the security company that's supposed to be protecting the pastor."

"Is there a problem?" Pris asked.

"Yeah, a big problem. Both guards are missing."

Pris sounded shocked as she gave him the code.

He began to type in the code when he heard Isaac's voice from his bedroom, "Disconnect, Greg. I dismissed the security guards. I don't need them any longer."

"What the hell do you mean you don't need any security," yelled Greg towards Isaac's bedroom. "You're the prime target, you need—"

"You're correct," interrupted the pastor. "I need security. However, I have already arranged for a much better security service."

"Oh really?" Greg said sarcastically as he swept the room for any type of surveillance hardware. "I don't see any indication that you have *any* protection at all."

"I need you to give me ten more minutes of meditation," requested the pastor. "Then I will fill you in on all the details.

During those ten minutes why don't you take out your Taser-12 and you can provide my protection."

Greg mumbled something unintelligible. He drew his weapon from its holster, clicked off the safety and began scanning the apartment as he watched the timer on his com unit counting down from ten minutes.

Just as the timer chimed that the ten minutes was up, Isaac appeared in the doorway to his bedroom and smiled at Greg. "Thank you for granting me the extra ten minutes," he said with a cheery voice. "I feel I have a much better grasp of my last vision. How was your trip to the armory with Pris?"

Greg really wanted to hear about the new security company, but he knew better than to push it. "It went well. We got all the body armor we need and we both of us qualified with the VOG weapons. Oh, and by the way, I've still not heard back from my two special agents. They could be dead by now."

"Do not worry about them," replied the pastor. "Whatever happens to them is God's will."

He didn't bother with a comeback. Instead he said, "Are you finally ready to share your information about this new security company? You could start with the name of the company. I want to check them out."

"Why don't you have Pris join us?" asked Isaac. "She should be kept informed as well. It will only take a few minutes to explain."

Greg contacted Pris and asked if she could join them for a few minutes in the apartment. She got approval from her boss for a fifteen minute break. She was breathing heavily as she approached the open doorway. Apparently, she had run down the rather long hall. "What's this all about?" she asked as she sat down next to Isaac. Greg closed the door behind her and joined them at the kitchen table.

Isaac smiled warmly as he said, "I no longer need to have security people hovering around me all day and night. I was made aware of another form of security which is superior to any organization I've ever heard of."

"So what's the name of this great security company?" asked Greg sarcastically. "I really want to find out all about them."

The pastor thought for a moment before he answered, then said, "I guess you could call them God Inc. They've been around for a very long time."

Greg was upset. "What are you trying to pull, Isaac? Are you just making up stories so you don't have to put up with people protecting you?"

The pastor's expression turned from a smile to a very stern look. "It's been a long time since I've told a lie. I'm not telling one now. Do you remember me saying to you that God was protecting me?"

Greg was very agitated and his voice became angry as he said, "Yes you did. You told us you couldn't die. You didn't say you would be protected from people who would enjoy the opportunity to inflict unbearable pain on you or smash your hand with a hammer or perhaps cut out your tongue, maybe gouge out your eyes."

Pris put a hand on Greg's arm, her voice was shaky. "That's enough, Greg. Please calm down. You don't have to go into the gory details."

"No Pris," the pastor interrupted. "He's correct. I should have explained this differently." He took a deep breath then said, "While you two were at the armory, I had another vision. This one was crystal clear. God assigned an angel to be my guardian. His name is Uriel and he has been given the assignment of assuring nothing will harm me, not even demonically possessed humans. Nor will he permit Satan or any of his demons to approach me, let alone to injure me. An added bonus is he will protect both of you while we are together."

There was total silence as Pris and Greg sat stunned, starring at the pastor's face. It was obvious they'd like to believe him, but it seemed impossible. Isaac broke the silence and said, "I know how difficult it is to believe what I just said. I made arrangements for you to see Uriel for a few moments. Watch the center of the living room."

The room seem to darken a bit and then a light began to form. It gradually materialized into a creature almost as high as the ceiling. The angel had androgynous features and wore a long white robe tied at the waist with a golden cord. He moved toward them slowly and came to a stop a few feet from them. When he spoke, his voice had a deep, resonant tone. "It is a pleasure for me to reveal myself to you. It will be my great honor to protect you from every type of danger. All three of you will become very important in the time to come. You may not see me again, but I will always be with you until the end of time."

Uriel took two steps backward and his image began to fade until, after a few moments, it disappeared entirely.

If they had been stunned before, it couldn't compare with what they were feeling now. They didn't have any words that could express the awe they felt. Tears were streaming down Pris's cheeks. Greg bowed his head and appeared to be sobbing.

Then they heard Uriel's voice once more, he said, "I'm still here. I will always be with you."

They rose early on the Sabbath, had breakfast in the cafeteria, then ordered an Uber/Lyft transport van. Fifteen minutes later, the auto-drive van pulled up at the entrance to Angel of Mercy Assisted Living Complex. It was early June and the temperature was already in the nineties in Gilbert, Arizona. It would be in the hundreds before the day was through. They knew they had to get started now to get through this challenging day.

They loaded all the duffels into the back of the van, climbed aboard and strapped in. The van didn't move. After a moment, Greg said, "Isaac, you have to tell the van where to go before it will move."

"Oh, you're right, I was lost in thought, sorry." He leaned forward and said, "Grace Community Church in Gilbert, back parking lot, please."

Pris giggled, and said, "Pastor, you don't have to be polite to the van. It's just a machine."

The pastor sighed, and meekly said, "Right again. My mind has been preoccupied with what lies ahead."

"You don't have to worry, Uriel will protect us," she added.

They rode the rest of the way to the church in silence. They arrived at the back parking lot at 10 AM, within easy walking distance to the church. Once the van came to a stop, the doors opened as well as the back hatch. Greg was the first out and did a quick scan of the empty lot before he let the others step out. As the pastor began to get out of the van, Greg leaned toward him and said in a whisper that was loud enough for Pris to hear, "Don't tell the van good bye. It won't be offended."

Pris giggled again, but Isaac just glared at Greg and said nothing.

They all picked up the duffels and headed to the front of the church. To their surprise, Bud was waiting for them. He stood up from his powered wheelchair and smiled broadly. "It's so good to see you all again," he said with a huge smile.

"What are you doing out of the hospital?" asked Greg. "Did they release you already."

He nodded, then replied, "Actually, I snuck out. I told the head nurse I was the only one who had the church keys. I have an orderly here somewhere. I sent him to the office to get the master key for the door locks. Unfortunately, I'll have to return to the hospital as soon as the doors are unlocked. I just wanted to see you all again and thank you. I owe you my life."

"To the contrary," interjected the pastor, "if it hadn't been for you challenging the men with the bomb, we would have all been killed and many others would have died. You're the hero here, not us."

Bud blushed. "Thank you for your kind words, but I still..."

A large, athletic looking man in hospital scrubs came walking up behind Bud and glared as he shook his head. "Mr. Clark! You're not supposed to be standing up. Here are the keys," he said as he handed them to Bud. "Give the keys to the pastor and then it's back you go to the hospital."

Bud sat back down in his wheelchair and the orderly used his remote to turn the chair back toward the parking lot. Bud turned and yelled over his shoulder as the chair took him away, "It was so good to see you. I hope to see you one more time before you leave for Israel."

The pastor walked up the steps to the middle entrance doors to the lobby and unlocked them. Pris held the doors open for Greg to muscle all the duffels inside, all three paused just inside the lobby to scan the area for danger. After seeing Uriel, Greg held no more doubt in his heart, and the feeling of strength and assurance that ran through him as he glanced around assured him even more that his old pastor was blessed and the three of them were doing God's work.

Leaving the duffels in the center of the lobby, Greg and Pris each took Semtex sniffers from one of the duffels and did a thorough inspection of the entire church. They were confident no one had planted any bombs within the church during the night.

As they were doing their bomb search, Isaac carried two of the duffels to the front row of pews. One contained the two VOGs and all the equipment that went with them, the other held their body armor.

The pastor took off his sport coat and shirt then slipped on the large body armor and covered it with his shirt and coat. It was lightweight and he hardly noticed it once he had finished dressing.

Greg and Pris joined the pastor at the front pews and put on their own body armor and covered it with lightweight shirts. Pris took one of the VOGs and slung it behind her on her right side and hid it with a long, black lightweight cover that looked quite stylish. The color matched the black of the VOG and helped to hide the weapon. She placed the muffs in one deep pocket and the visor in the other.

She walked to the left side emergency exit and made sure the door was locked. There was a tall plant close to the exit door which might provide cover from the back of the sanctuary. She would stand behind the plant once the service began.

Greg went to the right side emergency exit and confirmed it was locked. He also slung his VOG on his right. He wore a lightweight gray shirt and a long, loose fitting darker gray jacket that also covered his weapon. Instead of the muffs he opted for high-tech ear buds which canceled the sound of the VOG and permitted communication between himself, Pris, Isaac and all the troops.

Pris and Greg both wore their Wireless Taser-12s on their left side to keep them out of the way of their VOGs. They would cross draw their dart guns with their right hands. Pastor Isaac placed his dart gun on a shelf below the top of the pulpit. He clicked the safety off so he wouldn't forget when the shooting started.

At 10:30 AM, the six men and women selected for guarding the doors showed up at the lobby. Each one was given a dart gun along with several extra magazines of darts. They all had their own body armor on and waited for their instructions.

"You two will be outside next to the two emergency exits," ordered Stone pointing. "The other four will be inside in the lobby. When people start showing up for the service, the three sets of exterior doors will be unlocked and opened. The doors to the sanctuary will also be opened. You," he pointed at the shortest one, "will be standing in front of the wooden cross, as a backup if any problems occur. You others will be stationed at each of the three entry doors. When the troops have entered the sanctuary and the music begins you will lock all of the exterior doors as well as all the doors to the sanctuary. Two of you will be facing toward the exterior doors and the other two will be watching the sanctuary through the windows next to the doors. Are there any questions regarding your orders?"

There were none. Stone continued, "If you need to use the head, do so now. Once our troops begin showing up, you can't leave your posts. There are Semtex sniffers installed in the lobby area. If they detect any Semtex, a klaxon will go off and you need to secure all the doors immediately and prepare for a fire fight. The same goes if you see anyone carrying a small metal suitcase.

"There will also be sniffers outside the two emergency exits. Those doors should remain locked unless we need to empty the sanctuary. At that point the emergency exits will be opened. If you see anyone trying to get back inside and they have a small metal suitcase, take them out."

Stone slowly looked at each one of them and was satisfied they were professionals. They had the look of being combat ready. In closing, Stone added, "Let me make myself very clear. This is not going to be an easy two hours. Get frosty and stay that way until I tell you to stand down. It's time for you to command your posts. Once there, report to me on channel 17A on your com units. They should be secured. One last thing, if you see anything hinky you com me immediately." Several left for the restrooms as Stone walked through the middle doors into the sanctuary and down the aisle to the pulpit.

"Are they ready?" asked Isaac.

"Yes sir, I believe they are," replied Stone. "They've just started to check in with me as they settle into their assigned areas."

They waited. A few minutes later, Stone relayed, "All six are in position and the coms are working fine. How about you, Pastor? Are you ready?"

"Absolutely, Greg. I can't wait for this to begin."

"Really?" Pris sounded surprised. "I always get butterflies just before a gunfight."

Isaac smiled at Pris and said, "I didn't say I wasn't anxious. I just said I was ready."

One of the security team reported, "I've got ten men and women climbing the stairs into the lobby, no metal suitcases."

"Let them through," ordered Stone. "They're probably the choral group. I also expect two techs to show up soon. They will be handling the sound system and the vid screens."

After that there was a steady stream of people, mostly men, but also some women, who walked down the aisles and took seats in the pews. None of them were younger than 18. By 11:00 AM, Pastor Silberman stood and walked up the steps to the pulpit and said, "Let's lock it up. It's time to begin."

Stone relayed the message to the security team and they all reported back, everything looked okay. The exterior doors were shut and locked and the lobby doors to the sanctuary were also locked.

Pastor Isaac Silberman stood and looked out over the small congregation. He smiled broadly and said in Hebrew, *"Happy Sabbath! Thank you all for volunteering today. Let us begin!"*

The pastor looked out at the faces of his audience. They were a strong looking group of men and women. When they were recruited for this mission he and Stone checked their military records. All of them had served in combat, either in the Israel Defense Forces or the US Army or Marines Corps. They were all seasoned veterans.

They had been briefed the day before by Lieutenant Colonel Stone. He'd passed out all of the Wireless Taser-12 dart guns available at the armory with the understanding they would be returned when the mission was completed. Those who did not have weapons were to assist in restraining the enemy until someone with a Taser could stun the demon controlled attackers and drive out the demon. Killing was a last resort, to be used only in self-defense. Stone reminded them the nine Jewish Marines were not the enemy, it was the demons who were controlling them. And they had no idea how to destroy a demon, the best they could do was drive them out.

Several of the unarmed Jews were trained in Krav Maga. They declined the Tasers and one of them had said, "We don't need no stinking Tasers," in a poor attempt at a Spanish accent. The pastor hoped they had enough combat trained soldiers to deal with six demonically possessed Marines carrying two Semtex bombs.

They'd filed into the church not wearing uniforms. Instead they walked down the aisles in casual clothes, some with body armor under their shirts and blouses. They sat in the pews with as much distance between each other as possible. They were focused on the pastor standing behind the pulpit. They occasionally glanced at the man and woman next to the two exit doors near the stage. A few of the troops sitting close to the stage thought they might have caught a glimpse of a VOG.

"How many of you know the meaning of the word *Shalom?*" asked Pastor Isaac, his voice low and rough.

Everyone raised their hands.

"Excellent! *Shalom* is a word with many meanings, but today I want you all to think of it as meaning peace." His voice was becoming deeper and stronger as he went on. "Because for the first time in recent memory there is peace in Israel. Praise God for His blessing!

"Those we will be fighting today would like to destroy this peace, to destroy the chosen people, to wipe us from the face of the Earth. This will be the first of many, many battles. May God grant us a victory today.

"I'd like to begin with our first hymn, actually it's an Israeli folk song written over 200 years ago. The choral group will sing the first verse, then feel free to join in on the next two verses. It's a song of rejoicing, perfect for rejoicing the peace in Israel. It's called *Hava Nagila* which translates in English to Let Us Rejoice."

The choral group stood up in the loft area behind the pulpit. The tech at the back of the room cued up the musical sound track and the intro music began. The choral group went through the first verse and did a pretty good job, considering none of them spoke Hebrew. However, when the second verse began, the voices of the Jewish men and women were much stronger and more powerful. Some of the men spontaneously stepped into the space in front of the pews and began to perform the traditional dance that went with the song. They were cheered on by the rest of the Jewish troops, including Pastor Isaac. When the third verse began, the pastor could wait no longer. He jumped down from the stage and joined in the dance, singing along with the rest of them.

Pris and Stone were overwhelmed by the effect the song had on everyone, even those who didn't speak a word of

Hebrew. It took a while for everyone to get seated after the song ended. The dancers were met with hugs and praises as they returned to their pews.

The pastor climbed the steps to the pulpit and wiped away the sweat from his forehead with a tissue. Pris thought she saw him wipe away a tear or two as well.

Standing at the pulpit, he said, "Now *that* is the right way to praise! I will always remember this moment. Let me catch my breath." He glanced over at Stone who was speaking on his com unit.

His acolyte spoke into the com mic, "Nothing yet."

Turning back to his audience, the pastor announced, "Our second song is to remind us what Christianity is all about. It's titled *Amazing Grace.* It was written by John Newton, a British captain of a ship involved in slave trafficking. Ashamed of the pain and suffering the slaves were put through, he gave up slave trafficking and became a minister. He wrote this song almost 400 years ago and it is still as meaningful today as it was centuries ago. There are 10 verses to the song. We will sing the first, second and last verses with the choral group singing the first. The congregation will then rise and join them in the last two verses. If you are not familiar with the song, the words will be projected on the two big vid screens behind me."

The choral group stood, the tech put up the lyrics and the background music began.

"Amazing grace, how sweet the sound that saved a wretch like me…"

The choral group finished the first verse and everyone stood and began singing the next one when Stone received a com from the security guard outside the left emergency exit.

"A small yellow school bus just pulled up in the back parking lot on my side of the church. It has Gila Springs Indian Reservation written on the side. It's just sitting there. Orders?"

"Standby," replied Stone. He contacted the security guard near the right emergency exit, "Do you have a visual of the school bus too?"

"That's a negative, sir. I think it's too close to the left side of the church for me to see it. If I walk about 50 feet to the back of the church, I would be able to confirm it."

"Go ahead, but return back to your emergency exit quickly," ordered Stone.

A few seconds later, the guard replied, "I confirm the bus. It's just sitting there. Back at the exit door."

"Roger that," Stone replied, then he tapped the ALL button on his com unit. "Go to Alert Status 1. It looks like we may have company,"

Inside the church the singing stopped, but the music kept playing. On the two vid monitors behind the pulpit the lyrics disappeared and large flashing red letters spelled out ALERT STATUS 1. The choral group immediately stopped singing and ran to the music room and locked the door behind them.

Everyone went to their assigned positions and made sure their weapons were active and the safeties were clicked off. Pris and Stone inserted their magazines into their VOGs, powered up their weapons and waited until the blinking green light came on indicating they were ready to fire. They knew the VOGs were a last resort, but they wanted to be prepared for any surprises the demons might try.

"I've got movement in the school bus, the door is open and I see people ready to exit," reported the guard to everyone at the church. "Here they come! I count... I count six men running towards me all in a line and all of them are carrying... carrying metal suitcases and it looks like they all have Glocks."

The other outside guard asked, "CO, do you want me to assist?"

"Negative," ordered Stone. "Remain at your post until otherwise ordered."

The first guard came back on the com. "They're running right by me, like they don't even see me… no! they see me, but they keep on running… they're shouting at me… they want me to kill them! This is nuts, what should I do?"

"DO NOT! I REPEAT, DO NOT KILL THEM," shouted Stone. "If they attack you, you are cleared to stun them."

"They're running right by me… they're at the front of the church now. I've lost contact… No wait, I see three more men leaving the school bus. Two are wearing civvies, the other one in Marine fatigues… each of the ones in civvies are carrying a metal suitcase… one is heading to the right side… the other two are heading towards me…t hey pulled their weapons…"

"This is the lobby, all six men in dark blue overalls are at the exterior doors. They split up, two to each door. They tried the locked doors… it looks like they have breaching tools."

"Shoot them with darts as soon as you have a clear shot. Don't wait!" ordered Stone.

Stone switched his channel to the left exit. "Status check."

At first there was only static, then he heard a shrill scream. "It's got me. I shot the bastard with the dart gun and the man dressed in Marine fatigues with gunnery sergeant stripes fell to the ground twitching. Before I could get to the man in the civvies, the demon left the downed man and took control of me. He doesn't want me talking to you… he's shutting down my voi—" his voice made a strangled squeak, then nothing more.

"Lobby is under attack," shouted the guard. "We dart gunned them through the broken windows in the doors, but as soon as we did, the demons took over the guards who shot them… I'm the last…"

Once the demon guards had neutralized the four Jewish lobby troops, the demons dropped their metal suitcases, drew their Glocks and headed toward the three sanctuary doors. Stone was pretty sure they were carrying the Glock-22. Those were one of the standard sidearms for the Marines. They probably stopped at the armory to pick them up before driving to the church.

"Has anyone heard a klaxon?" shouted the pastor as the doors to the sanctuary burst open.

"Negative, nothing through the front doors," yelled Stone. "It had to be a fake to draw us away to the front of the sanctuary. The metal suitcases were all empty. No bombs through the front so they have to be coming through the side exits."

The first order of business was to disarm the demon controlled Glock shooters. The Krav Maga troops were instrumental in disarming the demons as they entered the sanctuary. As they passed through the doorways with gun hands extended, the KM troops grabbed the guns and twisted them out of the hosts' hand before they could get only a few shots off. The demon hosts couldn't react fast enough because the guns were thrown as far away from the demons as possible and before the demons could determine where the guns went, they were captured. Other people stripped the guns down into parts and scattered them throughout the church so any body-jumping demons wouldn't be able to use them.

There were only six demons armed with guns coming from the lobby now. The other three were outside, waiting to get in.

Fortunately, the KM troops were fast enough to take all six guns away. Two of the troops were shot, but not fatally.

The sanctuary looked like a grade B western movie set. Everybody was shooting everybody and nobody died. However, once a demon's host was shot with a dart they were out of commission for at least fifteen minutes. It looked like there were six demons against a little over 200 of the Jewish soldiers.

The fighting was intense, but the demons were making steady progress, even after all six of the Glocks were out of the picture. Slowly, very slowly, the demon controlled Marines continued to push forward as the demons bounced from one host to another, leaving the stunned hosts shaking on the pews and the church floor. As they reached the front row of pews, they broke into two groups of three and made a rush toward the two emergency exit doors. If the demons could get the emergency exit doors opened, the demon possessed person waiting outside would be able to get the bombs into the sanctuary and detonate them. If only one side was opened it would be enough to kill everyone inside and destroy the entire church.

The six demons selected the largest, strongest Jewish men available and took control of them. All six of them looked the size of defensive linemen on a pro football team. Somehow the demons had discovered a way to shield the behemoths from the effect of the stun darts. Each group of three began moving steadily toward the exit doors.

Stone, Pris and Isaac were protected from stray darts by their body armor and being on the stage they were pretty much out of the line of fire. However, with the two teams of demon controlled Jewish men moving steadily towards the emergency exits, it was time to intervene. Stone and Pris moved to opposite sides of the stage and began firing darts from their own Tasers at the respective teams to shut the big men down. They quickly discovered they had no effect and they both quickly moved to plan B.

After Pris's sixth dart hit home, and the three-man team on her side continued to push away anyone who tried to stop them, Pris swung her VOG around to a firing position and screamed for everyone to get clear of the door. No one seemed to hear her, so she fired a warning shot into the ceiling. That got their attention, but before she could aim the weapon at the real target, a demon possessed her.

Her prostheses continued to function and she managed to fight back, resisting the demon's control. However, it was a losing battle. She fought against the demon's power, but the VOG started to move upward toward the emergency exit. "Shoot me!" she shrieked. "For God's sake, shoot me now or we'll all be dead."

She knew if the demon who was controlling her made her shoot the door, the demon waiting outside the exit would crash through the pile of door dust and immediately detonate the bomb. She screamed again as a dozen darts hit her. They hit her all over her body, some on her body armor, but more on her arms and legs. She was vaguely aware the pastor had shot her twice. For some unknown reason, the darts had no effect on her. Somehow the demon who controlled her had blocked the effect of the darts

Both teams of defensive linemen suddenly collapsed onto the floor less than six feet from the exit as the demons deserted them. That left a clear shot at the emergency exit door. The barrel of Pris's VOG continued to move upward inch by inch.

"Kill me, Stone. I can't stop this. Use the VOG or this will all be for nothing. Please, kill me," she cried.

There were tears in Stone's eyes as he brought the VOG up to the shooting position and pulled the trigger.

* * *

For an instant, everything went dark. Slowly, it began to get lighter, Pris, Stone and Isaac heard a deep familiar voice. It was unmistakably Uriel's voice, "Why were you so frightened? I told you no harm would come to you. Have you lost faith in me so quickly?"

The pastor spoke up, the others were too stunned too speak, "It wouldn't hurt if you were a little quicker."

Uriel didn't reply at first and as the light got brighter, they became aware he hadn't materialized, but they could clearly hear his voice. Pris was checking to see where he might be when she noticed something odd. "Wait a minute. Nothing is moving. What did you do?"

"The easiest way to describe this phenomena is to say I froze time. By the way, don't walk through the VOG beam. It could hurt you."

Pris looked toward the left exit door and saw herself with her own VOG almost pointing in the direction of the door. She turned quickly to the other side of the stage to see Stone firing his VOG at her. The sonic beam seemed to be frozen half way from his weapon to her body. In the middle of the stage, standing behind the pulpit was the pastor holding both his hands up to signal Stone from firing.

"This is too much," she whimpered as her legs began to buckle. Stone managed to grab her before she fainted.

She was mumbling something, then they could make out her saying, "This can't be real. I can't be in two places at the same time. Maybe I'm dead and this is my spirit. How could this be real?"

Uriel whispered something in an unfamiliar language to Pris and she seemed to be back to normal.

"Do you remember the Bible verse which says God's ways are not the ways of man?" asked Uriel.

They all nodded.

"This is one of those times," said the angel. "I've shown you this so it won't be so disorienting when we reset the last few seconds. Did you notice your dart guns appeared to stop working?"

"Yes," answered Stone. "What happened to them? I can't believe they all stopped working at the same time."

"They did stop working, but it was not due to a flaw in the weapons. You see, a very high ranking demon who has more…abilities than the average demon, manipulated the dart guns which permitted one of the six demons to take control of Pris. To correct that, I have to briefly rewind time. As to why I waited before stopping time, it was necessary to wait until the last possible second to minimize the changes in the time flow I would have to make. First, I needed to… lock out the super demon."

He paused for a moment then added, "I hope you understand the words I use to describe what is happening are symbols of what's *really* happening. Once the super demon is removed, I can rewind time and the dart guns will work correctly. The six behemoths will be shot with the darts and they will cease their push toward the exit doors. When the demon merges with Pris, you will be stunned by the darts you requested. The demon will abandon you and Lieutenant Colonel Stone will fire his VOG at the exit door, disintegrating it. One of the demon hosts will quickly throw in the suitcase bomb with the time set for 10 seconds, then quickly step to the side. Stone will fire a second blast from his VOG vaporizing the bomb. He will quickly fire his weapon on the opposite exit door with the same results. The remaining demons will sense the presence of an angel. Me. They will sense I was protecting the three of you. With the bombs being vaporized by Stone's VOG, the demons will realize they are defeated and will attempt to… disappear. I will make sure they are restricted."

"How can you be so sure it will happen just as you described it?" asked Isaac.

"Because it already happened. When I shut down this vision, everything will be *exactly* as I described it. Unfortunately, you will remember little of what you just experienced, but you will be content with the outcome."

He waited for a moment, then added, "This vision is ending now. Have faith that I will always protect you."

* * *

The battle ended, but the Invisible War was becoming slightly more visible. The Jewish service ended early and those who were able, quickly cleaned up the sanctuary as best they could. They also recovered most of the parts of the Glock pistols, however one pistol was not found.

The two special agents along with Gunnery Sergeant Crow from the armory were discovered outside the emergency exits. Fortunately, they were out of the line of fire or they would have become dust piles. They had suffered concussions from the VOG blasts and would have only vague memories of the last night and day. All that remained of the doors and the bombs were piles of dust.

The three sets of front exterior doors were severely damaged. The Jews for Jesus organization apologized for the damage to the church and indicated they would replace all the doors in time for Sunday services. When questioned about the damage, they said they got carried away and out of control when they celebrated the end of the war in Israel. One of the Jewish attendees said, "Taking part in the singing and dancing to *Hava Nagila* really got my juices flowing," then he sheepishly added, "I think I lost my Glock somewhere in the sanctuary. I'd like to get it back."

By 12:30 Pastor Chen Liu was welcoming the Chinese Christians to the service. As they walked down the aisles to the pews, they heard the recorded voice of Harry Belafonte singing *Hava Nagila,* the one who made it a world-wide hit. A few of the older Chinese recognized the song and sang along with Harry as they found their pews. With the church doors missing, it turned out to be an open-air service.

The next few days were for recovery. They gathered at the armory to return the borrowed equipment. All of the dart guns, VOGs, Glocks and body armor were cleaned, serviced and accounted for before being stored in the appropriate areas.

Once that was accomplished, there was an After Action Report to be written. Actually it was more like a subdued party, hosted by Lieutenant Colonel Gregory Stone with the assistance of Pastor Isaac Silberman and Sergeant Priscilla Wright.

There were lots of aches and pains to be attended to as well as a few cases of severe injuries. A medical team from Mercy Hospital treated all the injured. It was a miracle no one was killed. Before the AAR could be approved and released to the bosses at NCIS, Stone asked for volunteers to speak one-on-one with the three of them. They were looking for specific answers to a single question: What is it like to be possessed by a demon, or in some cases, possessed by multiple demons, one after another?

Before the three began their interviews, Pris and Greg wanted to meet privately with the pastor. Pris was the first to volunteer. Stone was never demonized, but asked for a session with the pastor anyway. His issue was the guilt he felt for almost killing Pris. He was torn between the old adage *the mission always comes first* and the thought he was ready to kill Pris, someone he had become very fond of.

Pris met with the pastor in one of the armory's breakout rooms. They sat facing each other. The pastor spoke first. "Pris, I want you to know this conversation is between you and me." His voice was soft and calm and Pris thought it seemed like the way her dad spoke to her many years ago when she was seriously troubled about something. "You may speak freely and nothing we say will be shared with anyone else. Tell me what you're feeling now."

"I feel so confused," she manage to say, her voice barely a whisper. "I felt totally in control during the battle, right up to the moment the dart guns stopped working. My first reaction was that this can't be happening. Then the demon took possession of me and I totally lost all control of my body. It was like the demon could make me do anything it wanted no matter how much I tried to resist it. All I could do was speak, scream actually. I realized the only way we were going to prevail was if someone killed me. I knew it had to be Greg. There was no other way. It was the most terrifying moment of my life."

She stopped speaking as she began to tremble and tears streamed down her face. The pastor reached out and placed a reassuring hand on her shoulder. She was surprised how much his touch calmed her.

"Then Uriel appeared," she began again. "I think that was a bigger shock than when the demon controlled me. As much as I believed in angels and demons, I was not emotionally prepared to accept what was happening to me. Uriel said something to me in a language I didn't understand. I wasn't sure what it was, maybe some kind of vocal potion which took me back to some semblance of reality. But it was so unreal at the same time."

She stopped again and looked pleadingly at the pastor. "Pastor Isaac, I need something to help me through this, but I have no idea what it might be." She slid out of her chair and kneeled in front of the pastor and begged, "Please... please help me!"

The pastor reached down and placed his right hand gently on the woman's head. He began speaking, but not in English. She thought it might be Hebrew but it also reminded her of when Uriel spoke to her. She realized the pastor was chanting, it was almost lyrical but then she began to feel as if a weight was being lifted off her shoulders. When he stopped his chant, there was restful silence that swept over her. She opened her eyes, she didn't remember closing them, and smiled up to the pastor.

He smiled back and said, "You are very important to me, Pris. You will be joining Greg and me traveling to Jerusalem a week from now. God has plans for you, important plans. However, once we are done with our interviews and our AAR is completed later today, I want you to retire to your condo and rest. Remember, Uriel will be protecting you. You will not fear anything."

When Pris left the room, she smiled at Greg. He had been waiting outside for her to finish her session with the pastor. As he walked passed her, she touched his hand briefly and said, "Don't worry Greg, everything is going to be all right between us."

Greg paused a beat, he had a surprised look on his face then he nodded and gave her a brief smile. He entered the room and the pastor closed the door behind him. Pris headed out into the large central bay of the armory and began her interviews.

Greg sat in the same chair that Pris had occupied. He looked pensive, unsure of himself, a very unusual expression for him. As the pastor walked by Greg, Isaac reached out, gave his shoulder a brief squeeze then sat down.

"What would you like to talk about Greg?"

"I was not prepared for today," he replied with a tremble in this voice. "I thought our planning had covered all the bases. It turns out I had no clue what was going to happen."

"No one was killed," said the pastor. "Your planning couldn't have been too bad."

"I thought I had prepared for every contingency," he said as if he hadn't heard Isaac's comment. "If Uriel hadn't saved us, we'd all have been killed and the church destroyed."

He paused, but the pastor said nothing. "I was within a hair's width of killing Pris. Do you realize how that made me feel? I don't think I could live with myself if I'd killed her. I told her once I wasn't going to do any more killing. I was supposed to be done with that… forever. I saw you try to stop me from firing the VOG, but I felt I had no choice. It never dawned on me Uriel would save us all."

He was sobbing now and the pastor waited for him to regain control. When he had, Isaac asked him, "Do you remember when I introduced you to Uriel and he told us he would protect you, keep you from being killed no matter what the situation was? Did you not believe him?"

"I kind of believed him." The sobbing had stopped and Greg answered sheepishly, "But when things went sideways and I didn't see him stepping in to protect us, I felt I had no choice but to act."

"And if you could do it all over again, what would you do now?"

"Have more faith in Uriel protecting us," Greg answered firmly.

"One last question. Do you think Pris hates you now for trying to shoot her? Remember, she was begging you to kill her."

Greg considered the pastor's question for a moment then answered, "She smiled at me as I was walking in. I don't think she hates me, but I never want to be in that situation again."

Isaac nodded, then said, "Pris is a long way from hating you. She's going to be joining us in Jerusalem."

Greg looked surprised, then smiled. "I'm really glad she'll be with us."

* * *

The armory had a huge open bay, about the size of a football field with offices and storage rooms along one side. Tables were set up to accommodate all the troops who had participated in the battle. There was a serving line and most of the 200 plus troops were moving through the line, filling their trays with wide varieties of food. As they ate and talked about the fire fight, those who volunteered to speak briefly about being possessed by demons were called into one of three rooms.

Most of those who did not volunteer were so badly traumatized they reported they had no memory of the experience. Others were terrorized and wished they hadn't experienced demon contact at all. Some broke down as they attempted to describe the total lack of control they had once the demons took possession of their bodies. A few, as they relived the experience, were so terrified they had to be sedated.

It took less than an hour to finish hearing the comments of a little less than a 100 troops. Once they were done, Lieutenant Colonel Stone made closing comments to the entire room. "Ladies and gentlemen, we had a victory today, an incredibly important victory. To the best of my knowledge, what you experienced today was unique. Without you, all of you, we would not have won the battle. I hope and pray there will never be another battle like it."

He paused and looked at the battle weary troops, then added, "I need to remind you of one very important fact: You cannot share anything about this battle, especially anything that includes demonic possession. The population is not ready to deal with it, so you can't tell your loved ones, your friends or especially any reporters. If you post anything on social media you will be arrested and placed in prison. This has to be a secret, at least for the foreseeable future. To encourage you to keep that secret, each of you will receive an incentive package of $10,000. The source of this funding is also a secret. See Captain Grant on your way out today to receive an envelope."

"That's all I have to say, except this: If we ever go to war again, I want to fight alongside each and every one of you. Captain Grant?"

The captain stood at ridged attention and shouted in this best officer voice, "Atten…hut!!!... Salute!"

There were crisp salutes from every trooper. When the hands came down, Lieutenant Colonel Stone ordered, "Dismissed!"

After the Jewish troops left the armory, Stone met with the two special agents, Harris and Glenn. Pris and the pastor also sat in, but they let Stone ask all the questions.

"So tell me what happened," said Stone. "The last I heard from you was in the middle of the night. You said you'd located the bombs, but you thought the demonized Marines were on to you, is that correct?"

"Yes, SAC," Harris answered somewhat sheepishly. "As soon as I said that, those damned demons were on us. I couldn't even punch the End button on my phone and I couldn't speak until one of the demon hosts shut off my phone. I had no idea how powerful they were. I couldn't move, not a muscle. How about you, Glenn? Could you move?"

"Same for me," answered Glenn. "For me, the worst part was having one of the demons materialize right in front of me. I think it may have been one of the demons from the mega church attack. When you shot the three hosts, the demons bugged out and they hadn't taken any new hosts until we showed up. One of them materialized just before it took me for its host. It was the scariest thing I'd ever seen, a nasty, ugly creature eight or nine feet tall. It had to walk bent over in the abandoned house they commandeered."

"How did you feel when it joined with you?" asked Stone.

"It felt freezing cold," interrupted Harris. "I could feel the cold move through me as it took complete control of my body.

My brain worked fine and I could still speak, at least a little bit. I had a friend who had ALS. As the disease ate at him, he continued to gradually lose control of all body functions, but his brain remained completely intact. It was terrible to watch and it finally killed him. With the demon it took me about five seconds to lose complete control. It was the worst feeling I ever had. Oh, I saw my own demon materialize too. It was big, just like Glenn's demon but it was transparent. I could see right through it which really freaked me out."

"What happened when the demons left you?" Stone asked them.

"I wasn't shot by the dart gun, neither was Harris," Glen answered. "I think it would have been easier if we were. When we talked with the Jewish troops who had been shot by the dart guns, it was like they'd been knocked out. When they woke up, their demon was gone. They were groggy and disoriented, but not feeling any pain."

"Yeah," interrupted Harris. "When my demon left me it was like my body was being ripped apart. I felt this terrible pain, then a hot flash and then I blanked out. When I regained consciousness, I hurt all over for several hours."

There was a pause, then Stone looked towards Pris and the pastor and asked, "Any questions you'd like to ask of the two special agents?"

There were no more questions for the special agents. However, the pastor asked Stone, "When you write your After Action Report, do you plan on including the demons and the part Uriel played in saving us all?"

"Absolutely not!" he replied emphatically. "The NCIS big wigs would think we were crazy. I don't plan on mentioning the Jewish troops either. I will do my best to be as vague as possible without outright lying to them."

He looked towards the two special agents and then back at the pastor. "I will recommend Glenn and Harris are awarded Citations of Valor for their role in finding out where the Semtex bombs were being stored and warning us of the incipient battle."

Glenn and Harris looked up in total surprise at Stone's mention of awards. They looked at each other, wide smiles forming on their faces. Glenn said, "Thank you SAC. I'm not sure we deserve this, but we really appreciate it. We both promise the word demon will never again be mentioned by either of us."

NCIS After Action Report
Submitted by
Lieutenant Colonel Gregory Stone
Temporary Special Agent in Charge
Submitted 3 June 2101
This NCIS Report is classified Top Secret

Nine Marines reservists on active duty at the Armory in Gilbert, Arizona, were involved in attacks on two separate church facilities located at the Grace Community Church Complex. The first attack came on Saturday, 22 May 2101, on the larger of the two churches.

Two services were held at that church on Saturdays and the attack occurred during a thirty minute break between services. Three unidentified attackers destroyed the church by a Semtex bomb. Three of the Marines who were present at the church were killed in the explosion as they attempted to apprehend the bombers. Several of the civilians who were still in the lobby when the bomb exploded were severely injured. One of the church employees was shot in the back by a sniper who was supporting the bombers. The bodies of the bombers were never recovered. Either they managed to escape or were consumed by the fire caused by the explosion.

The second bombing occurred the following Saturday on 29 May 2101. The attack was carried out by nine individuals on a smaller church also located at the Grace Community Church Complex. The smaller, older church was used primarily by church members who spoke foreign languages. This attack began after a Jewish Christian service had begun. Six of the attackers were armed with Glock-22 sidearms and entered through the lobby.

The six Marines who survived the first church attack were present at the second attack, along with two NCIS special agents and a gunnery sergeant from the armory. They all fought bravely against the attackers as did many of the Jewish Christians. Many of them sustained injuries as they fought the attackers in hand-to-hand combat, slowing the advance of the attackers.

There were three additional attackers who attempted to gain entrance through the two emergency exits. It turned out these attackers possessed two Semtex bombs and were waiting for their cohorts to open the side exit doors. If they had succeeded, they would have placed the bombs inside the church then detonated them. We believe their goal was to kill everyone inside the church and completely destroy the facility.

Fortunately, Marine Lieutenant Colonel Gregory Stone and Sergeant Priscilla Wright, acting as part of the security team used their VOG weapons to vaporize the two Semtex bombs before they could be detonated. Due to the quick thinking of the NCIS SAC, no one was killed in the attack and the church experienced minimum damage. There were minor shootings which wounded two of the Jewish Christians. The damage to the church was minimal allowing the next service to be held as originally scheduled.

Although none of the attackers were captured, it is believed they may have made their escape in a small school bus belonging to the Gila River Indian Reservation.

After a rigorous search of the church complex using advanced technology Semtex sniffers, no additional bombs were detected. However, it is recommended private security be put in place to guard against further attacks at the complex.

The next two days were for recovery. Pris and Greg spent most of the time sleeping, napping and visiting the physical therapists at the Angel of Mercy facility. Pris needed the most attention. She was beaten up both physically and emotionally. It was going to take a while to get over being possessed by demons. Greg had his own emotional trauma, but on a scale of 1 to 10, his issues were a 5 and Pris's were more like 11.

Pastor Isaac seemed not to have any lingering issues. Perhaps one of his visions revealed the outcome of the demon battle, or maybe his faith in Uriel's promise of protection was so strong he knew he would not be harmed. In retrospect, Greg wondered why none of the demons attempted to take control of the pastor. Perhaps the demons realized it was a waste of their time to approach a human protected by an angel.

Whatever the reason, Pastor Isaac's rating on the trauma scale was more like a 2. After a good night's sleep, he put it all behind him and began planning for their trip to the Holy Land. A day later, he had their trip all planned out. They met in the pastor's apartment after lunch, three days before their departure.

"Come in, you two," said the pastor, a note of happiness in his voice. "It's been too long since we've had the chance to get together. How are the therapy treatments going?"

Pris replied first. "I feel much better, Isaac. It seems like I've slept too much and too often, but I feel so much better. The physical therapy has really helped too."

"Any problems with your prostheses while you were under the control of the demon?" the pastor asked.

"No, not really," answered Pris. "I think that was more mental than physical. How are you holding up?"

"Tip top!" answered Isaac with a smile. "I just finished 100 pushups and 100 sit-ups right here in my living room."

"Really?" exclaimed Pris.

"Isn't it sin to tell a lie?" teased Greg.

"That wasn't a lie, more like a fib," laughed the pastor. "Truthfully, I did 20 pushups and 30 sit-ups. Not bad for an old man who just recently passed his 100th birthday."

"Except you have the body of a man half that old," injected Greg.

The pastor turned his head toward Greg and gave him a pretend glare. "Aren't acolytes supposed to support their masters, not give away their secrets?"

"My apologies, Master Isaac, I misspoke," replied Greg with feigned humility.

The pastor began to chuckle at Greg's theatrics and Pris joined in.

"Enough of the comedy hour," said Isaac. "How are you feeling Greg? Judging by your antics, I'd say you were feeling well."

"You're right. In addition, I'm no longer the temporary NCIS SAC. I'm still a Marine lieutenant colonel, but no longer on active duty. My official status is inactive reserves. I'm back to normal and anxious to see what you have planned for us," he replied.

"And I'm anxious to share with you, have a seat. Here's our itinerary. Tomorrow morning we will travel to the Phoenix Maglev Station and board a train to Denver. Have either of you been on a Maglev train?"

Both of them nodded their heads and Greg said, "I think both of us have been on Maglev trains several times. Have you ever been on one?"

The pastor shook his head. "No, this will be my first time. I'm looking forward to it. I remember the last time I drove from the Phoenix area to Denver to attend a seminar. Traveling in the express fast lane at 100 mph it still took us eight hours to make the trip. We'll do it in two hours on the Maglev."

"Why are we going to Denver?" asked Greg. "Why can't we just board a plane at Phoenix Sky Harbor? The new supersonic airliners can get us to Israel in eight hours."

"Because we aren't going by a commercial supersonic airliner," replied the pastor with a grin. "Were going on a sub-orbital rocket. That gets us to the Middle East in just two hours and Denver has the only sub-orbital launch facility in Western America."

For a moment, Pris and Greg were speechless. Then she looked at Greg and shook her head. Turning back to the pastor she said, "Pastor, I've been on military sub-orb flights during the wars, twice in fact, and they are not fun to ride in. When they launch, they pull 5 Gs. Greg weighs about 200 pounds. At 5 Gs he would weigh 1,000 pounds. He remains at that weight for at least 15 minutes during climb out to the fringe of outer space traveling at 15,000 knots. About half the troops passed out and a few died from the stress and these men and women were in their early 20s. During the wars, we lost several vehicles. Many soldiers and marines died just getting to the war zones."

She paused for a moment before continuing. "In spite of your desire to get to Israel in a hurry, I don't think the sub-orb is an acceptable answer."

The pastor had sat quietly until she finished, then said, "You haven't been on a sub-orbital flight in several years and when you were it was always on military vehicles. Things have changed during that time. First of all, this will be on a commercial flight. Secondly, propulsion systems have been advanced. Using clean fusion reactors to superheat the water to provide the thrust, they can accelerate a little slower and take a little longer to reach 15,000 knots. The maximum load will be around 2 Gs which may be a little uncomfortable, but not dangerous to even someone my age. Lastly, the seats we will be riding in will fully recline during the boost phase which results in less stress on the body and less chance of losing consciousness."

He paused for them to process the information he just dumped on them. Before they could ask any other questions, he added, "And most importantly, I've already bought the tickets and they're not refundable."

That evening, after they packed everything they thought they needed, they relaxed a little. They met in the pastor's apartment before heading out for a nice dinner at Abuelos (Spanish for grandparents). The restaurant served delicious Mexican food and everyone seemed to be looking forward to getting away for a few hours.

When Pris entered their apartment, both men did a double take. "You're wearing a dress!" said a surprised Greg. "I didn't know you had any dresses... wait, that didn't come out right. What I meant to say was, this is the first time I've seen you in a dress. You look..." he fumbled for the right word. "You look terrific," he said at last.

Pris giggled at Greg and said, "Good save. So I gather you like my outfit?" She spun around slowly to give both of them the full view. Her dress had a scoop neck and was cut diagonally just above the knees. As she spun, the skirt flared out showing a little bit of thigh. The dress was white with colorful flowers that went well with the spring season. She was wearing matching high heel shoes, but not too high. Her hair, usually pulled back into a pony tail, was now full of curls that framed her face. If she was wearing makeup, neither man could tell, but she was radiantly attractive.

"A very attractive outfit on a very attractive young lady," commented Isaac.

She looked at Greg and waited for him to say something. The best he could come up with was, "What he said," gesturing toward the pastor.

"I guess that's the best you can do," she said with a coy smile.

Before they left, Isaac handed out their boarding passes to the Maglev and the Sub-orbital Rocket. He also handed them new diplomatic passports. "How did you manage these?" asked Greg. "Are we diplomats now?"

"Of course," answered Isaac. "They were issued by our State Department. We are officially ambassadors of goodwill. Consider us as diplomats."

"Does that entitle us to first class seats, great food and cocktails?" enquired Greg.

"Absolutely, but you need to dress the part as diplomats, no jeans and sweat shirts allowed, just business casual," the pastor replied.

"If we are supposed to be diplomats, why are we taking VOGs and Wireless Taser-12s?" Pris asked with a smile.

"Sometime diplomacy requires a little encouragement," answered the pastor with a straight face.

They took an Uber/Lyft to the restaurant located on Chandler Boulevard in the city of Chandler, a city adjacent to Gilbert. It was a fifteen minute ride to a full parking lot. They were fortunate to have reservations. As they walked toward the entry, the pastor pointed out the two large grandparent statues on either side of the doors.

"This was my favorite Mexican restaurant when I was younger," said Isaac as they walked through the double doors into the lobby area.

"It must be very popular," commented Pris. "Did you notice the long line waiting to get in?"

The pastor replied, "That's why I made us a reservation. I invited a few friends to join us." Then he added, "Have either one of you been here before?"

They both shook their heads.

"Then you are in for a real treat," smiled the pastor.

They were escorted by a server into what appeared like a large, open-air patio. The domed ceiling looked like a powder blue sky laced with a few puffy white clouds that seemed to move slowly across the sky. The sound of a few chirping birds could be heard along with a slight breeze.

Two things caught the eye as they entered the patio. The first was a huge Mexican stone fountain in the middle of the patio. The second was the Mexican hand-painted mural which ran the full width of the back wall.

At least twenty heavy, hand carved tables with matching chairs sat on the Mexican tiled floor which encircled the fountain. Several booths ran along the side wall. There was also a bar area off to one side of the restaurant, but completely out of view of the patio.

The server seated them at a patio table that could accommodate eight people. Pris seemed to be awed by the detail of the restaurant. "This looks similar to a restaurant I ate at in Mexico City. Only this one is bigger. I noticed all the people who work here are dressed in traditional Mexican outfits." She paused then added, "Who did you invite to the dinner, Isaac? Do we know them?"

"I think you know most of them," Isaac answered. "Bud will be joining us. He was recently released from the hospital. You know Dr. Dennis Goodman from Angel of Mercy and his wife Jean. I don't know if you've met his wife. The last two you met at my second sermon at Grace Community Church. That would be the psychiatrist, Dr. Christopher Suan and his fiancé Esther."

While they waited for the rest of the group, two young Hispanic servers dressed in colorful traditional dresses brought out several bowls of tortilla chips and four different types of salsa. Others brought out large ceramic cups and pitchers of water. Pris was surprised when the pastor ordered a pitcher of margaritas.

"You look mildly shocked, Pris. Does it upset you I ordered an alcoholic beverage?"

"Maybe," she sheepishly replied. "I guess I thought all church leaders were forbidden to ever drink… adult beverages, even beer."

"Have you never heard of sacramental wine used in the Lord's Supper?" he asked.

"Sure, but I never heard of replacing it with sacramental tequila," she answered.

"If it offends you, I won't drink it. However, my intention was to have one margarita, not to get roaring drunk."

"I'm embarrassed, Pastor, please forgive—"

"Nothing to forgive, would you like me to pour you a drink?"

"I wouldn't mind if you poured *me* a drink, Pastor," interrupted Greg.

Pris gave a nervous laugh, then said, "Okay, pour me one too."

Isaac poured drinks for the two of them and one for himself as well. He raised his glass and toasted them with, "*La Heim!*"

They repeated it back to the pastor, then Pris asked Isaac, "I know it's a Hebrew toast, but what does it mean?"

"It means To Life! a good life, a life blessed by God, and life eternal with God. So I say again, *La Heim.*" He took another sip and heard a familiar voice behind say, "*La Heim,* Pastor, to life!"

It was Bud and he sat down with them and poured himself a margarita and took a sip. "I've heard it is bad luck to toast without taking a drink." His eyes widened as he licked his lips and said, "This is really good!"

During the next few minutes the rest of the party joined them. Greetings were made, margaritas were poured and tortilla chips were consumed dipped in a variety of salsas.

One more round of *La Heim* for everyone then orders were placed.

Just as the food arrived, the patio sky darkened. Within a few minutes the sky became black, filled with a thousand twinkling stars and the occasional meteor streaking across the night sky.

Torches were lit around the patio giving it a subdued, romantic feeling. Then the Mariachis began to perform. There were four men playing a variety of guitars and singing romantic ballads in Spanish, joined by the voice of a lovely *señorita* named Carmelita. They moved from table to table playing requests as they went. They were all dressed in black with white shirts and bright silver accessories adorning their clothes. They all wore huge, black sombreros. They were excellent musicians and their guitars blended seamlessly together to match the voices as they sang. They played all types of music, from ballads to *cumbias* to salsas and many at the tables got up and danced.

The pastor and his friends finished their meals and waited. It took the Mariachis another ten minutes to reach their table. Isaac stood up as they approached and said, *"Buenas noches, señores y señora,"* in perfect Spanish. He spoke back and forth with them for a few minutes, then joined them as they sang a famous romantic ballad, titled *Volver.* In English it means 'to return,' to return to a past love and never be parted again.

It was beautifully done, and everyone in the restaurant joined them in singing, including the servers and cooks. Many slow danced to the song, cheek to cheek including everyone at the pastor's table. Even Bud grabbed one of the server girls and they danced like they had known each other forever.

When they came to the last verse, the guitars stopped and Isaac and Carmelita sang a duet, standing face to face, holding each other close, singing in perfect Spanish harmony, blending his deep resonant bass with her beautiful soprano.

They held the last note for a good ten seconds, then stopped and embraced. There wasn't a dry eye in the restaurant. There was cheering and applauding that seemed to go on forever. Finally, Isaac took the girl by the hand and they faced the audience and bowed. They repeated the bow several times as the applause continued. Then Carmelita pulled him into another embrace and kissed him on the cheek. There were tears in her eyes as she whispered into Isaac's ear. She kissed him once more to the delight of the crowd then parted.

On their way home, Pris snuggled up to Greg in the back seat of the taxi and said, "This had to be the best day of my life. I've never felt so happy. How about you?"

Greg didn't speak at first, he just pulled her close and kissed her passionately on the mouth. She kissed him back just as passionately.

Sometime later, just before they dropped Pris off at her condo, Greg asked, "What did Carmelita whisper to you at the end of the song?"

Without pause, Isaac answered, "She wants me to join the band."

Pris began laughing hysterically. "What did you tell her?" she asked after she stopped laughing.

"I told her I had another gig scheduled in the Middle East."

It was Greg's turn to laugh. Before he could ask another question, Isaac said, "She gave me her com code and asked me to get in touch with her as soon as possible. I told her I would. She seemed like a really nice girl."

Isaac and Greg checked out of Angel of Mercy Assisted Living Complex and loaded their luggage into the Uber/Lyft. They said their goodbyes to the staff, then met Pris at her condo. They had all dressed in comfortable clothes for the trip and Pris was back to wearing her hair in a ponytail. Once they loaded Pris's luggage and strapped into the van seat, Isaac ordered, "Phoenix Maglev Station."

It took 20 minutes to get to the station. On the way, Pris asked, "How are we going to get the weapons through inspection?"

"Diplomatic luggage does not go through inspection," answered Isaac. "I hope you packed all you weapons. The only ones permitted to carry weapons on board are Maglev security. The same goes for the sub-orb flight."

The Uber/Lyft opened its rear hatch and drove through the luggage drop-off ramp. All their luggage was automatically removed from the vehicle and their bar codes were scanned. The AI scanner read data on each bag. It determined the luggage was for diplomats which resulted in the bags bypassing inspection and routed them to luggage storage on the Denver Maglev. Once in Denver, it would be sent to the Western Sub-Orbital Launch Port where in turn it would be directed to the sub-orbital space craft heading to the Middle East Port. When they arrived in the Middle East, all the luggage would be waiting for them. At least that's what they were told.

Their taxi dropped them off at the entrance to the maglev station and it took them a few moments to determine which one of the 10 departure portals would take them to the Denver train.

As they walked towards their portal entrance, a larger than life woman appeared on the numerous vid screens mounted on the edge of the second floor balcony which surrounded the station entrance. Her rich contralto voice announced, "Welcome to Phoenix Maglev Station. Please select your portal and hop on the slidewalk to take you to your train. If you've arrived early, please feel free to check out all our shops and places to eat. I hope your enjoy your trip."

That image faded to be replaced by a Hispanic woman who made a similar announcement in Spanish. When she finished and faded to black, a young Japanese man was shown. He bowed deeply then said the same message in Japanese. Followed in Chinese. As they stepped onto the Denver portal slidewalk, an image of a Native American followed. They assumed he would repeat the message in his native tongue, but once they were in the portal, a cacophony of voices and a variety of sounds drowned out the announcements.

Pris said, "This place is enormous. It's like a small three story town imbedded in the city of Phoenix."

"I thought you said you'd ridden on the Maglev before?" asked Greg.

"I did, but the last time was almost five years ago. This is a new station and it's a lot bigger. When I arrived from one of the SoCal Maglev stations there were only five portals with a few shops and restaurants. This new station has everything. I just noticed it even has a hotel to accommodate passengers who have to wait for a connecting train."

The walls of the portal tube were covered in a wide variety of vid displays trying to catch passengers' attention as they moved rapidly toward the Denver boarding port. That included numerous advertisements and information regarding the status of various Maglev departures and arrivals. They were happy to see their train was on time and would be boarding soon.

As they got closer to the boarding port the tube began to spread out. The adjacent tube which transported arriving passengers back to the center of the station began to fill with passengers. A few minutes later they saw their Maglev train standing in the port with the doors open and a trickle of people still exiting.

They stepped off the slidewalk and found the lane that led to their seats. A quick check was made to ensure the train was empty followed by a chime that indicated it was time to board. They flashed their boarding cards at the card reader, stepped inside the train and took their seats in their first-class private compartment. Within ten minutes, everyone was aboard and seated. All the doors closed and sealed and a different chime sounded followed by an announcement, "Welcome aboard. This is your captain speaking. We will be leaving Phoenix Maglev Station in a few minutes. Please make sure you have secured any carry-on luggage in the overhead compartment above your seats. Then sit back, relax and enjoy your brief trip to Denver. Remember to strap in with your seat restraints. The train will not move until everyone is strapped in. Once we have attained our cruise speed, I will announce when it's safe to move about the train."

There was a brief pause, then the captain's voice said, "We are cleared to depart. Enjoy your trip."

The train began to slowly move out of the station and into Phoenix's hot spring weather. The Maglev train ran on a track elevated two stories above the street and was restricted to a speed of 150 mph until cleared of the tall buildings downtown. Once outside the city, the train accelerated smoothly and quietly until it attained its cruise speed of 400 mph. The Phoenix to Denver trip was one of most recent routes established. It involved boring a number of tunnels in the mountains to keep the train on a nearly flat trajectory.

"This is so cool!" exclaimed the pastor. "Even though we're traveling at an incredible speed, It feels like we're hardly moving."

"Did you look out the side window?" asked Pris. "Everything is a blur."

"These seats are great, really comfortable," exclaimed Greg. "I may recline and take a nap for at least a part of the trip. When will they serve us our first class meal? I don't want to miss that."

Pris frowned. "You may want to rethink eating a big meal. When we launch on the sub-orb you don't want to have a full stomach. Going form 2 Gs to zero Gs can mess you up."

Greg reclined his seat until he was almost horizontal just as the captain announced they were at cruising speed and were free to move about the cabin area. He unstrapped his belt, blew Pris a kiss, then closed his eyes. A few minutes later he was gently snoring.

Both Pris and the pastor sat quietly watching the countryside fly by. After a while, she turned to Isaac and asked, "Have you had any further visions which could explain why we're going to Israel?"

Isaac closed his eyes and pursed his lips together before replying. "I'm not sure," was his answer. "The last few days I've either been dreaming or having very strange visions. They seemed sort of bizarre and unrelated, so I don't know what to think."

Pris thought for a moment before speaking again, then asked, "Do you think Satan or one of his super demons could be feeding you disinformation to confuse you?"

"That's an excellent question," he replied. "It never occurred to me, but I feel it's highly unlikely."

"Why's that?"

"I was led to believe part of Uriel's protection was to keep Satan or any of his demons from messing with my mind as well as not being able to injure me physically. I believe that applies to you and my acolyte as well."

"Okay, that sounds reasonable, so what do you think those dreams or visions are trying to tell you?"

The pastor closed his eyes and thought for several minutes before responding. He waited so long, Pris was beginning to think he was taking a nap along with Greg. However, he finally opened his eyes and said, "I think it has to do with End Times. The war in Israel is over and there was considerable damage, especially in Jerusalem. But the damage was limited both in scope and location. However, I keep seeing images of modern day Jerusalem in ruins, total ruins. Just like it was laid waste by the Babylonians in 586 BC or when Rome destroyed the city in 70 AD. In both of those instances, Jerusalem was uninhabitable for a long period of time."

He stopped speaking and this time, Pris waited with him. "I had another, completely different dream or vision. It's been a recurring event with me and I see it very clearly. Are you familiar with the Dome of the Rock? It's an Islamic shrine that was built around 700 AD and has been considered a holy place for Muslims all over the world. It was built on land called the Temple Mount, a Jewish holy place where Solomon built the first temple and Harrod the Great built the second one. Both were built on the same site as the Dome of the Rock."

"I've heard of it, but I'm not familiar with its history," answered Pris.

"Well in this vision I'm standing on the Temple Mount and looking at the Dome of the Rock. The sun is shining brightly on the golden dome, when all of a sudden it explodes into a million tiny pieces. As far as I know, the Dome of the Rock is completely intact and has never been destroyed. It did collapse in 1015 but it was rebuilt in the early 1020s. It's gone through a number of upgrades, including the gold plating of the dome's roof in 1960 and again in 1993."

"How did it survive the Jerusalem wars? I thought that might be a prime target."

"Another excellent question, Pris. I don't have an answer. Although, there are several possible answers. For example, the Muslims suggest Allah protected it. Another possible answer was the Jews never tried to destroy it. The best guess I heard was the Temple Mount was Holy Ground to many religions and none would risk desecrating it."

Before they could continue their conversation, there was a soft chime followed by the captain's voice. "In a few minutes we will be passing through our first tunnel. It will get very dark very fast, but don't worry, we do this all the time."

At the sound of the chime, Greg's sleepy voice asked, "Is it time to eat?" At the same time they were plunged into complete darkness except for the lights of their cabin. Greg yelled, "What the hell just happened?!!" as he brought his seatback to the upright position, his eyes wild with fright. He reached for a weapon to protect them, before he remembered their weapons were locked away in the luggage.

Pris laid a comforting hand on Greg's arm and said in a consoling voice, "It's okay, honey. We just went into our first tunnel, nothing to worry about. Go back to sleep. I'll call you when the food is here."

About an hour into the trip, a robo food cart arrived with their first class meals. Greg smelled the aroma of the food and came awake abruptly. "This smells terrific. I'm starving."

Greg took a full meal from the food cart and placed it on his tray. Isaac and Pris did likewise. However, both of them ate a small portion of the food. Greg totally ignored Pris's warning regarding the upcoming sub-orb flight and ate the entire meal.

Shortly after the meal was finished, they felt the Maglev very gradually begin to decrease their speed. The robo food cart collected their trays as the captain began speaking. "We've begun our approach to Denver Maglev Station. Please return to your seats to a fully upright position and strap in. You'll have to remain in your restraints until the train comes to a complete stop."

The train came to a complete stop in the station and just as they left their compartment, the captain made his last message. "Thank you all for riding with us to Denver. You may notice Denver is slightly cooler than Phoenix so make sure you take your coats and other belongings with you from the overhead. Have a pleasant stay in Denver or wherever your next trip may take you. Good day!"

As they left the train and headed to the slidewalk to the central station, Pastor Isaac commented, "I'm really impressed with the way the captain kept us informed during our trip. He has a very dynamic voice. I'd really enjoy meeting him."

Both Greg and Pris stopped walking on the slidewalk and the pastor had taken a few steps before he turned back. "Is everything all right? Did we forget something in the overhead?" he asked with a hint of concern.

Greg turned to Pris and asked, "Do you want me to tell him or do you want to do it?"

"You're his acolyte, it's your responsibility to keep him informed," she replied.

Greg nodded and turned back to the pastor. "Isaac, there is no captain driving the train. In fact, there's not even a computer controlling the train. There's a super AI computer located in Kansas City which controls the all Maglev traffic in the U.S. The voice you heard is a recorded synthetic which is triggered by the main computer at appropriate times."

Isaac's expression was one of sadness. "I find that disappointing. I should have known the captain was too good to be true."

He turned and continued walking on the slidewalk to the central station. Pris and Greg hurried to catch up with him. They had taken a few steps before the pastor stopped and turned around again. "Does this mean the sub-orb is also controlled by computers?"

Greg nodded. "I'm almost certain they are. It's been five or six years since I've ridden on one. Even in those days, multiple computers controlled every aspect of flight from launch to landing. In those days of continuous wars, our sub-orb transports had to not only fly the craft from A to B, they also had to protect themselves from attack by the enemy. I'm pretty sure the current computer systems, as well as the vehicle technology, have made significant advancements."

With a slight smile, Pastor Isaac said sarcastically, "I can't wait to put the fate of my life in the hands of a machine. Oh, wait. Computer's don't have hands… I must be doomed."

It was indeed cooler in Denver than Phoenix. In fact, it was downright cold. Before they stepped outside, they were all bundled up in their coats. Pris put on gloves and a wool knit hat and she claimed she was warm as toast. The two men didn't respond. They just stuffed their hands deep into the pockets of their coats as their ears began to turn red. Fortunately, they only had to wait a couple of minutes before their ride pulled up.

They climbed inside the warm cabin of the taxi, and once seated and strapped in, they began their ride to the Launch Port.

It was a 20 minute ride from the Maglev station and the Denver Launch Port. It was mid-afternoon when the taxi began slowing and the road to the spaceport began to curve. There was a three-story-high rock formation on the left side of the vehicle blocking their view. When they cleared the largest of the rocks, they pulled into a parking lot several miles from the end of the runways and stopped to check out the view. Directly ahead of them was a series of huge buildings located at the foothills of the Rocky Mountains. Extending out from the terminal buildings were three parallel runways that had to be nearly three miles long. The road from the distant parking lot where their taxi had stopped to the terminal buildings was about five miles away.

As they continued on towards the terminal, a flashing red light signaled them to stop before they were close to the runways. They waited for an approaching mothership to land. It was an ungainly looking vessel used during launches of the suborbital spacecraft. As the mothership approached the north runway, it became apparent how huge it was. Greg estimated it had to be doing at least 200 knots or maybe a lot more, but the landing was flawless as it touched down at the far east end of the runway. It continued to decelerate as it moved further down the runway and stopped a few hundred yards from the terminal. The traffic light signaled it was safe to proceed and they watched the mothership as it slowed to a stop on the runway and then turned to the right onto a taxiway that led to an enormous hanger. The taxi dropped them at the entrance to the terminal and they checked in at the reservation counter.

As the young woman behind the counter began to confirm their flights, Isaac leaned over and whispered to Pris,

"Do you think she's real or a humanized android? It's so hard to tell these days."

Greg heard Isaac's comments and moved away from him as if he didn't know him. Pris smiled at the pastor and whispered back, "Behave yourself, pastor. Of course she's a real person."

Before the pastor could respond, the ticket agent quickly raised her head and stared intensely at Isaac. Her face was expressionless and her eyes never blinked. Pris began to feel uneasy, but didn't say anything. After an undetermined amount of time, the agent leaned forward towards the pastor and said in a mechanical voice, "I am not human. I am a cyber 17 construct. How may I help you? How may I help you? How may I…" then her head slowly dropped down until her chin rested on her chest.

Isaac moved back a step and was totally confused, as was Pris. After a long moment, the girl jerked her head up with a big grin on her face. "Gotcha, didn't I?"

All the passengers who were waiting in line to check in for their launch were laughing and clapping. Even Greg was now smiling. "That's the best impression of an android I've ever seen. You must shock a lot of people."

"Thanks for your compliment," she smiled back at Greg. "I've always wanted to become an actress. I took this job to see if I could entertain my customers. Who knows, maybe a producer or director will see me perform and offer me a job in Hollywood." The young woman scanned their passports then looked up with an expression of concern. "All three of you are diplomats? I'm so sorry for messing with you. I hope I haven't offended you. Here are your clearances for your diplomatic sub-orb flight. You have one spaceship ahead of you. You can wait in the VIP Lounge until you're called."

Isaac smiled and said, "Don't worry. We're all fine. In fact, not only us, but everyone at the check-in counter were entertained by your impression of a cyborg. I believe your dream of becoming an actress will be fulfilled in the near future."

Isaac turned and headed for the VIP suite with Pris following him. Greg hesitated a moment then said to the young woman, "Just so you know, when Isaac makes a prediction, he's always right. You're going to be a big star." Before the agent could respond, Greg turned away and hurried to catch up with his friends.

When they entered the VIP lounge, there were about a dozen people sitting at the bar or watching vid presentations on several of the large screens. Their sub-orb ship wouldn't launch for at least an hour.

There were huge floor to ceiling windows that looked out over the runways. Pris and Greg stood close to the windows to admire the view. It was breathtaking. The land was open range and they could see for mile after mile into the barren plains. As they watched, they heard a soft chime followed by an announcement in a woman's voice, "The spacecraft from Tokyo, Japan, will be landing shortly."

"Do you think that's a real woman's voice?" asked Greg.

Pris elbowed him in the ribs then replied, "Enough of the computer versus human comments, please."

"Look!" said Greg. "Do you see that black dot directly in-line with the center runway? I think that's the flight from Japan."

The dot got bigger quickly and within a few minutes they could see the spaceplane touch down on the end of the runway. It seemed it was moving much faster than the mothership had been. Then the maneuvering jets reversed, slowing the vehicle dramatically. It came to a stop at the same place the mothership had stopped and turned off the runway onto the taxiway, but entered into a different hangar.

Another chime sounded and the woman's voice announced, "The spacecraft to Stockholm, Sweden, is boarding. This is your last call. Please board through gates 1, 2 and 3 on level 5."

It seemed like only a few minutes had past when a set of hanger doors opened and something slowly taxied out. It looked like a different vehicle, but Greg finally recognized it. "It's a spaceship connected to a mothership," he said.

Isaac had moved up behind Greg and asked, "Are you sure? It looks much bigger than I... imagined."

Pris turned to look at the pastor and said in a quiet voice, "Did you see something different in a vision?"

"I think so," he replied. "It's becoming more difficult for me to tell anymore."

Before he could say anything, he was interrupted by the roar of the six hybrid engines on the mothership. Slowly, very slowly at first, the combined vehicles began to move down the runway gathering speed at an incredible rate.

Greg noticed a vid screen that showed readouts of the vehicles' performance. He looked back and saw the combined ships lift off the runway as they neared the end. Looking back at the vid screen, it showed they were already traveling at 300 knots just as they went airborne. Their speed increased as they climbed almost vertically. They could hear the muffled sound of the shock wave as they passed Mach 1 at an altitude of 5,000 feet. Soon they were out of sight, but Greg continued to track the flight data. Five minutes after takeoff they were at 60,000 feet traveling at Mach 4 as the engines transitioned to the scramjet mode. Another 5 minutes later they were at 100,000 feet traveling at Mach 10. At that point the spaceship fired up its rocket motors and decoupled from the mothership. The mothership began its return trip to the Denver Launch Port. The spaceship continued to accelerate to over 10,000 knots and climbed to the sub orbital altitude of nearly 100 miles above the Earth.

At that point, the spaceship began it hypersonic decent back to the Earth to land at the Stockholm Launch Port two hours after its takeoff. By then, Greg had lost interest in tracking the spaceship and decided to have something to drink and a few snacks. Pris joined him, but Isaac seemed to be meditating, trying to figure out his latest vision.

It wasn't long before they heard another announcement. "All those who are traveling to the Middle East Port, please gather your belongings and move to the boarding area at level 6, gates 2, 3 and 4. If you are traveling under diplomatic credentials, please proceed to level 3D, gates 1 and 2 for immediate boarding."

It was a 10 minute trip on two slidewalks and an elevator before they arrived at level 3D, gate 1. It was a small room that could hold no more than a dozen people. As they waited in line to show their credentials to the boarding agent, Pris looked out the picture window to the hangar below. She watched as a crew of technicians finished coupling a smaller mothership to a sleeker looking spaceship. She turned to Isaac and said, "Take a look at the hangar." She gestured. "Does that look anything like your vision?"

The pastor looked and a grin started to spread across his face. "Yes," he said ecstatically. "It looks exactly like my vision. Thank you so much, my dear."

One by one the line moved forward. It turned out the boarding process for diplomats was much more thorough. In addition to showing the agent their cred packs, they also had to show the documents ordering them to travel to Israel, followed by a retina scan of both eyes. When they were finished, they headed down to the boarding ramp, then into their spaceship. They found their assigned seats, then had to figure out how they worked. A flight attendant had to help them.

Pris shook her head in disbelief. "This is nothing like the military sub-orbs I've traveled on." She smiled at her two male companions and added, "This should be a piece of cake."

"We'll be taxiing out of the hangar in a few minutes," said one of the flight attendants. "I want to make sure you know how to operate your seats. These seats are designed to minimize G force during acceleration. When our ship exceeds 1.5 Gs, your seat will automatically recline and rotate so your body is perpendicular to the line of force. That way, you are very unlikely to lose consciousness. In addition, the seats will mold to your body shape as the G force increases to minimize any discomfort."

They followed the flight attendant's instructions and felt they were ready for the flight. A few moments later they began to taxi to the runway. Once into position on the runway, it came to a stop and waited for a moment. A synthetic male voice announced, "We are cleared for takeoff. Rolling now."

As the combined ships began to move, everyone aboard could hear the sound of the hybrid jet engines spooling up to full speed. There was a deep rumbling roar inside the cabin and they could feel a slight vibration. The artificial captain, or maybe his fake copilot, began calling off velocities as the ship quickly accelerated down the runway.

"One hundred knots... two hundred... 275, rotation, liftoff. Up, up and away!"

As the spacecraft lifted off, it rotated to a near vertical climb and the passengers were being pressed into their seats. When they passed 1.5 Gs, their seats rotated to minimize the added weight caused by the acceleration. The synthetic captain announced, "We are approaching 2.5 Gs. That should be our maximum G force. Try to relax. Don't fight the strain."

The three newest diplomats lay stationary in their seats doing their best to breathe. It was a struggle. It felt like an elephant was sitting on their chests. Pris had the most experience with G forces. In the military sub-orb craft, the Gs were higher and the seats harder. She thought flying in this new state-of-the-art vehicle should be relatively easy. She was wrong. Her body had lost a lot of its fitness during the five years since her last sub-orb flight and she fought to breathe. She wondered how the pastor and Greg were doing. However, it was a struggle to even turn her head to see if they were okay, so she didn't bother, she would find out soon enough. She also wondered how her prostheses were handling the G force. It was too late to do anything about it now. She'd just have to wait and see.

After what seemed like an eternity, the faux captain made an announcement. "In a minute from now we will reach our planned altitude of 100 miles above sea level. We will be shutting down our rocket motors and maneuvering into our descent mode. During that time you will instantly go from 2.5 Gs to zero Gs. You will feel like you're falling and it may cause some of you to experience vertigo. However, it will only last for about 15 seconds. After that, the rest of our trip will be conducted at 1 G. I'll let you know when you can unstrap and move about the cabin."

The voice paused for a few seconds, then began counting down. "Here we go, 5…4…3…2…1…weightless!"

Greg thought it would be a relief to be weightless after weighing 500 pounds for what seemed like forever. He was wrong. His stomach began doing flip-flops and he was afraid all the food he'd eaten on the Maglev was going to exit his mouth. After fifteen seconds, his weight began to return to normal. After a few quick swallows, his stomach calmed down.

Now that he was able to move his head without straining his neck, he turned to see how Isaac was doing. He seemed to be sleeping, but he wasn't sure. Who could sleep through the ordeal they just experienced?

The pretend pilot voice made another announcement. "We are now flying at one G. You may remove your restraints and move about the cabin. We should be landing at Middle East Port in a little less than two hours from now. Meals, drinks and snacks will be available until 30 minutes before touchdown. Just place your order from the menu display on the right arm of your chair and our robo food cart will bring your order to your seat. Enjoy the rest of your flight. Don't forget to check out our vid screens, they display spectacular views of space. You can also see the big blue marble called Earth. Look closely. You might be able to see your house."

Greg shook his head in amused disbelief. He thought he'd seen and heard pretty much everything. However, this was the first time he'd heard a computer doing stand-up comedy.

He unfastened his seat restraint and stood up. He joined Pris standing next to Isaac's seat. The pastor appeared to be completely relaxed with a hint of a smile on his face. Pris reached out and gently squeezed his arm. "Are you okay, Isaac?" she asked quietly.

His eyes opened and his smile got bigger. "I'm fine Pris. How are you and Greg doing?"

Greg said, "We're both okay. Did the G force hurt you in any way? How about when we went weightless ?"

The pastor shook his head briefly. "To be honest, I don't remember any of those things. After I strapped into my seat I had this vision. When it ended, I meditated on what the vision was about."

"Could you tell us about the vision?" Pris asked.

"Of course," the pastor replied. "But first, I need to use the restroom, then have something to eat. I'm starving. How about you, Greg?"

The acolyte swallowed twice at the mention of food. "I'm not hungry right now, maybe later."

After Pris and Isaac had eaten, the pastor told them about his most recent vision. The part of the spaceship reserved for diplomats had three small rooms for private meetings during the flight. One of those rooms was vacant and they went inside and locked the door behind them. Pris had brought a mini signal jammer in her purse to insure their meeting was not overheard by any of the other passengers or even snooping AI computers.

"Part of this vision was very specific. The events I saw were presented in chronological order. Unfortunately, the actual timing of the events wasn't disclosed except for one event."

"What event would that be, pastor?" asked Greg.

"Our spaceship will be attacked before we land at Middle East Port. No one will be seriously injured and the attacking aircraft will be destroyed by the weapons of an American fighter plane."

Pris looked surprised. "I wasn't aware there were any American fighter planes based in the Middle East. Perhaps it will be a fighter from one of the Navy's super carriers. I believe there's one stationed in the Mediterranean."

"Or maybe it was a fighter stationed at the Middle East Port," replied the pastor. "Several of the ports near war zones have fighters available to handle the type of attacks I saw in my vision. Remember, the wars in the Middle East have been going on for almost two years. Even though there is a truce in Israel, much of the surrounding countries are still at war with each other. Attempts are being made to expand the truce to include all the countries from Turkey in the north to Yemen in the south, but that could take years to negotiate."

"What about the other parts of your visions?" asked Greg.

"They're all centered around Jerusalem. I see myself trying to convince leaders from various nations that the Dome of the Rock will be destroyed soon. Unfortunately, they want proof that it will happen. They also want to know who will be responsible for its destruction and lastly, they want to know how I know this. Was it a threat handed down to me by my leaders? Am I looking for a bribe to keep me from destroying the shrine? I didn't think telling them I had a vision from God was going to convince them."

"Would it help if we could find out who's behind the planned destruction?" asked Greg.

The pastor shrugged. "I don't know. Maybe it would, but I need to examine my vision in greater detail first. I need to meditate on the existing vision. It would also help if there would be other visions to augment the last one."

"What else did you see, pastor?" asked Pris.

"That was the worst of the visions," he said slowly, his voice filled with anguish. "I was in the spirit as I watched from the top of the Mount of Olives, or what was left of it. I was looking across Kidron Valley and watching the sun begin to set behind where the Dome of the Rock once stood. All of a sudden there was a blinding white light, a deafening explosion and a searing wave of heat ripping through everything, vaporizing whatever it touched. As the brightness faded, I saw Temple Mount was also gone. In its place was a molten crater that engulfed most of Jerusalem. There was no crying or wailing in pain, only the silence of death and destruction."

"Do you think it was a physical representation of a reality which must happen or symbolic of what might happen?" asked Greg.

"I wish I knew, Gregory," replied the pastor. "I truly wish I knew. This was not the vision of End Times that I expected. I will meditate on this. Please don't disturb me until we land."

Pris and Greg returned to their seats and rested quietly, both lost in their thoughts of what Isaac had revealed. Greg reached over and took Pris's hand and gave it a reassuring squeeze. They sat that way until the computer generated voice of a non-existent pilot announced, "We've just fired up our maneuvering jets and began our final approach to the island of Cyprus. The Middle East Sub-Orbital Port is located close to the city of Limassol. Please return to your seats and fasten your restraints for the remainder…"

There was a pause, then the synthetic voice stated in the same calm tone, "We are currently under attack. We will need to maneuver to survive the attack. I will keep you informed of the status of our counterattack."

There was a large explosion behind the rear of the spaceship, drowning out the roar of the maneuvering jets and yawing it from to side of side. A second explosion was heard, but farther back than the first. That was immediately followed by the spaceship nosing over into a dive toward the Mediterranean Sea then pulling several Gs to level out only a few feet above the surface of the water. The spaceship was still traveling at greater than Mach 1 and the trailing shock wave was kicking up a tremendous amount of spray.

Greg's head was on a swivel checking the windows from one side of the ship to the other. "I see at least two attack fighters. I didn't see any markings on either bird," he said to Pris.

"I think I saw a third one," shouted Pris over the sound of the battle and panicked fellow passengers.

One of the three jets was following directly behind the spaceship, trying to get a bead on the maneuvering rocket. All at once the ship pulled up abruptly into a vertical climb and went to full power on the previously idling rocket engines. The fighter jet could not respond quickly enough to avoid the fiery plume. Instead, it was driven down into the sea and exploded on impact.

One down.

Two to go.

The rapid maneuvering of the spaceship had a very adverse effect on its passengers. Even though they were strapped in, the G forces were higher than expected and the gyrations required to avoid the attacking jet fighters resulted in injuries to the diplomats, some quite severe.

One of the two remaining jets climbed vertically before the spaceship performed its pop-up maneuver. As the spaceship continued to climb, it was a sitting duck for the enemy jet to takeout with an air-to-air missile. Unfortunately for the jet, the pilot locked on to the spaceship and never saw the on-coming F-39. The American fighter made short work of the enemy aircraft using its laser cannons.

The third enemy decided he was out-gunned and bugged out on full burners.

The sub-orbital spaceship returned to the landing approach and made an excellent landing at the Middle East Port. Cypriote medical personnel swarmed over the diplomats to offer assistance where they could. Of the 28 diplomatic passengers and their aides, 15 had to be taken off the ship in gurneys and then hospitalized.

Fortunately, neither Pris nor Greg were injured. Isaac had been so deep into his meditation and strapped into a conference chair, he didn't even realize they'd been attacked.

As they moved to the exit hatch, the faux pilot's voice announced, "Thank you for flying with us. We hope you enjoyed the flight. Please take a minute and fill out a short survey on how we could improve our service. Thanks again, we look forward to serving you on your next flight."

It took only a few minutes for the three of them to pass through immigration at the Middle East Sub-Orbital Port on the island of Cyprus. They just had to show their diplomatic passports to an AI reader and do a quick retina scan. They collected their baggage and had it forwarded to the American Embassy in Tel Aviv by secured transport.

Greg decided to remove three of the Wireless Taser-12 dart guns from the luggage before it was shipped. He didn't want to be weaponless in Israel, a country where everyone else was weaponized. At first, Isaac didn't think it was necessary, but Pris and Greg ganged up on him and he grudgingly accepted the inevitable.

To avoid any further argument, Greg secretly brought along the Glock-22 he had found at the church after the demons were driven away. He brought two fully loaded magazines as well, just in case things got really rough. He wished he'd designed a pistol sized VOG, but the Glock would have to do.

Once outside, they hailed an old fashion taxi with a real human driver to take them to Limassol, a commercial seaport on the south side of the island. They paid their fare in credits and tipped the driver who seemed very pleased to get the extra money.

As they walked down a long dock to Jet Boat Station, Isaac commented, "It was nice to interact with a real human being for a change. I really enjoyed our conversation with the taxi driver."

Greg looked annoyed. "So, you don't consider Pris and me as human? We talk to you all the time. Doesn't that count?"

"Of course you're human, and yes, we do speak frequently. I was referring to interacting with strangers."

Pris smiled as she said, "Well, Greg is kind of strange at times."

Greg changed the subject. "How long will it take us to get to Israel from here?"

"I'm not sure," answered the pastor. "The last time I left Israel, I used the Israeli Sub-orbital Port. However, that was destroyed in one of the wars and never rebuilt. We can ask one of the human agents at Jet Boat Station."

"Why do we have to go to Haifa instead of directly to Tel Aviv? They have a seaport, don't they?" asked Pris.

"Unfortunately, their seaport is not for commercial shipping, only for private power boats, yachts and sailboats," replied Isaac.

They entered the building that housed the Jet Boat Station office and made arrangements to board the next boat to Haifa. The ticket agent sold them reserved seats on the next boat leaving for Israel. When Greg asked how long the trip would take, the agent said in heavily accented English, "It is 205 nautical miles from our seaport to Haifa's. If the sea is calm, our jet boat will travel at 80 knots. So the trip should take a little less than three hours."

Pris asked the agent, "Is the sea calm today?"

"It is a very calm sea near Cyprus today," he said with a slight smile. "However, that can change quickly."

"Isn't 80 knots too fast for a boat?" Greg asked with a frown. "I thought the drag on the hull would prevent that much speed."

"It would be impossible in a traditional boat," agreed the agent. "However, our jet boats are hovercraft which ride above the surface of the sea. On a good day, a very good day with a sea like glass, our boats can top out at 100 knots. Unfortunately, the Mediterranean Sea is rarely like glass. Any other questions?"

There were none and they left the office and walked down the wharf to board their jet boat. The cabin of the boat had a 100 passenger capacity plus a crew of 10. They were booked in the first class section of the boat and their seats were in the front row. Looking forward through the large windows gave them an excellent view of the sea and surrounding small islands. Fifteen minutes after they boarded, they were on their way to Haifa.

The sea was almost like glass for the entire trip and their jet boat averaged almost 90 knots. It took them another few minutes of dead slow speed as their boat wound its way through the extremely busy port. The Haifa port was the biggest and busiest port in Israel, located in the northern part of the country. Isaac had vague memories of an excellent seafood restaurant and after a quick search on his wrist smart com, he was able to find its location in a matter of seconds. They walked the four blocks to the restaurant for a wonderful brunch before boarding a self-driving electric limo to Tel Aviv.

The road was a pleasant hour's drive down the coast. There was some noticeable war damage, however, it was a lot less than they had imagined. Repair crews seemed to be repairing damage almost as quickly as it occurred.

Isaac turned to Greg and asked, "Do you think we could watch the local news for the rest of the trip?"

"Sure, Pastor," he replied. "Go ahead."

"I wasn't asking for permission," he said in an annoyed tone. "I don't know how to turn on the car vid. Would you please do it for me?"

"Oh, sorry, of course," Greg answered sheepishly. "Vid on. Local news."

"I'd like it in Hebrew please, with English captions."

"Your wish is my command," he said with a smile. "Hebrew audio, English captions."

Pris suggested, "Perhaps you should practice improving your vid skills, just in case there's no one around to help you."

"Excellent idea, Pris." The pastor turned to face the vid screen and said in a loud voice, "Vid off!" He waited a beat then said still in a very loud voice, "Vid on. Local news. Hebrew audio. English captions."

Instantly, the vid showed a news anchor speaking in Hebrew with English captions scrolling across the bottom of the screen. However, the volume was way too loud.

"Why is the volume so loud?"

Greg shouted to the vid, "Vid audio normal," and the sound level dropped to a comfortable volume.

Pris answered, "Because you shouted your commands. The vid receiver has excellent hearing. Whatever level of voice you use to place your command is the same level the vid will use, assuming you are either hearing impaired or in a noisy environment."

The rest of the trip they watched the local news at a comfortable volume level with the English captions scrolling across the bottom of the screen. The news anchors were discussing the new change in the location of the nation's capital. Prior to 1980, the capital resided in Tel Aviv. However, in February of 2018, it was moved to Jerusalem and had remained there until the Middle Eastern wars started. The capital then bounced back and forth between Jerusalem and Tel Aviv for over a hundred years, depending on the status of the wars. Frequently, two capital locations were used simultaneously with one location being referred to as the main capital and the other as a branch office.

Some, but not all, of the various foreign embassies in Israel had followed that trend. With the recent peace treaty, the Israeli main capital was changed back to Jerusalem and the branch capital to Tel Aviv. Many Israelis thought the move was premature as did some of their allies. However, the American Embassy followed the current trend.

The three new diplomats would be making their first stop at the American Embassy in Tel Aviv, meeting with Deputy Ambassador Miriam Levi. She'd been an old friend of Isaac's when he was a seminary professor. He hadn't seen her for many decades and he looked forward to renewing their friendship and finding out if she had any information regarding his mission.

It was almost noon when their limo turned off the coastal highway onto the city streets and made its way to the embassy. As expected, there was a platoon of Marines providing security inside the gated grounds. After their IDs and diplomatic documents were checked, they were escorted into the ground floor lobby.

The lobby was spacious with paintings of moments in American history decorating the ten foot high walls. There were also numerous large photographs of high-level American politicians posing with Israeli dignitaries.

They were offered refreshments while they waited for the deputy ambassador to finish with other business. They sat in comfortable high-back arm chairs with side tables to place their drinks and small plates of pastries. When they finished, a young man dressed in a gray suit with a white shirt and red tie escorted them to the deputy ambassador's office.

Miriam Levi strode across her office floor to shake the hands of the three new diplomats. She was an attractive woman, dressed professionally in an expensive pantsuit which her position required. Her dark curly hair was beginning to show traces of grey, but she looked younger than her reported 50 something years.

"Pastor Silberman," she said smiling, as she gripped Isaac's hand in both of hers and shook it. "It's so good to finally see you again." She paused for a moment as she studied Isaac then let go of his hand and said, "I'm so sorry, I think I've confused you with your father."

"Don't be sorry, Miriam," said the pastor. It's a long story, I'll share the details with you later. But for now, let me say I'm the real Isaac Silberman with a few improvements."

She gave him an embarrassed smile and said, "You look exactly like you looked when I was your student. I can't wait to hear your story. You were such an inspiration to me and your other students at Dallas Seminary. I was fresh out of high school when I met you and was sure I was going to get my Master of Divinity degree. Unfortunately, that didn't work out. My parents had other plans for me."

"I'd say you've done very well for yourself. I'm sure your parents are very proud. Your year in seminary gave you a strong Christian basis. I thought you were an excellent student."

Before the deputy ambassador could reply, Isaac said, "Let me introduce my acolyte." He motioned for Greg to step forward. Isaac continued, "This is Marine Lieutenant Colonel Gregory Stone, retired. He has been my acolyte for the last five years."

He gestured for Pris to come forward. "This is Priscilla Wright, a relatively new addition to my team. She acts as my aide and is in charge of my security."

Miriam shook hands with everyone and asked them to sit down. "How can I be of service to you and your team, Pastor?"

"Have you received any communications regarding our diplomatic mission?"

"Unfortunately, no I haven't. I was contacted by State that you would be arriving sometime today. The message said you'd be continuing on to our embassy in Jerusalem. That was about it. I assumed you'd have been briefed before you left the states."

The pastor shook his head and said, "No we haven't. I guess we'll find out when we get to Jerusalem."

They spent a few more minutes reminiscing about old times and how Miriam had worked her way up to her current position. Greg and Pris sat quietly and listened intently on how the deputy ambassador had managed to be promoted to various government positions of ever increasing responsibility. She'd questioned Isaac regarding his career as a theologian and pastor. Their conversation continued until an aide reminded the deputy ambassador another appointment was coming up.

They said their good-byes and were escorted out by one of the Marines to their waiting limo. As they drove out of the embassy compound, Greg noticed a black SUV began to follow them.

He wasn't sure they were being tailed, so he didn't alert Pris or the pastor as their limo began their hour long ride to Jerusalem. He'd wait until he was sure they were being followed before he took any defensive action.

The pastor had been very quiet since he entered the limo and sat back in one of the vehicle's plush seats. Pris had noticed it too. He'd closed his eyes and they both assumed he was having another vision.

Taking advantage of the quiet ride through the surface streets of Tel Aviv, Greg accessed the limo's rear camera with the smart com function of his wrist chrono. For the next ten minutes, the black SUV followed them at a distance. They never got too close or had more than a couple of other vehicles between them. He was sure they were being followed.

Before he could warn Pris, the pastor sat forward, eyes open and said, "Limo, Holon Military Cemetery."

A soft chime sounded and the limo's voice repeated, "Redirecting to Holon Military Cemetery. ETA six minutes."

Pris and Greg stared at the pastor in surprise. Pris asked, "Why do you want to go there?"

"Two reasons," replied Isaac. "First, I want to visit the gravesite of one of Israel's famous prime ministers, Benjamin Netanyahu. Second, we need to acknowledge our escort from the American Embassy."

"Vision?" asked Pris.

"Of course," was his response. "At least, an important part of one. I didn't want Greg to act like we were in the wild west."

Greg looked confused.

"Oh, come on," challenged the pastor. "Have you forgotten the famous cowboy saying *shoot first and ask questions later?*"

Pris giggled and Greg looked mildly upset as the limo pulled into the cemetery parking lot, followed closely by the black SUV.

They met briefly in the parking lot with their two escorts. Both men were large and muscular with no sense of humor. One was an Israeli and the other an American. Before they introduced themselves, the American asked Greg, "When did you make us?" He looked annoyed.

"As soon as we left the embassy compound. At first, I wasn't sure you were tailing us, but you kept appearing in the limo's rear camera with every turn we made."

The American turned to his Israeli partner and said, "See Moshi, I told you not to get too close, not at the beginning. You need to give them some space then creep up on them."

Moshi didn't reply, he just looked away and shrugged.

The escorts followed them into the cemetery and they all paid their respects to the deceased prime minister.

They returned to their vehicles and continued their drive to Jerusalem with the black SUV right behind them.

It was a relatively short drive from the cemetery to enter a six lane freeway that led to Jerusalem. It would be a 59 mile drive. The elevation at Tel Aviv was only 50 feet above sea level, however, they began a gradual climb. When they had driven about ten miles and passed the Ben Gurion International Airport, the elevation had increased to 135 feet.

Not all of the freeways were free. Sections of the highway were high speed toll lanes however, the sticker on the limo's windshield let the group pass through the gates without even slowing down.

Pris noted what looked like a high speed railway and asked, "Why didn't we take the train? I'd think it would be a lot faster than the highway."

Moshi replied through his com link. "It would be a lot faster. Unfortunately, sections of the tracks have been destroyed. It seemed like a favorite target of our enemies. As soon as we repaired the track, another section was destroyed. Many Israeli's died in the ensuing train wrecks. The highway is slower, but safer."

Jeffrey Clark, the other escort from the embassy, added, "It's believed our enemies want to isolate Jerusalem from the rest of Israel and the rest of the world."

They continued on in silence for a while as the highway began a series of twists and turns. There were even several tunnels to go through. Greg noticed there was one tunnel that was covered with sod, plants and trees. He checked his wrist com then reported is was called an animal crossover. It's intent was to keep wild animals from trying to cross the highway, allowing them a safer path to use when they needed to migrate or find new feeding areas.

The climb became steeper as they got closer to Jerusalem. The peak elevation was 2,700 feet but by the time they arrived in Jerusalem it was down to just over 2,000 feet with sheer cliffs surrounding most of the city. It was a natural fortress used as such from before the time of King David.

They exited the freeway and continued on to the American Embassy. Both vehicles were inspected before being allowed into the embassy grounds by uniformed Marines who kept their weapons at the ready position. They were not allowed to proceed until they had surrendered all weapons. They would be returned when they left the grounds.

Jeffrey and Moshi said their good-byes and headed back to Tel Aviv. The three diplomats underwent thorough vetting of their documents in a foyer adjacent to the embassy lobby. As a Marine captain scanned their documents, well-armed Marines were apparently assigned to watch each one of them. They stared at them as potential targets and held their assault rifles at the ready position with safeties off.

When the captain was satisfied they were really the diplomats they claimed to be, he gave the order, "Stand down."

All three took a step back, safetied their rifles and pointed them at the ground.

The captain pushed a button on his iPad21, signaling for an escort to take them into the embassy lobby.

A young woman, tastefully dressed, opened the doors to the lobby and ushered them in. "My name is Claudia Johnson," she said in a pleasant, almost melodic voice. "I will be your hostess for this afternoon. It is lunch time and Ambassador Johnson will be joining you soon. Can I offer you some light refreshments until the ambassador is available?"

The branch embassy in Tel Aviv had been outstanding, but the American Embassy in Jerusalem was far beyond outstanding. The deep pile carpet was so deep and soft their shoes sunk about an inch into it as they gingerly made their way to an ornate low table surrounded by four high backed armed chairs.

Before they were seated, two servers entered, one carrying a variety of drinks and the other a tray of finger sandwiches and pastries.

It seemed like everything was at least twice as grand as the branch embassy. The grandeur of it all made it almost feel like a holy place. A place where people didn't talk, they only whispered.

Fifteen minutes later, Claudia returned and escorted them into a lavish dining area. Two men were standing at the double French doors to greet them. One was Ambassador Elijah Blake who was dressed immaculately in a thousand dollar suit and custom made shoes. He smiled broadly as he shook each of their hands and then introduced the man standing next to him.

This man also had a very expensive suit, as well as shoes. He carried a white cane and wore gold framed sun glasses. He was obviously blind.

"Gentlemen, lady, it is my great pleasure to introduce to you John Baptist, a close Jewish friend and the senior rabbi of the entire Jewish community, not just in Jerusalem, but throughout the entire world."

The man's expression changed from a stoic look to a slight smile as he turned toward the pastor and said in a quiet voice, "It is an honor to meet you at last. I so looked forward to meeting the last prophet. A man who returned from the dead to live again with visions from God. A man who speaks to the angels and casts out demons."

He paused for a long moment and they could see tears of joy running down his cheeks. "And most importantly, the prophet who will introduce to the world a new Messiah!"

There was a stunned silence. Everyone was shocked by what John Baptist just said. Even John seemed to be surprised by what he had said. As the silence continued, suddenly, John's legs began to shake, he dropped his cane and it looked as if he was going to fall. Greg quickly reached out and took his arm to steady him.

"Thank you," he said to Greg, his voice weak and raspy. "Perhaps it would be best if I sat down for a moment."

Pris took his other arm and they slowly guided him into the dining area. He almost collapsed into his chair. "A glass of water, please?"

Claudia was there in an instant with a cut crystal glass filled with water and ice. She took one of John's hands in hers and guided it to the glass. She kept one hand on the glass and helped him to take a sip, followed by a longer drink, then together they set the glass on the table.

"Thank you my dear. My thanks to all of you. I apologize for my weakness. I haven't had an event like that in years."

The ambassador finally found his voice. "My God, John! I've never seen you like... like that. Are you all right?"

"Not really," he answered weakly. "However, based on past events, my strength will return gradually. By tomorrow, I should be back to my old self, for whatever that is worth."

Isaac had not spoken once John had begun revealing all of his secrets. He asked softly, "John, do you remember what you said to us?"

"I think so, but could we put that discussion off for another day? I need to regain my strength before we speak together."

He slowly searched for the glass of water, found it, and raised it to his lips by himself. He took a long drink, then returned the glass gingerly back to the table.

His head was facing an empty chair across the table when he added, "Ambassador, could I impose on you for one night in one of your guest rooms?"

"Of course, John," he replied. "Whatever you need for as long as you want, old friend."

The ambassador nodded to Claudia and she returned with two male staff members and a wheelchair. The men placed him in the chair and Claudia picked up his cane and laid it across the chair arms. As they began to wheel him away, John said to an empty space, "I can't wait to speak with you again, Prophet. We have so much to discuss."

Instead of the sumptuous dinner the ambassador had planned, everyone sat at the table and picked at their meals. Halfway through his lamb shank, Isaac asked the ambassador in a calm, reassuring tone, "Has John ever mentioned these things before?"

"Never, at least not that I remember. I mean, they were ridiculous babblings about being resurrected from the dead and dealing with angels and demons. I have no idea where those came from. As the most powerful Jewish rabbi in the world, I'm sure he knows the Jewish Bible from front to back. On many occasions he even quotes from the Christian New Testament, but nothing like what he said tonight."

He paused for a moment and everyone could see he was having difficulty controlling his emotions before he said, "I'm so afraid he losing his mind or maybe it was a mild stroke. Tomorrow morning I will have him checked out by our team of doctors. They are the best in the world."

He stood abruptly, no longer hiding the tears or his anguish. Everyone stood with him as he said, "Please excuse my behavior, but I need to be alone. I will see you all tomorrow."

He turned abruptly and headed for the elevator to his quarters. He was sobbing loudly as the doors to the elevator closed.

Claudia escorted them to their suite. She was also distraught. "John is such a good man. He has been a dear friend to not only me but to all of us in the embassy. It breaks my heart to see him losing his mind. I feel so helpless."

Pris looked pleadingly at Isaac. He nodded and moved close to the young woman and put his arm around her and held her close, like a father comforting his child. Her crying stopped and she managed a slight smile. "Thank you so much for your compassion." She turned and left the suite, closing the door behind her.

The three of them stood silently for a moment, then Greg asked, "How could John know so much about you, Pastor? This doesn't make any sense."

"Do you think he was possessed by a demon who forced him to reveal all your secrets?" asked Pris.

The pastor shook his head. "Very unlikely. The demons who possessed the nine Marines and both NCIS special agents didn't speak through their hosts. In fact just the opposite. Also, I didn't sense any demon possession."

Greg seemed lost in thought for a few minutes, then said, "John summarized everything that happened to you from your death and resurrection, having visions from God, to casting out demons and working with angels. The only new thing was about a new Messiah, which to my way of thinking is not Biblical. Am I wrong about that, Isaac?"

"No, you're not wrong, Greg. The Bible teaches us there was only one Messiah and he lived over 2,000 years ago. He was crucified for all our sins, was resurrected three days after his death and now resides in heaven in a glorified, eternal body, sitting at the right hand of God the Father. That is basic to Christianity, even though there are some so-called Christian sects which do not preach this message. I feel it is an abomination they call themselves Christians."

"So why did a Jewish rabbi think a Messiah was coming?" asked Pris.

"There's one thing you need to know," said the pastor. "The Jews have always believed in a Messiah. However, not as a humble servant of all mankind as the Christians believe. The Jews have been waiting for thousands of years for a Messiah who will be a strong king. Someone who will lead Israel to become a powerful nation like in the days of Kings David and Solomon. I believe that is what John Baptist was speaking about, but I don't understand why he thought I was going to make that happen."

The pastor sighed. "It's been a very long and tiring day. We've been in almost every mode of transportation possible in the last 24 hours. I'm exhausted and you probably are too. I'll see you in the morning." He turned and walked into one of the suite's two bedrooms and closed the door behind him.

Pris looked at Greg and said coyly, "So where are you going to sleep tonight, cowboy?"

"On the couch with my six shooter, ma'am," he answered in his best cowboy impression.

Pris opened the door to the other bedroom and looked in at the king sized bed. She looked back at Greg and said, "The bed is huge and looks oh so comfortable, if you promise to be a good boy I don't mind sharing it with you."

"Well thank you ma'am, that's a mighty nice offer and I am kind of tuckered." He turned back and looked at the couch. "I reckon the sofa is a might small for a buckaroo my size. So I accept your gracious offer."

"Okay, but I shower first and get into bed, then you can shower and join me in the bed… way on the other side of the bed."

Fifteen minutes later everyone was snoring loudly. It really had been an exhausting day.

They were awakened early the next morning to the sound of an alarm and people shouting. Greg jumped out of bed dressed in his shorts, looking for his weapon before he remembered it was in the embassy lockup.

Pris joined him blurry eyed and hair disheveled. She was wearing a long T-shirt as her nightgown and had to grab Greg's arm to keep from losing her balance. "What's going on?" she asked. "Are we under attack?"

They cautiously walked out into the main room and saw Isaac sitting on a couch in his pajamas. His eyes were closed and he was gently rocking back and forth. He looked sad.

"Are you all right, Pastor?" asked a concerned Greg.

He opened his eyes, looked at them both and said, "They're both dead."

Before he could explain, there was a loud knock on the door.

"This is Marine Captain Black, open your door immediately." It was a wasn't a request, it was an order and from the tone of the captain's voice, an order that needed to be followed without hesitation.

Isaac went to the door and opened it a crack while Greg got embassy robes from the bedroom closet for Pris and himself.

"What's going on Captain?"

"Everyone is required to meet in the downstairs conference room. Please follow Lieutenant Connors now."

The captain turned and headed to the next bedroom door with the same message. The lieutenant waited for all the bedrooms to be emptied and then guided them to the conference room.

Within fifteen minutes everybody in the embassy, about 75 American citizens and staff, were seated waiting for someone to explain why they were rousted from their sleep. They didn't have to wait long before a Marine colonel entered the room and stood behind a podium.

"Ladies and gentlemen, the embassy is now on lockdown. No one will be allowed to enter or leave. Last night or very early this morning, two people were shot and killed in their bedrooms. Those killed were Rabbi John Baptist and Ambassador Elijah Blake.”

The announcement was shocking, like a hard slap in the face. Some couldn't believe what they just heard, many began sobbing and a few were angry, very angry. The colonel waited for the crowd to calm down and then proceeded.

“At the present time, we have no idea why they were murdered or who may have committed the crimes. As most of you know, the Israeli police have no jurisdiction here. The American Embassy complex is considered American soil. However, because of the nature of the crimes, we have invited an Israeli forensic team to assist us in the investigation. Our own team will be arriving later today from DC.

“Each of you will be questioned as to your whereabouts last night. This is just routine, we do not suspect any of you were involved in the killings. This will probably take at least a couple of days.

“A few final comments. First, Deputy Ambassador Miriam Levi is in route right now. For the foreseeable future, she will be the acting ambassador. The embassy staff will go back to work after this meeting is over. Embassy guests can do whatever they want, except they will not be allowed to leave the embassy or communicate with anyone outside the embassy. All vid coms will be collected until the investigation is completed. That's all I have for now. As soon as we have any details regarding the murders, we will keep you informed.”

Isaac stood and motioned for Greg and Pris to join him. They didn't speak to anyone on their way back to their suite, but both Greg and Pris couldn't wait to be alone with the him. They were certain he'd had a vision that would explain what happened.

They entered their suite, closed and locked the door behind them. Isaac placed a finger to his lips to signal no talking. Pris took the hint and searched through her luggage for the jammer. When she found it she placed it on the table in the living room and pushed the button. A blue flashing light indicated the jammer was doing its job of keeping anyone from hearing their conversation.

"I had a vision… No, that's not exactly correct. It felt like a vision, but it seemed more like I was watching a vid. It seemed I was in the ambassador's quarters. He appeared very distraught. He was sobbing over the condition of his closest friend. It seemed he couldn't be consoled. Then I heard a voice, a calm soothing voice that said, 'Your dear friend is waning, he will be dead within a month or two. He will suffer ever increasing pain from the disease in his brain. His memory will be the first to go. Within a few days, he will not recognize you ever again. He will be perpetually frightened and the drugs they give him will deprive him of his humanity.' The voice ceased for a moment, then continued, 'If you are truly his friend, the humane thing to do is to prevent his suffering. He will thank you for it in the afterlife. It will be like snuffing out a candle. All it will take is a single shot and he will be with his Lord. Do it now before he no longer recognizes you.'

"I watched in horror, not able to prevent what came next. The ambassador stood up and took a pistol from his nightstand, placing it in the pocket of his robe along with a master key card to all the rooms. He quietly opened his door to the hall and silently moved to John Baptist's quarters, inserted the card and opened the door.

"John was sitting in a chair in a dimly lit room facing the door, 'Who's there?' he called in a weak, distorted voice. 'Who are you?' He called again, this time his voice was full of fear. 'It's your best friend, John. Don't you know me?' the ambassador asked in a pleading voice. 'No, you are the evil one, the father of lies and prince of the air.' The fear in his voice becoming anger. 'Be gone from me, Satan. Let me die in peace.'

"The Ambassador pulled the Beretta M9 from his robe pocket, racked the slide and clicked off the safety. He raised his weapon and fired a single shot into his dearest friend's forehead, killing him instantly. 'Goodnight my friend. You are forever with your God now.'

"Most of the rooms in the embassy are soundproofed. Late at night, the gunshot was muffled and hardly noticed. Most of the residents were sound asleep.

"I watched him walk slowly down the hall to his elaborate quarters. He sat down in a soft, comfortable chair next to the bed with the Beretta lying in this lap. Then the voice returned. 'You fool! You insufferable, stupid fool! Do you realize what you have done? You've murdered your best friend. He was the hope of the future. He could have made Israel strong again. Whatever possessed you to murder someone so important?' 'But... but you said he was dying. You told me it was the humane thing to do, to keep him from suffering, you said...' 'Oh shut up. Don't you have a mind of your own? This is all on you. You are ruined. They will discover you are a murderer and they will strip you of all your wealth and power. I'm so glad your wife isn't alive to see you now. It's only a matter of time before you are executed. That's what they do to murderers in Israel. Why don't you just shoot yourself and be done with it.'

"And that's exactly what he did. He put the barrel of the gun against his temple and pulled the trigger."

"That's terrible," cried Pris.

"What happened next?" asked Greg.

Isaac paused, shaken by what he just relived, more so by what was to come. He tried to speak but couldn't make the words come out. Pris quickly brought him a glass of water and the pastor took a long drink.

"What happened next was that I saw a shadowy image materialize next to the body of the ambassador and it said to me in its smooth deep baritone voice, 'See how easy it is to manipulate humans? Even the smartest of humans.'

"I could see the beginning of a smile forming on the face of the shadowy figure, then it said, 'So you are the dreaded prophet we are supposed to fear. I don't understand why we should fear any human being. But we won't have to worry, you're next on my list to die.'"

Greg and Pris sat quietly on the couch, watching the pastor and having no idea how to respond to what he had just told them. He waited patiently for them to say something, but when they didn't respond he asked, "So, what do you think?"

Greg hesitated, then said, "I think nobody would believe you if you told them what you just told us."

Pris added, "I think the investigators will come to the conclusion this was a mercy killing followed by a suicide."

Greg built on Pris's comments. "Based on what you just told us, I think a demon or perhaps even Satan himself, was the voice you heard coercing the ambassador into murdering John, then getting him to commit suicide. It doesn't sound like demonic possession, does it to you, Isaac?"

The pastor shook his head. "No, but I agree with Greg. The demon had to be a very high ranking spirit to be so effective in manipulating the murders."

Aren't you concerned about the threat it made about killing you?" questioned Pris.

"No, not really, but let's contact an expert to be sure," replied Isaac. "Uriel, are you with us?"

"Always," was the immediate reply. His voice was so deep and strong it made the room resonate.

Isaac said, "Pris wants to know if you are strong enough to protect us from the demon who threatened to kill me."

"Wait a minute," protested Pris. "I said no such…"

"I know what you said, Pris," interrupted Uriel. "Don't worry, I know you don't doubt my ability to protect all of you, even against Satan himself. Please remember, Satan is just an angel, a fallen angel. I know he has powers and skills humans do not currently possess. But none of you can die unless my Lord wills it. I can assure you he does not will it."

Uriel's reassurance changed their entire attitude. Of course, they were saddened by the loss of the two men, but they felt encouraged they would persevere no matter what God had in store for them.

Isaac changed topics and said, "We will be questioned soon regarding our whereabouts from the time we left the dining room last evening until we were summoned to the conference room this morning. All of us should tell the investigators exactly what we did during that time interval. Of course, I will not share anything regarding what I saw during my dream. I'm not sure if that's what I had, but I know it was not a vision from God.

"In the meantime, we should continue to rest up from yesterday's travels, perhaps watch the local news vids and get a better feel of what's going on in Israel. I still don't have the foggiest idea what my mission will be here. I assume I will receive visions from God as he sees fit."

It took two days to finish the interviews. During that time, the two investigative teams came to the same conclusion. Ballistic tests confirmed the Beretta M9 found in the ambassador's quarters was the same weapon used to kill both John Baptist and the ambassador. Forensic evidence determined the only fingerprints found on the Beretta were those of the ambassador. The gun powder residue surrounding the entry wound on the ambassador's right temple supported the position he had committed suicide.

Piecing together all the evidence, the investigators concluded it was a murder/suicide. The only thing missing was a strong motive. Those present at the dinner the evening before the murders suggested the death of John Baptist had been a mercy killing. However, when the results of the investigation were released to the press, they took a different position.

The Israeli national news headlines read in bold print and large font:

AMERICAN AMBASSADOR MURDERS BELOVED RABBI IN COLD BLOOD

Every vid network in Israel condemned the United States for the actions of the American ambassador. Every hour some new approach to vilify America was introduced. Some suggested America thought of Israel as a second rate power who needed to be subservient to American needs. Others suggested it was a Christian coalition against the Jewish interests. Still others seemed to feel the Americans 'removed' a powerful Jewish Rabbi in an attempt to strengthen their relationship with the Muslims. It went on and on throughout the day.

Anti-American feelings exploded. Within a few hours, angry Israelis were preparing to storm the embassy gates. To protect the embassy in case things got out of hand, the Marines were placed on high alert. Their weapons were armed with rubber bullets to prevent any bloodshed, however, most carried additional magazines with live ammo.

At noon, Ambassador Miriam Levi spoke to the crowd from the embassy's second floor balcony. "Good afternoon, ladies and gentlemen, my name is Miriam Levi and I am a Jew."

She waited to see if those who were close to rioting would let her speak. When they had quieted to a dull roar, she continued. "I was born in Tel Aviv to Jewish parents. When I say they were Jewish, I mean they were born in Israel, but they were also religious Jews and worshipped at the synagogue every Sabbath."

The crowd had quieted considerably, waiting to hear what else she had to say.

"My parents and siblings migrated to New York when I was 10 where we continued to worship at the Temple Emanu-El in New York City. My parents and I applied for and were granted American citizenship when I turned 15. When I turned 18, I returned to Israel and joined the Israeli Defense Force fighting against Palestinian terrorists.

"Like many Jews, I have dual citizenship. I am a citizen of both the United States and of Israel. During my career at the U.S. State Department, I had the good fortune to meet with Rabbi John Baptist. Like many Jews, he was born in a foreign country. His mother was from Israel but his father was French, both were religious Jews.

"I became one of John's avid followers and attended many of his seminars." She stopped for a moment to regain her composure, then said in a ragged, angry voice, "And the murder of John Baptist was the worst atrocity I've ever heard of." She paused again, then began. "The Israeli and American investigators say his death was a mercy killing. I say there was no mercy in John's murder. Ambassador Blake had no right to end John's life. I think he came to that conclusion, but only after it was too late. He took his own life, but it wasn't enough."

The crowd was silent now and waited for her to continue.

"I've been chosen to be the acting American Ambassador to Israel. I have no idea how long I will be here in Jerusalem. The State Department may bring in someone else to replace me and send me back to the branch office in Tel Aviv. While I'm in Jerusalem, I pledge to you that I will do my best, my very best, to defend Israel's interests while at the same time, strengthening the bond between my two countries.

"Let me leave you with this thought. Do not blame America for the death of Rabbi John Baptist, all the blame should be directed on former Ambassador Elijah Blake, may he burn in hell forever!"

There was a smattering of applause as the ambassador turned and walked back into the conference room adjacent to the balcony. The ambassador in Jerusalem has a 50 member staff, however, there were only 10 of the highest ranking staff members present to critique her brief presentation. Pastor Isaac Silberman and his two aides had also been invited.

She walked in and took a seat at the head of the table. "Tell me what you think about what I just told some of our citizens. By the way, I want you all to know I don't tolerate ass kissers. Okay, let's hear it."

No one wanted to go first. After a moment of silence, the pastor said, "Madam Ambassador…"

"Don't get all formal on me, Isaac. Just tell me what you think."

Not many of her staff knew the pastor or his aides. In fact, only a few even knew the ambassador. None of them wanted to be the first to give their opinion to the ambassador in front of the rest of the staff for fear of saying the wrong thing.

Isaac smiled and said, "Okay Miriam, I thought your opening approach was spot on. You established you are first and foremost an Israeli citizen with strong Jewish religious beliefs. I especially liked the fact you added your service in the IDF. I believe that surprised many of the crowd who knew nothing about you. Next, you brought up your dual citizenship and how your job was to strengthen the ties between your two countries. You were very tactful in isolating America from the actions of Ambassador Blake. Lastly, it pained me greatly to hear you say Elijah was the sole cause of John Baptist's death. It was true and it had to be said, but it still grieves me to hear it." He paused for a moment then said, "That's all I have to say."

The room went silent as Miriam looked sadly at Isaac and gently shook her head and softly said, "It grieves me too, Isaac. It hurt me to say it, but it was necessary."

One of the senior attachés shifted in his seat.

"You have a comment Eric?" asked Miriam.

"No ma'am, two questions. First, who is this Isaac?"

"He's a close personal friend. He was my professor at Dallas Seminary and taught me Old Testament Theology. Isaac is recognized as one of the top theologians in the world. Any other questions? Anyone?"

"Do you really expect any of us to add anything to his comments?"

She smiled briefly then said, "I guess not, thank you all for showing up. Work starts tomorrow. You're dismissed."

When they all left, Miriam walked over and gave Isaac a hug while Greg and Pris looked on. "You will never know how much your being here meant to me. Thank you for your suggestions, Professor. You and your aides will always be welcome here as long as I'm the ambassador." She gave him a brief kiss on the cheek and said, "Now get out of here and go visit Jerusalem. See how things have changed since you were here last."

They made their way down to the main floor. When Greg requested their weapons, a Marine on duty contacted his captain.

"Mr. Stone, why do you think you need your weapons with you?" asked the captain. "Do you expect to be involved in some type of conflict?"

"First of all Captain, we aren't tourists, were diplomats," answered Greg in a no-nonsense, military voice. "We will be gathering intel in Old Jerusalem at the Temple Mount area. Secondly, I'm not Mr. Stone, I'm Lieutenant Colonel Gregory Stone. Thirdly, all three of us will be packing nonlethal dart guns, the Wireless Taser-12 model to be exact. Lastly, I will be the only one carrying a Glock 22. Now tell me Captain, what is the hold up in getting our weapons?"

When Greg mentioned his Marine rank, the captain stiffened noticeably to attention. After Stone had finished his tirade, the captain replied, "No problem at all, sir." He turned to the sergeant who had summoned him and ordered, "Get the Lieutenant Colonel his weapons."

The sergeant saluted and moved quickly, returning with all the required weapons. Stone did a brief check of each of them, then looked up at the captain and nodded. "It looks like you took good care of our equipment, Captain. I also appreciate your attention to protocol, carry on."

Both the captain and the sergeant snapped to attention and saluted Stone.

"I'm not in uniform, Captain. You don't have to salute me."

"Yes sir. I'm not saluting you sir. I'm saluting the creator of the VOG. You saved the lives of thousands of Marine jarheads like myself. God bless you sir."

Stone paused a beat, then commented, "Thank you, Captain. I hope you're right."

The three of them passed through the security portal, out under the portico where their limo was waiting. Stone and the pastor were silent as Pris commanded the limo to take them to the Temple Mount. It was going to be an interesting day.

During their relatively short ride to the Temple Mount, Isaac filled them in on what they were going to see. "Our first stop will be at the Western Wall. It is the only remaining section of the second Jewish temple. The first temple was built by King Solomon around 950 BC. It was destroyed by the Babylonians in 586 BC. A second temple began construction 70 years later. When Harrod the Great became King, he finished an extensive upgrade to the temple in 20 BC. In 70 AD the temple was destroyed by the Romans and never rebuilt. The only remaining portion of the temple is a section of a wall called The Western Wall.

"The dimensions of the exposed section of the wall that survived the Roman destruction are 160 feet in length by 60 feet high, although the wall goes much deeper into the ground. The Western Wall has existed for over 2,000 years and is considered a holy relic by the Jews. The wall is open to non-Jews, but there are some restrictions regarding dress and the touching of the wall.

"I see we are almost there; make sure your dart guns are hidden under your clothing. To the best of my knowledge we won't be scanned when we enter. Pris, make sure your legs, head and shoulders are covered before you approach the women's section of the wall. It's pretty much the same for men. If you don't have a hat, they will hand you a little paper equivalent of a *yamaka*. Some men use a bobby pin to hold the hat in place."

"What if they're bald?" asked Greg.

"Glue, maybe?" replied Pris.

"Stay focused," interrupted Isaac. "I suggest you approach the wall straight on, no talking and stop an arm's-length from the wall. Don't look around. Maybe close your eyes and pray or meditate. Jews sometime speak their prayers in Hebrew. Some Jews stand and pray for hours. Since you are not Jews, limit your stay for about five to ten minutes. Don't take any pictures of people praying. That's not tolerated."

"Is that all?" asked Greg somewhat sarcastically. "That's a lot to remember."

"Just follow me," replied Isaac. "But stay slightly behind me and an arm's-length away from me on my right. Pris, just follow one of the women who look like this isn't their first visit. Let's do it."

As they approached the wall, something unexpected happened. It was the voices of the Jews as they melded together speaking Hebrew. Some chanted softly, repeating the same words over and over. Others sang their prayers as they expressed their feelings in famous Jewish *zemirots* and other religious songs. In the men's section, some of the voices were deep and the sounds vibrated off the surface of the wall. Others, with a higher pitch, formed a moving harmony of religious emotions. On top were the light sounds of the women's voices migrating and blending into the sounds of the men.

To Greg, it seemed like the music went on forever and he never wanted to leave. When Isaac touched his shoulder he was startled. When the pastor backed away from the wall, Greg hesitated for a moment then followed.

They met up with Pris along a pathway leading to a colorful garden area and sat down at one of the many picnic tables. Greg noticed Isaac was strangely quiet, as if he weren't feeling well.

A young man wearing a *yamaka* wheeled a cart with various refreshments for sale and stopped at their table. Greg paid for their drinks and snacks and waited until he moved on to other customers before he asked Pris, "Well, what did you think of your first time at the Western Wall?"

She briefly hesitated then replied, "It was mesmerizing!"

"That's the word I was searching for, mesmerizing!" exclaimed Greg. "It was truly mesmerizing. I've never heard sounds like that before."

"I know, me neither," said Pris in a dreamy voice. "I could actually hear the sounds of tears running down the cheeks of the women, feeling the blending of so many levels of pain and suffering. It was excruciating, but at the same time I could sense their strength, their combined strength giving them hope for what lies ahead."

Greg stared, mouth open, an expression of amazement on his face. "I didn't hear anything like that. What I heard was completely different. Isaac, what did you fee... Isaac! Are you okay?"

In a low voice he answered, "Get me back to the embassy, please, as quickly as you can."

Greg helped Isaac to his feet as Pris used her wrist com signaling for the limo to pick them up. Once strapped in, the limo accelerated to the maximum allowable speed with its exterior red and blue lights flashing.

Once back at the embassy, a staff member escorted Isaac to a small clinic on the lower level. While the doctor began checking the pastor over, they waited impatiently just outside the examination room.

They were both worried, but had no idea what had come over Isaac so quickly. "The pastor was fine as we backed away from the wall," exclaimed Greg. "Did you notice anything unusual about our boss after we sat down at the picnic table?"

"Not at all," answered Pris. "He was just sipping his drink. I don't know if he had eaten any of the snacks or not. I was paying attention to you, sharing feelings about the wall."

Ten minutes later, the doctor came out of the examination room. "Isaac is resting now. I think he may have had a touch of food poisoning. He will be fine; however, he should rest for the remainder of the day. How are you two feeling? Did you drink the same thing Isaac drank?"

Greg looked at Pris. She shrugged her shoulders. "We don't know. I don't think we did, but I'm not sure. I feel fine. How about you Pris?"

"I'm okay," she replied.

They placed Isaac into a unmotorized wheelchair and Greg pushed him to the elevator. Pris looked concerned as they took him to their suite. Once inside, Isaac struggled to mumble, "Jammer."

It took both of them to get him out of the chair and onto his bed. Pris turned on the jammer and she and Greg pulled up chairs next to the bed. They sat there quietly for a moment then Pris whispered, "Say a prayer for him, Greg. You're good at prayers. I really liked hearing you pray at Grace Community Church."

Greg nodded, closed his eyes and bowed his head. "Dear heavenly father, we ask for your mercy for your servant, Isaac..."

"Wow! I'm glad that's finally over."

Their heads snapped up and their eyes opened to see Isaac sitting in the bed looking completely normal. Before they could gather their wits about them, Isaac added, "I hope that never happens again. Praise the Lord."

He noticed the shocked expressions on their faces and said, "I'm guessing you'd like to know what happened to me?"

Without changing their expressions, they both nodded.

He smiled broadly and began. "Listen my children and you shall hear, of the midnight tale full of fright and fear..." He chuckled and added, "I love the poetic play on words, however, I can tell you are not in the mood for poetry. So let me start from the beginning… again. Let me preface my story by saying, I am very happy to be alive.

"While Greg and I were standing by the wall, I had a vision. In the vision, I saw the Western Wall begin to crumble. Everyone turned from the wall screaming with fear and began running to escape the destruction. Then the wall looked like it was being assaulted by a hundred VOGs and in no time the wall and everything that surrounded it had disintegrated. There were no people, no buildings, no trees nor shrubs, only a flat barren desert as far as the eye could see.

"I meditated on the meaning of the vision as I walked back to the picnic tables. Then something completely unexpected happened. The vision returned, except it happened in a flash, as if time was being fast forwarded.

"On that barren desert plane a new temple was being created. It was larger and grander than the temple of Solomon and seemed to rise from the ashes. It was like the ash became the building material for not only the temple but also for the city as well. It all happened so quickly. It was difficult to keep up with the details of the various structures.

"All of a sudden, it was finished. It was as if I were sitting on a distant hill, looking down on not only the temple site, but also an incredible futuristic city and a flourishing countryside.

"I thought it was the new temple prophesized by Ezekiel. My heart was filled with a happiness I hadn't felt in so many years. I couldn't wait to share what I had just experienced with you."

Isaac stopped and seemed puzzled. "I can't seem to remember what happened after that. That's odd. The next thing I remembered was waking up in my bed feeling fine, but very tired. Perhaps my memories will come back to me after a good meal and eight hours of sleep."

Isaac spent the rest of the day recovering from whatever had been ailing him. He had his dinner brought to their suite in the embassy. Pris and Greg had their meals delivered as well. The pastor said he was fine and suggested the two of them eat in the embassy dining hall, but Greg disagreed.

"As your acolyte, I will not leave your side until I'm sure you don't have a relapse. Food poisoning can take a lot out of a person. I want you to eat your dinner and relax the rest of the evening where I can monitor you."

"I agree with the acolyte," added Pris. "You need us to keep an eye on you for the rest of the day."

"Since when did you have a say about my health?" the pastor teased.

Without missing a beat, Pris answered, "Since Greg appointed me assistant acolyte."

Greg looked surprised. "When did that happen?"

"A long time ago, but it became official when we were leaving the Temple Mount. Didn't it, Greg?"

He paused for only a split second then smiled and confirmed Pris's comments. "Yes, absolutely. I appointed her my assistant. I'm sure you don't remember. You weren't in any condition to hear about her promotion after you came down with your illness."

Isaac didn't say anything for a long moment, then nodded his head. "You're correct. I have no memory of anything after we walked back to the picnic area." He paused again then added, "Welcome aboard, assistant acolyte. Would you mind opening the door? Our dinners are coming down the hall."

A second later, there was a series of beeps from the other side of the door to their suite. She opened it and the robo food cart drove itself into the middle of the room and a synthetic voice said, "Your dinners are here. *Bon appétit.*"

When dinner was over, the cart returned and cleared the plates, silverware and glasses and closed the door behind itself.

"How are you feeling, Pastor?" asked Greg after they'd left the dining area.

"I didn't realize how hungry I was," he replied. "Whoever the embassy chef is, we should praise their talents. I thought the dinner was as good as any five-star restaurant. How about you two? What did you think?"

Greg gave the pastor a slight smile and said, "I'm not a big fan of French cuisine, but it was alright."

Pris giggled and said, "You probably prefer Q-paks"

"During my twenty years of service in the Marines, I grew to enjoy any food they gave me," Greg replied, somewhat indigent.

"Are Q-paks the same as MREs? I found them to be barely edible during my tour of duty in the Ukraine," Isaac added.

"Q-paks are much tastier and self-heating," answered Greg.

There was a short pause before the pastor spoke up. "How did we get off on this ridiculous food tangent? I find it very tiresome. In fact it was exhausting… I think I'll retire for the evening. Good night you two, sleep well."

The next morning, after an excellent breakfast (based on Isaac's evaluation) they moved to what he called the conversation area. It had to two loveseats facing each other and four very comfortable high-back arm chairs with well cushioned seats. In the center was a large, low coffee table that could also serve as a footrest. It was the perfect place for casual conversations, even unofficial government discussions.

"I'd like to address some issues I've been thinking about," Isaac began. "It seems like some of my missing memory has begun to return which has led to several questions."

"What kind of issues?" asked Pris.

"About my visions. They've led me to questions I don't have answers for and I thought you two acolytes might supply some answers or perhaps you have vision questions of your own."

"That sounds intriguing," said Greg,

Pris nodded her head enthusiastically. "Why don't you start with the first question?" Pris asked the pastor.

"Okay," he replied. He paused for a moment to collect his thoughts, then began. "My last vision was similar in some ways to other visions I've had. The main theme seemed to be the destruction of Jerusalem or at least a Jewish holy place like the Western Wall.

"In this last vision, we were at the Western Wall, the only remaining portion of the last temple. I was walking backwards, away from the wall when it began to crumble. The people who had come to pray turned and began running away, screaming in terror. As the wall continued to disintegrate, the people seemed to fade from sight and the screaming stopped.

"Then I noticed it wasn't just the wall, it was everything around it, like the adjacent museum that depicted the history of the temples, the picnic areas across from the wall, the tree lined streets with moving traffic, everything was turning to dust as if a million VOGs had been used to turn the entire city to powder.

"Eventually, the area looked like a wasteland as far as the eye could see, no temples, no buildings and no people. The only sound I could hear was the wind blowing across a deserted plane.

"That was the first part of the vision. Any ideas what it was supposed to represent?"

"The first thing that comes to mind is the destruction of Jerusalem, similar to when the Romans destroyed Jerusalem in 70 AD," offered Greg.

"I was thinking it was symbolic of the destruction of all of Israel," said Pris. "The lack of people in the vision could represent the elimination of all the Jews in Israel or perhaps the entire world."

Isaac put his half full coffee cup down on the table, sat up straight and said, "I never thought about what you just suggested. However, if this vision is truly about End Times, what you suggested is a distinct possibility."

"How many Jews are there?" asked Pris.

Greg said a few words into his wrist smart-chrono and got the answer. "At the last census, there were eight million Jews in Israel, over sixteen million in the entire world. Why do you ask?"

Pris seemed lost in thought before she asked, "What event would bring all those Jews to Jerusalem?"

Isaac answered immediately, "The dedication of a new temple on the Temple Mount."

"But they can't build a temple on the Temple Mount. The Dome of the Rock would make that impossible," said Greg. "In your vision did you notice if the Dome of the Rock survived?"

Isaac shook his head. "In my vision, I never saw if the Dome existed. However, it was never in my line of sight."

"I noticed we could see the Dome of the Rock as we entered the Temple Mount from the west side. However, as we walked down the steps from the parking lot, the Western Wall blocked the view of the Dome," added Greg. "Or maybe in your vision it was destroyed along with the wall."

"You've given me a lot to consider," said the pastor. "However, I'd like to move on to the second part of my vision. I feel I might regain some of my forgotten memories as I recount them to you."

Greg and Pris nodded their heads in agreement so Isaac continued. "The second part moved on very quickly, almost too quickly for the eye to see. A temple began to rise from the ashes. It appeared to be about 50% larger than Solomon's Temple. It grew in its stature and its majesty as the temple was completed. At first, I thought it was the temple described by Ezekiel, but it didn't seem to match the dimensions recorded in chapter 40 of his Old Testament book.

"When the temple was finished, a futuristic city formed around it which grew as far as the eye could see. It was a walled city with enormous gates on each of the four sides. Six lane roads led into and out of the gates and there also appeared to be maglev tracks. A large airport and sub-orbital port were just outside the walls. I almost forgot to mention, the city was situated between two large rivers with huge seaports only a short distance from the gates."

He stopped to gather his thoughts, then added, "There were so many colorful lights inside the city and on the tops of the walls. The lights were brighter and more colorful than anything Las Vegas, Tokyo or Macau had to offer, with elaborate, three dimensional moving displays and advertisements."

Isaac paused once more and his demeanor and voice changed. It seemed as if he could hardly speak. "On top of each of the four gates were enormous signs that scrolled across the gates in vivid red lights: Welcome to New Baghdad, Madinat al-Salām (City of Peace), The Home of the New Messiah."

He stopped talking as his memories flooded back into his mind. He swallowed twice and attempted to speak, but his voice had left him.

Pris handed him a glass of water and he drank deeply, nodding his thanks to her, then began again. "Once I realized this wasn't a Jewish city, it came to me in a flash. This was the city of the Antichrist and I was seeing into the middle of the seven year tribulation. I felt trapped. I desperately wanted the vision to end. But it was too late.

"I heard a voice whispering in my ear. It was the same voice I'd heard telling Ambassador Blake to murder his friend John Baptist, then to kill himself. 'You should not be seeing these things,' his voice was a searing wave of heat burning my ear. 'You will not share what you saw with anyone. It's not time for mankind to know about the future.' I could smell my flesh beginning to blister from the fire in his voice, my whole head felt like it was engulfed in pain and I knew what was to follow. 'You will be subjected to the full wrath of my master. Today you will die a most hideous death.'

"'No he won't,' interrupted Uriel. 'Be gone from here, spawn of Satan. Henceforth you are banished forever from the Earth and will suffer in the lake of fire for all eternity.'"

The three of them sat stunned, not only from the description of Isaac's vision, but also from the presence of Uriel. He had materialized and repeated his own message to the demon. "How many times do I have to tell you to call on me for help?" his deep, rumbling voice asked. "I am, and always will be, your guardian angel. Have you forgotten what that means?"

Uriel turned to face Isaac, his essence filling nearly all of the ten feet high living area. "If you'd called on me as soon as the demon showed up, I would have... made sure you didn't have to endure his torture. I wouldn't have had to block your memories at all, if you'd only called on me sooner. I was just waiting for you to ask for me, not only to save your life, but also to give me the opportunity to get rid of that particular demon. He's been a thorn in my side even before God banished Satan and his demons to Earth."

Before any of the group could respond, Uriel faded into invisibility.

They all sat mute, not having any idea what to say. Finally, the pastor said, "I'm so glad Uriel restored my memories. However, those memories have led to additional questions. Unfortunately, I'm currently both physically and emotionally drained. I need a nap."

He headed toward his bedroom, then stopped abruptly and said to Pris and Greg, "I almost forgot the short vision I had last night. You two are going to get married next week here in the embassy. Congratulations."

Pris and Greg were beyond stunned, they were almost comatose from all that had happened since breakfast. Time passed while the pastor's prophecy sunk in. When it did, Pris squealed with delight, hugged her now fiancé and kissed him numerous times. During all the kissing, Greg thought to himself, *what a crazy, mixed up, wonderful world we live in.*

After a two hour nap, Isaac was ready to go again. Pris and Greg were still excited about their wedding. Isaac decided that should be first on their agenda.

"Greg, during the shortest vision I have ever had, I learned you were going to propose to Pris tomorrow. Let me give you the wedding details you haven't seriously thought about yet, but were considering. Of course, since I'm an ordained minister, I will be the one marrying you two. Miriam will agree to be your matron of honor and Marine Captain Black will be your best man. Miriam will provide your wedding ring as her gift to the bride. I was able to see the engagement ring in my vision. I think you will be pleased."

Pris just sat on the couch smiling and shaking her head in disbelief as Isaac went over the wedding plans.

Greg didn't seem as pleased. "Do I get to say, 'I do' or are you going to handle that too?"

Isaac stared at him briefly before continuing. "If you feel I have usurped your responsibilities, I apologize. However, in light of how quickly things are moving now, I thought it best to make some of your wedding arrangements. I'm afraid we don't have a week or two to plan a wedding. If it pleases you, I will step back and scrap all the things I've mentioned. It's your choice."

Pris turned to Greg, took his hand and said softly, "Please, dear, if you think I'm not happy about the plans he's made for us, don't be concerned. I learned in combat, life can be short. From my perspective, the sooner we're married, the happier I will be."

Greg looked at his future wife and kissed her on the cheek then said, "If it pleases you, it pleases me. Sorry for giving you a hard time, Pastor. What's next?"

"During my nap, I had another vision. It seems like the visions are coming faster now. The questions we had regarding the Dome of the Rock are partially answered. The Dome of the Rock is going to be destroyed in the very near future, less than a week from now."

"What?!!!" yelled Greg in disbelief as he jumped to his feet. "If that's true, everyone is going to think it was the Jews who did it. Israel will be back in a war again. This is terrible... Why are you smiling?"

"Because in my vision, I was able to determine it wasn't the Jews."

Greg sat back down next to Pris and asked, "If it wasn't the Jews, who was it?"

"Strangely enough, I don't really know, at least not yet. It may show up in another vision," answered Isaac.

"What do you think the Jews will do once the Dome is gone?" Pris asked.

"I'd guess with the Dome gone, the Israeli's might attempt to build a third temple on the Temple Mount."

"Do you think the Muslims will permit that?" questioned Pris.

"It depends," Isaac answered. "I can see one scenario where the Muslims would support the Jews in constructing a third temple."

"I find that very hard to believe," countered Greg. "I'd think they'd want to build a new Dome of the Rock instead."

"You could be right, Greg," Isaac replied. "That's another possible option."

Pris looked puzzled when she asked the pastor, "Why would you think the Muslims would even consider letting the Jews build another temple, especially on the Dome of the Rock location?"

"Because if the Jews build a new temple, the vast majority of the worldwide Jewish population would come for the dedication," replied Isaac. "With one nuclear weapon, the Muslims could eliminate the entire Jewish race."

Both Greg and Pris sat silently considering what the pastor just suggested. They never imagined genocide would be an option. Isaac spoke up, "These options are just speculations. At this point, I feel additional visions will occur to allow us to see more details of what will happen in the near future." Then he added, "I think I need to inform Miriam of exactly who I am and what I can do. I don't want her to get blindsided. Do you two agree to that?"

They both nodded as Greg said, "I hope she's prepared to hear the truth about you."

"So do I, Greg," he said. "So do I." He sat down in one of the comfortable chairs in the conversation area and changed directions. "After dinner, I think we should discuss my vision of New Baghdad and the new Messiah."

Pris contacted the kitchen to see what was on the menu for tonight's meal. There were a few options, but all of them sounded good. She took their orders and passed them on to the kitchen. It would be delivered within 30 minutes by the robo food cart as usual.

"What does the Bible tell us about the tribulation?" asked Isaac as the robo food cart cleared away the remains of their dinners.

Pris answered first. "I'm afraid I don't know much and I'm not sure what I know is accurate. Doesn't it happen just before the second coming of Jesus?"

"That's a good start, Pris," encouraged the pastor. "How about you, Greg?"

"If I remember correctly, the Book of Daniel in the Old Testament says it's a seven year period of time which ends in a huge battle between Jesus and Satan," replied Greg. "I think the Book of Revelation in the New Testament has even more information, but much of it is written allegorically. I found the symbolism very confusing."

Pris shook her head and said to Greg, "I found what you just said confusing. What does allegorical mean?"

"Perhaps it would be better if I just explained my understanding of what will occur during the seven years of tribulation and where my latest vision fits in. Would that be okay with you both?" asked the pastor.

They both agreed and Isaac began with a disclaimer, "What I'm about to share with you is my own interpretation. Many knowledgeable theologians do not agree with my opinions on certain details; however, I believe we all agree on the big picture.

"As you both said, the tribulation is a seven year period of time that occurs at the end of this age. Based on other Biblical predictions, this could occur at any time. All other Biblical predictions have already come true. The seven years is divided into two parts, each lasting three and a half years. The first part will be a unification of the world. A charismatic leader will come upon the scene who convinces all the nations of the world to unite into a world government. All war will be abolished forever and economically the world will prosper like never before. As part of this unification, all the major religions will consolidate into a unified system of beliefs and worship based on the principle there is only one God. Of course, this unification will require many compromises.

"By the end of the first half of the tribulation, the majority of the population will believe this approach has led to a perfect world. But that belief will quickly change.

"The charismatic leader who claims no national citizenship, denies he ever wanted to be the world's leader. He will claim it was forced on him. As World Leader, he oversees all facets of the world government, including religion. Some religions, Judaism included, will reject the unification of the church. Their rebellion leads to conflict. Martial law is required and the leader is given the power of a supreme dictator. Many of the previous member-nations wish to withdraw from the world government, worldwide war ensues and the supreme dictator is assassinated. Three days after his death, he rises from the dead and claims he is now the new Messiah, a divine leader with powers only a god can claim.

"He establishes his kingdom in a fantastic city, complete with a huge temple located between the Tigris and Euphrates Rivers. He abolishes the world church; all traditional religious worship ceases. Anyone who violates the law and fails to worship him, and only him, is publicly executed."

"The world is in complete chaos, but there remains a remnant of true believers. At the end of the seven years, the true second coming occurs, Judgment Day is at hand. A new heaven and earth are created and sin is abolished. Satan and all his demons, along with those who chose not to believe Jesus was God in human form, are sent to hell."

He paused and his expression turned to a look of great sadness. "This will be very difficult for the majority of the world to accept. There are three major religions that believe there is only one God, that would be Judaism, Islam and Christianity. Each of those religions have millions of believers who honestly believe they, and only they, know the correct way to worship God. In addition, there are millions more who believe there is more than one god and others who believe there is no god at all.

"Only the Christian religions believe Jesus Christ is God in human form. However, there are a variety of beliefs as to how we are to interact with Jesus, and even within those calling themselves Christian a great many have a different way of understanding the nature of Jesus and the Trinity. Again, those people are dedicated in their hearts and minds that they know the true path to salvation. However, there can only be one true path. I strongly believe that during the tribulation dramatic changes to religious beliefs will occur. When the World Religion collapses, the minds of many people will be opened and new Apostles will arise to preach the truth, the real truth, whatever that may be. As a result, many more will be saved. To me, saved or not saved is a choice. It is up to mankind to choose wisely."

"What happens to those who choose not to be saved?" asked Pris.

"Once they have made that choice, there is no turning back. They will all go to hell," replied Isaac.

"Exactly what is hell?" asked Greg.

"There are a variety of views on what hell is about due to the allegorical nature of the way Revelation is written. To some, hell refers to instant and permanent annihilation. To others it means suffering forever in a burning lake of fire. Still others believe only Satan and his demons will suffer for eternity in a lake of fire while other humans suffer for varying periods of time depending on how many sins they accumulated, followed by annihilation."

Greg and Pris sat quietly, processing what Isaac just taught them. After a long moment, Greg asked, "So your vision of the City of Peace occurs towards the end of the tribulation?"

The pastor nodded. Then Pris said, "Then the reason the demon wanted to kill you was to prevent you from sharing your vision with the world's current population? If they were forewarned, they might not be so gullible about this new Messiah?"

Greg added, "Then maybe your visions about the Western Wall being destroyed and the Dome of the Rock being blown up was to clear the way for this world religion. The new Messiah would want them worshiping only him at *his* temple."

"You both could be right. I feel I now know why I received my visions and I recognize what I should do about it. It all begins with me sharing with Ambassador Miriam everything that's happened to us since I was reborn. If she believes me, she might be able to get me an interview with the Israeli Prime Minister. If I can convince him my visions are true, perhaps we can at least delay the end of the world and give more of mankind the opportunity to be saved.

"I'd like you both to join me for that meeting. You two can verify my death and resurrection and the fact I do have visions. If I were in Miriam's place, I'd want a couple of witnesses to confirm what I was telling her."

Later that evening, Isaac contacted the ambassador's private secretary and requested a private meeting for no more than one hour. The pastor assured the young man it had nothing to do with the upcoming wedding, but it was very important. The secretary indicated the ambassador was completely booked for the next two days. Isaac thanked the secretary and hung up.

The pastor sat and waited ten minutes with his eyes closed, breathing calmly for the entire time. When his com unit beeped, he touched the speaker button so they all could hear and said, "Hello Miriam, thank you for your com."

"My secretary told me you'd called for an appointment for tomorrow. I hope you can wait a few days. Ordinarily, I'd cancel one of my meetings for you, however, I have one important meeting after another for the next two days. Two of them are with the Israeli Prime Minister, one on each day with some important politicians from America and France."

"Don't be concerned, Miriam. Your 10:00 A.M. meeting for tomorrow is going to be canceled."

There was the muffled sound as if the ambassador was holding her hand over her com unit's speaker. When she came back on line, she said, "I just spoke to my secretary. He said our meeting was confirmed two hours ago. We will be hosting the American Secretary of State. He will be arriving early tomorrow morning by a government Mach 2 Cruise Liner. His Maglev train has already arrived at the Dulles High-Mach Airport and he will be boarding soon. There's no way this meeting gets canceled. I'll work you in as soon as I can. I have to leave now. Good-bye Isaac, I'll see you soon."

She hung up and Isaac looked at his two acolytes with a sly smile. "You had another vision, didn't you?" accused Pris.

"Whatever gave you that impression?"

"Because now that I'm an acolyte, I can read your mind," she answered.

The pastor began to laugh as Greg stood up in mock anger and growled, "Wait a minute. I'm a full acolyte and you're only my assistant. Why do you get to read his mind and I don't?"

"Oh Greg, isn't it obvious?" she replied. "I'm a woman. Everyone knows women are more sensitive than men. I don't need to have visions to see mysterious things."

Greg picked up a cushion from one of the arm chairs and hit her softly in the head saying, "That's the last straw. You're fired. You're no longer an assistant acolyte!"

Isaac spoke out in an official voice with a laughing undertone, "I override you, senior acolyte. Pris is promoted from assistant acolyte to associate."

They were all laughing now. With all the insanity going on around them, they needed a good laugh. Pris threw the cushion back at Greg and asked, "Do I get a raise in pay?"

"No," laughed the pastor, even harder now. "However, you have my undying gratitude."

The rest of the evening went by quickly. Isaac was the first to head to the bedroom. He wanted to plan out what he was going to say to Miriam. Shortly after the pastor retired, Greg and Pris headed for their shared bedroom. They changed into their night clothes, but before they got into bed, they both checked the charges on their respective dart guns. Greg pulled the Glock from under his pillow, ejected the magazine and checked the load. He inserted the magazine into the butt of the Glock's hand grip, chambered a round, then clicked on the safety and slid the weapon back under his pillow.

They turned out the main lights speaking softly with only a nightlight shining from the bathroom. Pris snuggled up to Greg, gave him a hug, then kissed him on the cheek. She placed her mouth close to his ear and whispered, "I love you, my future husband. I can't wait to get married, but if you ever hit me in the head with a cushion again..." She paused and then in a little girl's sing-song voice said, "You'll be sorryyyy."

They were sound asleep when Isaac burst through their bedroom door. "Wake up! I've just had another vision. Everything fits together now... Why are you pointing your gun at me?"

Pris reached out and placed her hand gently on top of the Glock Greg was pointing at the pastor and said softly, "It's okay, Greg. It's only Isaac. Go back to sleep. He can brief us in the morning."

She carefully took the weapon from her fiancé's hand and watched him as he laid back down. In a few minutes he was snoring softly. She turned her attention to Isaac and whispered in an annoyed tone of voice, "Do you realize how close you came to getting your head blown off?"

"But this is really important," Isaac whispered back in his defense.

"It will be just as important tomorrow morning after we get up, and a lot safer," she whispered back. "Good night, Isaac. Close the door on your way out."

They rose from bed early the next morning, dressed for the important meeting and ate a light breakfast. When they'd finished, Isaac apologized for interrupting their sleep. Then the pastor shared the details of his latest vision and things became much clearer. When Isaac was finished, Greg stared at his pastor for a moment then turned to Pris and said, "I thought all that was a dream. Did I really almost shoot my pastor?"

At 9:30 A.M. Isaac's com unit beeped. He touched the speaker button and greeted the ambassador.

"How did you know, Isaac?" Miriam asked in a quiet, partially muffled voice as if she was covering the com unit so no one would hear what she was saying. "How could you possibly know? Five minutes ago the Secretary of State's flight was diverted due to a massive thunderstorm. His plane was grounded and he's unlikely to arrive until tomorrow. I want to know how the hell you knew about this!"

"If you permit me and my team to meet with you privately in a small, secure conference room, I'll tell you everything. It will take only one hour. I'll answer all your questions truthfully."

She gave him the location of the conference room. Promptly at 10:00 A.M. the meeting started.

The meeting was held in a modest sized, secured meeting room. There were no windows and Greg swept the room for any secret recording devices. There were none, but Pris took a small electronic jammer from her purse and placed it on the table, to be doubly careful. There were no computers in the room, however, Isaac placed an air gapped laptop computer on the conference table facing toward the ambassador.

Before Isaac began, Miriam said, "With all the security precautions, I assume this meeting is classified Top Secret."

Isaac replied, "Not really, Miriam. It's mainly for my protection and the protection of my two acolytes. I'd like to begin by telling you something about myself that you will find very difficult to believe. However, I swear everything I tell you is the truth and I have evidence that supports what I tell you."

"Let's get on with it," Miriam said, a bit impatiently.

"When we met in Tel Aviv you thought I was my father's son. You thought I was too young to be your seminary professor, I told you I would have to explain later. Well It's later and I need to explain. Please listen to me with an open mind."

Isaac went on to explain about his death and resurrection as a man half his age. He provided vid coverage from the morgue's surveillance cameras. He went on to provide the results of the examining doctors and how everyone involved had to sign affidavits they would not reveal this knowledge under severe penalties.

He watched the ambassador closely to see how she reacted to the first step in his reveal. However, she just listened quietly and gave no indication if she accepted what he had presented.

Then he told her about his visions, "Miriam, do you remember when I was your professor at Dallas Seminary?"

She nodded and replied, "That was over 30 years ago. I was in your Introduction to the Old Testament class. I never mentioned it to you, but when my parents found out I was attending a Christian seminary, they were not pleased, to say the least. That's why I had to withdraw after only one semester."

"How much do you remember about that class, specifically about the prophets?"

"They were people chosen by God to pass along information to various kings. I remember Isaiah passed on God's words to five different kings before the last one had him killed."

"Excellent memory, Miriam. One last question. How did God communicate his will to the prophets?"

"If I remember correctly, through dreams and visions," she answered.

"Excellent," Isaac exclaimed. "No wonder I gave you an A." He paused for an instant then said, "I'm like the prophets of old, God gives me visions to share with all types of people including world leaders. When I requested a meeting to meet with you today, I had a vision the night before that the Secretary of State would not be able to meet with your Prime Minister today.

"The Lord gave me other visions to share with you, important visions that I was to share with you today. I was directed to share the same visions with your Prime Minister as soon as possible. Eventually, I am to expand revealing specific visions to the High Priest of the New Sanhedrin, the chief rabbi, and a variety of world leaders."

"Can you give me any details regarding these important visions intended for me?" Miriam asked.

"Of course, Miriam. They're about the destruction of the Western Wall, the Dome of the Rock and then the building of a new temple on the Temple Mount."

She sat silently for a moment, her eyes opened wide with surprise. When she spoke her voice quivered a bit. "Well, Isaac, I never saw that coming. However, you now have my complete attention. I want to hear everything you have to say about these visions right now. If you need more time to get through them, I'll cancel my other meetings today. It would really help if you can supply me with evidence any of these visions have come true. I don't doubt your veracity, but others may question it."

"I anticipated this request, actually I saw myself sharing what I'm about to tell you," Isaac said. "There are two parts to the vision and they are very specific." Isaac glanced at his wrist chrono, then back at the ambassador. "Exactly seven minutes and forty three second from now there will be an earthquake with the epicenter located at the center of the Temple Mount. It will be rated a 3.7 on the Richter Scale and will last for 26 seconds. There will not be any deaths and hardly any damage, but it will be strong enough to feel it here in the embassy."

Greg began to verbally count it down. When he reached zero, the vibrations began and a mild roaring sound filled the air. Alarms went off inside the embassy and alert sirens could be heard coming from various locations throughout the city. There were several small pictures on the conference room walls that fell crashing to the floor. A small serving cart with silverware, coffee cups and crystal glasses began to shimmy and shake. A large glass water pitcher cracked in two, dumping water and ice cubes onto the carpeted floor.

The chairs they were sitting in also began shaking hard enough to make Mariam shout, "Oh my God! It's really happening!"

When Greg's wrist chrono hit 26 seconds, it all stopped. Almost as if it never happened.

Miriam's hair was a little disheveled and she used a finger to push her curls back in place as she said, "That was some demonstration. What comes next?"

"I think it best if you attempt to speak to the Israeli Prime Minister as quickly as possible. He needs to be warned about the next quake. Precautions need to be put in place."

"You're scaring me, Professor. What's going to happen? How much time do we have?"

Isaac stared at Miriam with a sad expression and said, "Twelve days from now, on the second Sabbath, a second quake will hit at the same spot, the Temple Mount. It will be much stronger, a 7.8 and it will last for 14 minutes. Many buildings will be destroyed." He paused not wanting to tell Miriam how bad it would be, but he knew she had to know.

"I'm truly sorry to have to tell you this, but I must. The American Embassy will be completely destroyed… and so will all structures on the Temple Mount… including the Western Wall and the Dome of the Rock. Many people in Jerusalem will be killed if we don't evacuate the city."

Miriam was terrified. Based on Isaac's demonstration of the validity of his vision, she had no doubt a second earthquake was coming. She needed to speak with Prime Minister Elisha Cohen as soon as possible. They would need to evacuate the city and surrounding area. Then she realized the first thing that had to be done was to convince the PM Isaac really was a prophet and his visions did come true.

While the prophet and his acolytes remained quietly waiting, Miriam stepped out of the conference room and contacted the PM's office. An assistant came on the line. "I'm sorry, Ambassador, the PM is tied up in very important meetings all day and most of the week so I can—"

She cut him off. "Listen Todd, I know how busy he is, but we had an appointment scheduled with him for lunch at noon."

"I thought that was canceled," he replied.

"It was, but something much more important has come up. It's literally a life or death situation that will occur in less than two weeks," she argued.

"Do you mean the earthquake? That was only a minor tremor, no one was hurt and the damage to property was hardly noticed. I wouldn't call that an—"

"Stop Todd!" she interrupted, her frustration showing in her voice. "There will be another, much stronger earthquake less than two weeks from now. I need to explain all this to Elisha. If you don't notify the PM immediately, I will come over there and rip your heart out. Do you understand me?!!!" She heard a few muffled words over the com followed by a voice she new well.

"Hello, Miriam, you've certainly got my attention now. My assistant is cowering in the corner. It seems you've put the fear of God into him."

"I will apologize to him later Elisha, but you must know I would never act like this over some trivial issue. I've been made aware that a second one, a much more powerful earthquake, is coming soon. I need this meeting to prove to you this is really going to happen."

There was a short pause, followed by more muffled conversation. "I assume you have a team of seismologists available to prove a second quake is coming?"

"Much better than that."

Another pause before the PM said, "All right, Miriam. If you believe it's that important, I suggest you and your team come to my office a half hour from now."

"We'll be there, Elisha. Thank you so much."

Fifteen minutes later, the limo pulled up to the Prime Minister's office, called in Hebrew *Biet HaMemshala* (House of the Head of Government). An aide met them in the lobby and escorted them to the PM's office.

The office was spacious and well decorated with a blend of historic items combined with advanced technology. As the prophet entered the office, he noticed an ancient copy of the Torah next to a large picture window showing a view of Old Jerusalem. The holy book was preserved in a glass-covered, nitrogen-filled case atop a bronze pedestal. On the other side of the office was a bank of numerous electronic items, a few of which the prophet recognized. Near the electronics was a rectangular conference table that could accommodate up to twelve people comfortably in high-back leather covered arm chairs. A long narrow side table was next to the wall with silver trays, coffee urns and plates filled with pastries.

Israeli's Prime Minister shook the hand of Miriam and gave her a warm smile. "It's so good to see you again, Ambassador." He was in his late fifties, a tall man, a little over six feet and very trim, wearing a very expensive suit with expensive shoes to match. His hair was dark brown with a touch of gray and he had a very disarming smile.

The PM glanced at the three people standing behind Miriam and said, "Ambassador would you introduce your people to us first? Then I will introduce you to two gentlemen who will be interested in hearing about possible future earthquakes."

"Prime Minister Cohen, this is Doctor Isaac Silberman, he's the one who will be discussing the upcoming earthquake. With him are Lieutenant Colonel Gregory Stone, the creator of the Voice of God weapon that was instrumental in ending a number of recent wars. Next is Sergeant Priscilla Wright, an American who fought in the War on Rome. Both Gregory and Priscilla are aides to Dr. Silberman."

"Welcome to Jerusalem," the PM said, then turned to the two men who were standing behind him. "These two gentlemen play a very important role in the culture of Israel. The first is Rabbi Jacob Abrams, the High Priest of the New Sanhedrin. He is the leader of all the synagogues in Israel and soon to be the leader of all the synagogues throughout the world. Standing next to him is Hans Jacob Choi, the man who negotiated the Middle East Peace Treaty which was ratified a little less than a month ago."

They took their seats at the conference table, with Elisha sitting at the head, and began the meeting. "Dr. Silberman, can you tell us a little bit about your background?"

"I'd be happy to Prime Minister Cohen. I don't want to mislead you or your guests. My degree is not in seismology. In fact, I know nothing about earthquakes. My degree is in theology and for three decades, I was the Department Chairman at Dallas Seminary." Isaac paused to weigh their reactions. Both the prime minister and the high priest looked very surprised, however, he noted a slight smile form on Mr. Choi's face.

Isaac decided on a frontal attack. "Mr. Choi, have we met before?"

"No sir we've never met, but I've had a number of conversations with a medical doctor who knows you quite well. Please continue your presentation. I look forward to hearing what you have to say."

The high priest said, "Can you briefly tell us more about yourself, especially as it pertains to this so called future catastrophic earthquake."

"Certainly, Rabbi. Let me give you the bottom line about myself then step back and answer any questions you may have. Is that acceptable?"

They nodded so he began. "Two weeks before my hundredth birthday, I died. After spending three days in a morgue waiting for my body to be identified, I woke up again and I was fifty years younger, to everybody's surprise, I might add, including myself. Since that time, I've been receiving visions from God showing me things about the future. It was very confusing at first, but as the months went by, it became easier to interpret the meaning of the visions. Two very important visions came to me early. The first was, I was going to Israel six weeks after a specific vision. The second was, the war in Israel would come to an end two weeks before I would arrive."

"Can you verify that claim?" asked the high priest.

"Yes, but I don't think you would accept the testimony of my two aides," he replied.

Miriam said, "I can verify his vision of the first earthquake was right on to the second, told to me a minute before the event."

"Really?" exclaimed the prime minister.

"Absolutely," replied Miriam. "Pris, would you please show the vid leading up to the first earthquake?"

"Of course, Ambassador." She turned to the PM and asked, "Sir, would you enter the code to download my file to your large vid monitor?"

Elisha recited a long line of Hebrew characters and the monitor turned on, flashing the word READY in English, Hebrew and a few other languages Pris didn't recognize. She powered up her laptop and said, "Download encrypted file 0278 and decrypt."

A wide-angle still shot of the ambassador, prophet and his two acolytes were pictured on the monitor. "Play file 0278," she ordered.

It took only a few minutes to show what transpired in the ambassador's office. It began with Isaac revealing to the ambassador he was a prophet, to Greg counting down to the beginning of the small earthquake, followed by the slight damage of Miriam's office and finishing with the earthquake ending the exact second Isaac said it would.

Pris stopped the vid at that point Isaac had instructed her. There was more to the file; however, he wanted to see their reaction before giving them even more to digest.

"Very impressive," said Elisha. He turned to the high priest and asked, "Your thoughts, Rabbi?"

"I agree, it was most impressive. I believe it validated the man as a prophet or that he is an exceptional charlatan."

The PM faced the negotiator. "How about you, Mr. Choi? What do you think?"

"I agree with you, Rabbi, and I'm sure he's not a magician; however, I was expecting something more substantial. Do you have more, Prophet?

"Sadly, yes I do," Isaac answered. Pris played the rest of the file. When it was over, Mr. Choi was first to speak. "When I said I'd like to see more, I had no idea what I was asking for. Can you explain why there were going to be two earthquakes?"

"Yes," Isaac replied. "The first earthquake had two purposes. The first reason was to validate me as a prophet. To the best of my knowledge, there hasn't been an acknowledged prophet in over two thousand years. The second reason was to warn the people of Israel of the impending doom; to let them know a disaster is coming and to give them time to escape what will happen very soon."

The rabbi was the next to speak up. "Just because you got it right the first time doesn't guarantee there will be a second earthquake."

"You're correct, Rabbi," the prophet replied. "However, I'm sure you're aware of the Old Testament writings regarding the test of a true prophet. He speaks the words God has given him and he never makes mistakes. Every vision I've had has come true. Are you willing to bet I'll be wrong? Think of the consequences if my vision is correct like all the other ones were. Just to add to what I've already said, this vision is the first one to be so specific about time, intensity and the damage which will occur. I am convinced that is so we can help people."

The meeting ended.

Unfortunately, the prime minister was not willing to make an immediate judgment regarding a mass evacuation. He cautioned both the ambassador and the prophet not to make any public announcements before he made a decision which he promised would be made in a day or two. The ambassador was concerned. She indicated she would be closing the embassy in Jerusalem and moving back to Tel Aviv as soon as possible. She invited the prophet and his acolytes to join her. They accepted her invitation.

Two days later, the PM held a press conference. He announced scientists from the Seismology Division of the Geological Survey of Israel were warning of a possible strong earthquake in the Jerusalem area following the earlier mild quake. Based on that information, the PM ordered an immediate evacuation of Jerusalem which might last for approximately two weeks. He also mentioned the Western Wall and the Dome of the Rock would be closed indefinitely beginning no later than the next Sabbath.

The ambassador was upset. "Why did he not give you the credit for predicting the earthquake, Isaac? Don't you find that at least annoying?"

"Not at all. I don't deserve any credit. The words I speak are not my words. I just repeat what God tells me to say," he replied with a smile. "The population of Israel is made up of many diverse beliefs. God's objective is to save all of them from being killed in the coming quake. If the PM were to suggest a Christian Jew had a vision everyone in Jerusalem will die if they didn't evacuate the city, many nonbelievers would disregard the warning. However, the PM rightly chose to say the scientists predicted the quake, now many will leave. Even the most religious people would rather hear it from the scientists than a rabbi, a minister, a priest or an imam."

Just as the prophet indicated, the earthquake hit the Temple Mount area, leveling the Western Wall and totally destroying The Dome of the Rock. For miles surrounding the epicenter, not a building was standing. It took several months to remove all the debris. One of the cleanup crew was quoted as commenting, "The war was bad, but this was worse, much worse. It looks like a wasteland as far as the eye can see."

The leader of the seismology team indicated this was the worst earthquake ever recorded in Israel. "Our data recorded the quake was measured at a magnitude of 7.8 and lasted for 14 minutes. While we get frequent seismic events every four years or so, none of them were even close to this one. If it hadn't been for our Prime Minister's quick evacuation order, Israel could have lost millions of souls."

There were two other interesting events that followed closely behind the earthquake. The first was announced by Rabbi Abrams, the High Priest of the New Sanhedrin. "I am pleased to tell you we will be building a new temple on the Temple Mount. The New Sanhedrin has been planning for this opportunity for decades. The plans for the temple are already completed. It will be an exact copy of the second temple. A scale model of the new temple is currently available for viewing. The project is fully funded and the completion date for the construction is only twenty months from now. Construction of the foundation has already been started."

There was considerable push back from the Muslim community. However, Mr. Choi was able to convince the Muslims not to blame the Jews for the earthquake. He pointed out the damage to the land on which the Dome of the Rock was built was so severely damaged it wouldn't be feasible to attempt to rebuild the Dome of the Rock shrine. Instead, he convinced them to build several new replica shrines throughout the Muslim world. He sweetened the pot by volunteering his organizations to help fund seven of the replicas.

The second event was the announcement by Mr. Hans Jacob Choi, the negotiator of the Middle East Truce. "I'm pleased to inform you of a new city being built. With the end of the violence in the Middle East, I've decided to build The City of Peace. It will be the cornerstone of peace throughout the world. Through generous donations of land, materials and construction funding, we expect the city will be completed four years from now. I will be continuing my efforts to eliminate wars wherever they currently occur and find a better way, a peaceful way, for everyone to live."

The prophet and his acolytes remained in Israel for a year. Pris and Greg were married in the Jerusalem embassy just before the evacuation to Tel Aviv. As a licensed minister, the prophet was able to legally marry them. Miriam was the matron of honor and Captain Black was the best man. It was a simple wedding attended by several dignitaries including the Prime Minister and the High Priest.

Mr. Choi did not attend. He was busy negotiating peace treaties. In his congratulatory message to the newly married couple, he shared his belief there would be complete world piece within three years.

Miriam asked the prophet and his assistants to become consultants; he'd agreed but the ambassador was usurped by the prime minister. He accepted the PM's offer; however, it was with the understanding he would keep the ambassador informed as well.

He continued to receive visions from God. He shared them as required, including informing the rabbi when appropriate. Very few people knew about the prophet. Shortly before the major earthquake in Jerusalem, Isaac had another vision, or perhaps it was just a dream.

He met with Uriel, who strongly suggested it would be better if the world at large didn't know about him being a prophet. "The world is not ready to know about you, Prophet. That will come later. Future visions will reveal to you whom you should share them with. Your friend, the high priest, is one of those people. When the new temple is completed, make sure the high priest is aware there are those who would use the time of dedication as an opportunity to annihilate the Jewish race."

The first order of business was to assist the ambassador in moving the embassy from Jerusalem to Tel Aviv before the major earthquake hit. Most of Jerusalem was destroyed, however, the damage to Tel Aviv was minor.

Unfortunately, the American embassy in Jerusalem was only 2.7 miles from the epicenter of the quake. It sustained major damage and would take nearly a year before repairs were finished. The Church of the Holy Sepulcher, traditionally the place thought where Jesus was crucified and buried, was completely destroyed along with almost all of the buildings, shops and homes within Jerusalem.

It would take years before the city could be rebuilt. The new third temple would be the first major construction project. It was scheduled to be completed in a little less than two years.

Mr. Choi and his world-wide organization titled Peace and Prosperity Now were largely responsible for accelerating the restoration of the city. Thanks to their quick response, the debris and rubble was cleared in record time, followed by the building of the major city structures. Much of the expense was covered by various property protection insurance policies.

During their time in Tel Aviv, Isaac and his acolytes kept busy. The prophet wanted to find out how many places of worship were lost due to the quake. Pris asked Isaac, "Can't you request a vision to give you that information?"

"It doesn't work that way, Pris," replied the prophet. "I can't order up a vision."

"Okay, when do you need it?" she asked a bit sullenly.

Sensing her discontent he asked, "Do you have something planned?"

"Greg and I have a Krav Maga class scheduled in 30 minutes. I'd prefer not to miss it."

"Then don't miss it. You can start on my request after your class. Is that okay with you two? By the way, how long have you been training? I hear it's a very violent form of self-defense."

"It can be," she answered. "But it's pretty effective. We've been training ever since we moved to Tel Aviv, about three months ago."

Ten minutes later Greg met her and they both headed out to the training area. "Why don't you join us, Isaac? It's a really good way to exercise and learn how to protect yourself."

He smiled and shook his head. "I have you and Pris as well as Uriel to protect me. I'll do some walking, push-ups and sit-ups to keep in shape. You to go ahead and beat each other up."

For the next couple of months there was a noticeable lack of visions and Isaac was wondering if God still had a use for him. Then late one afternoon, God spoke to him. It was a strange vision, but who was he to question God?

While Pris was busy in the embassy office providing some information the ambassador requested, Greg decided to jog on the quarter-mile track at the high school across the street from the embassy. She had just finished up and was heading out to join her husband when she saw a van pull up on the street next to the track. Six large men jumped out of the van wearing masks, their pistols drawn as they ran toward Greg.

"Look out behind you!" Pris screamed as loud as she could.

As Greg turned, he drew his Taser-12 and fired darts at two of the men, hitting them in the chest. Neither of the men were affected by the darts. A third man was trying to disarm Greg and the fourth was struggling to put a black bag over Greg's head.

Even though Greg couldn't see, he could feel the man standing behind him attempting to drag his body into the van. Greg snapped his head backwards into the face of the man. There was the sound of the man's nose breaking followed by screaming. The attacker momentarily lost his grip on Greg but he could hear two other men coming. Greg slammed his elbow into side of the head of the broken nosed man and he went down. Before Greg could get the bag off his head, another attacker grabbed at Greg but the Krav Maga kicked in and Greg began swinging wildly as that attacker came close. There was contact and the sounds of ribs breaking and a man screaming in pain. The ex-marine manage to pull the bag off his head just in time to see a third attacker closing fast. Without conscious thought, Greg kicked at the man's knee as hard as he could.

The man screamed in pain and fell to the ground clutching his broken knee cap as the fourth attacker grabbed Greg from behind pinning his hands against his body, his head tucked down so Greg couldn't strike him in the head.

Three of the men began stunning Greg with Tasers, rendering him unconscious and then threw him into the back of the van. Pris was almost at the van with her Taser drawn when a man on the passenger side, stepped around the back of the van and fired two quick shots at her with his Glock.

Both shots missed. Pris quickly kneeled and fired two darts at the man hitting him in the face. One dart hit him in the eye and the man fell convulsing onto the sidewalk as the van accelerated away with tires squealing.

She stood over the injured attacker as she heard the sound of police sirens. She debated whether to finish him off, but decided she needed to question him. They needed to find out where the men in the truck were taking him and why.

Ten blocks away, the van stopped to change vehicles. The three remaining men were replaced by four other men also wearing masks. The new van drove for fifteen minutes then pulled into an old warehouse near the Tel Aviv docks. Greg was still unconscious.

Pris was questioned at the site by local police. She identified herself as a member of the American Diplomatic Corps and showed them her permit to have a non-lethal weapon. She gave them a description of the van and the license plate number, followed by a description of the other attackers. She asked to be present when they interrogated the attacker she shot. After some debate, she contacted Miriam who in turn contacted the PM. Less than an hour later she was at the Tel Aviv police department.

When the injured man had regained consciousness, he was in extreme pain. They gave him a shot of lidocaine for the pain in his ruined eye and placed a patch there to cover the blindness. He was still suffering from the side effects of the darts. His whole face was an ugly shade of red and purple.

"What happened to me?" he said in very broken English. They tried a variety of languages, beginning with Hebrew and running through about a dozen more. He only spoke to them in English.

The detective answered, "You and your buddies kidnapped this lady's husband. You attempted to kill her with your Glock 22, but apparently you are a terrible shooter. However, your kidnapping victim's wife shot you in the face two times with a dart gun. I bet that hurts… a lot."

"I want a lawyer," was his response.

"Really? That's all you got to say to us and this lady?" asked the detective. He leaned forward and said in a low voice, "You are going to answer every question we ask you. If you answer with 'I want a lawyer' again, me and my detective partner are going to leave you alone with her. Not only is she an excellent shot, she's also a Krav Maga expert. She can make your death look like a suicide and there will be no questions asked. So, what's it going to be? You answer my questions or you die a terribly painful death."

The man jumped up and protested, "You can't do that. I have rights."

"You got shit. You understand me jerk face?" answered the detective calmly. "First of all, this is Israel, not the old U. S. of A. Our laws are different here." The detective nodded toward Pris and said, "Why don't you give him a taste of what Israeli law is all about?"

That was all it took for Pris. She stood up and kicked the man in the groin with her prosthetic leg set on full power. It lifted the man off the ground and over the desk screaming all the way to the floor.

"That was a very impressive kick! I'll bet that hurt a bit. Last chance. Tell us what you know or we're going to get really tough."

* * *

Greg regained consciousness strapped to a chair with a black bag over his head. "If you want me to answer your questions, take the bag off my head."

"If we take the bag off your head we will have to kill you."

"Are you really that stupid? Why don't you just wear the ski masks you were wearing when you kidnapped me?"

Greg heard someone walking toward the chair then stop. He could sense the man in front of him was getting ready to hit him in the face. He preempted him and kicked him hard in the leg. He heard the man cry out as he fell to the floor. A few minutes later someone removed the bag.

The room was full of at least a dozen men, all wearing knit black ski masks.

Before anyone could speak, Greg said in a strong in-charge voice, "Ask your question and be quick about it."

"You are Major Gregory Stone, the inventor of the Voice of God weapon," came a voice from the crowd.

"Wrong! I'm Lieutenant Colonel Gregory Stone. You are behind the times."

"Do you know why you are here?" came the voice again.

"Of course I know, do you?" Stone sneered.

"We have some of your VOG weapons—" the voice began, but Stone interrupted.

"You can't make them work, can you?"

Another voice, a stronger voice said, "You will show us how the VOG works or we will kill you."

"If you kill me, you still won't know how to make them work. However, if you cut me in for a piece of the action, maybe we can both win."

There was a long pause with muffled conversations. "You will instruct one of my men how to operate your gun."

"No I won't. It doesn't work that way. I need to show you how to do it. Bring me a weapon and a new magazine," he ordered. "First you need to untie me. I need to use my hands to program the weapon. Once it is correctly programmed it will only work for the person who programmed it. Do you understand?"

They reluctantly handed him a brand new VOG from a crate of 25 weapons. He noticed there were four crates plus another crate filled with new magazines.

Stone took the weapon with both hands, placing his right hand on the pistol grip with his index finger resting on the outside of the trigger guard. "Watch me closely now. First insert a new magazine and lock it in place. Look for the blinking green light just above the trigger guard. Does everybody see that?"

He glanced around the room and saw most of the men nodding their heads and heard a few men murmur yes.

"Next, touch the button marked PRGM and a red light should start blinking." He held the weapon high overhead so everyone could see the blinking red light.

"Enter the weapon code by speaking the number in your regular voice. The code is written on the weapon's butt plate. Once you've entered the code, a blue light will blink next to the magazine. Then release the safety and the weapon is ready to fire."

Greg slid off his chair to the floor as the screaming of multiple VOGs filled the room.

In a matter of seconds the room was littered with the dust of dead bodies.

"Greg? Where are you my husband?" cried out Pris.

"Here, my wife. Lying on the floor, out of the line of fire. You and the Marines from the embassy made it just in time. Thank the Lord for that blinking blue light signaling me to get down."

"We were on the move as soon as we saw the blinking green light on the magazine."

"When did you arrive at this room?" Greg asked.

"We were here before they brought you here. The guy who tried to shoot me in front of the embassy spilled his guts. I can be pretty persuasive when I need to be."

"I'm well aware of all your powers," he said as he smiled.

"Why didn't you call on Uriel?" she asked.

"The prophet said it was a dry run for something bigger in the future," he replied then added, "Let's get out of here. There's dust everywhere."

The prophet and his two acolytes returned to the United States after their year in Israel. There were several reasons for their return. One was to visit with their friends in Gilbert, Arizona. Repairs to Grace Community Church were completed and they were invited to attend the rededication of the church.

They visited The Angel of Mercy Assisted Living Complex first, and met up with the staff and the medical team, including Dr. Goodman, the doctor who tried to save the prophet's life. They spent the better part of the day at the complex getting reacquainted with old friends and new friends as well.

Pris excused herself to visit a new woman doctor she'd heard about from the medical staff. She hadn't been feeling well during the flight back to Phoenix in the Mach 2 airliner. When she returned to the group along with Dr. Pam Lawson, the doctor asked, "Who is Gregory Stone?"

"Right here, doctor," Greg asked. "Is my wife okay?" he asked with a look of concern.

"She's much better than okay. She's two months pregnant."

Greg had been standing up when he heard the news. His legs buckled and the prophet had to assist him into a chair as people began cheering and offering their congratulations. Almost an hour later, when Greg regained the ability to walk and talk, they said their good-byes and took an Uber/Lyft to the Gilbert Hilton, a short walk to the recently refurbished Grace Community Church.

It was Sabbath afternoon and the prophet checked his wrist chrono and noted it was time between services at the church. "How about we attend the second service at the church?" Isaac asked. "You can announce your pregnancy."

Pris was very excited, she was so happy as if she were the first woman in the world to be with child. "Can we go, my husband, my darling father to be?"

"I guess when you say it that way, I have no choice, my beautiful glowing mama," answered Greg.

As they walked up the garden path to the refurbished main sanctuary, Bud was the first one to see them. He did a double take before he recognized them, then dropped his clipboard and ran down the lobby steps. He sprinted to them with arms stretched out, a huge smile on his face.

Greg was able to shout a warning, "In coming!" before Bud grabbed each one of them with a strong hug, tears running down his face.

"I can't believe you're here! I've prayed for you every night, asking God to protect you. When I heard about the devastating earthquake in Jerusalem, I was so worried about you. I can't thank you enough for sending me the email you were all right. I read it to the congregations at all five services, as soon as I found out you were okay."

Bud looked at his wrist chrono and said, "The first service is just letting out. Let me tell everyone on the plaza you're back." He grabbed Pris by the hand and pulled her toward the crowd on the plaza.

"Wait a minute, Bud. That's my wife you're yanking on," Greg protested as he and Isaac hurried after them. They recognized many of the congregation as they walked quickly up the lobby steps.

"Could I have your attention, please?" Bud projected to those gathered near the lobby. "I want to reintroduce you to old friends, first is elder Greg and girlfriend, Pris."

Before Bud could introduce Isaac, Greg interrupted, "Excuse me, things have changed a bit which Bud's not aware of. Pris and I were married about a year ago." Before he could say any more the crowd erupted with cheers and congratulations.

When they had calmed down to a dull roar, Pris added, "It's so nice to be able to visit you all and our church. But it is my great pleasure to tell you all... We just found out, I'm pregnant!"

The crowd had increased in number as a new group of people was getting ready to enter the church for the second Sabbath service. When Pris broke the good news, the roar of the crowd was almost overwhelming. The start of the second service was delayed, but under the circumstances, nobody cared, especially Bud.

When Bud introduced Pastor Isaac, it was bedlam on the plaza. There was so much love shared amongst everyone there. It would be an event the three of them would cherish forever.

When it was time to leave for the hotel, they were approached by many people asking them to sign their church bulletins. Some said they were going to frame the signature and every time they looked at it, they would say a prayer for all three of them and the future baby too.

They ate dinner in the hotel dining room and then retired to their separate suites. They decided to retire early. They were all tired, not only from their trip with its time zone changes, but also for Greg and Pris and the emotional roller coaster ride of finding out they were going to be parents.

The prophet sat quietly in a recliner chair in the living room of his suite. He noted it had a small kitchenette and a separate bedroom with a king sized bed and an adjacent master bath. He was tired, but not really sleepy. So he sat in his recliner with his eyes closed and let his disconnected thoughts run through his mind as he breathed slowly and deeply. He let the fatigue drift away and, in a few minutes, he was completely relaxed.

Time passed; subconsciously he noted the sunlight through the living room window began to fade until the room was in total darkness. Then it got darker, so dark, he couldn't tell if his eyes were open or shut.

In the dark, he was able to hear the small sounds people usually ignored, the air conditioner turning on when it got too warm, the sound of the fan circulating the cooler air, the occasional muted sound of a door in an adjacent suite opening or closing and all the other numerous whispers one can't even identify.

Isaac sat quietly and waited.

Slowly, all those minute sounds disappeared.

He continued to wait.

After an indeterminate amount of time, a voice spoke to him out of the void. The voice was deep and powerful.

"Isaac, you have done well, my good and faithful servant."

He wasn't sure if it were truly a voice or just the thoughts of God projected into his mind.

"Thank you, my LORD. Thank you for all your blessings to me and those around me," he thought back to God as if it was a prayer.

"Time is on the verge of the last years. Since your rebirth, you have been exposed to both good and evil people.

It can be difficult to tell them apart. Within a year, a seven year period of time will commence that will lead to the end… and to new beginnings. During that year, you will continue to be my servant. Your task is to assist in the salvation of those who are currently unsaved, to give them one more opportunity before the Book of Life is closed forever. The visions you will receive from me will be focused on specific people I have chosen for you to assist.

"Your two acolytes will assist you; however, only you will receive my visions. The three of you will be protected by Uriel, but only if you call on him. Neither Satan nor his demons will be able to prevent you from communicating my visions.

"There are things I want you to be aware of regarding the next year. They will become permanently imbedded in your mind and you will recall them as needed. You will need this knowledge to prepare you for things to come.

"Most of this knowledge is found in the last book of the New Testament. It speaks of things that will happen in the last days. Much of what John wrote about was intentionally confusing. I will clarify it for you.

"When Satan and a third of the angels I had created, rebelled against me, they were banished to Earth during creation. They retained the powers I had granted them. I also permitted Satan to communicate with me. He attempted to bargain with me, claiming he should have power to rule over one infinitesimally insignificant planet in all of my creation. His major premise was, if all my created sentient beings could choose between obeying me or not obeying me, it was inevitable they would all chose not to obey my wishes.

"He suggested I consider a test using human beings as the test subjects. If he could prove his premise, he thought it only fair he and his demons should be reinstated.

"Lucifer, the name I gave to Satan before the fall, had been my best creation and my worst. I accepted his terms, but there was a time limit involved. That time limit will be coming to an end shortly."

There was a brief pause.

Then he continued, "I want to clarify something for you. What I just described was done in a manner you could understand. However, the spiritual creations that make up a substantial portion of existence, the angels and demons for example, function at a higher level than physical beings. Of course, all that will change once the test is over. Those who pass the test will be given an existence superior to the angels and demons. They are referred to in the Bible as Glorified Bodies.

"I want to inform you of what Lucifer is planning for his final attack. He will adopt the Holy Trinity approach, but from a perverse perspective. The real Holy Trinity has God the Father, God the Son (God in human form named Jesus), and God the Holy Spirit, one God in three persons. Lucifer's trinity has Satan, the Antichrist and The Beast. Satan is spirit, the Antichrist (a satanic form of a demon in human form) and The Beast.

"Both Jesus and the Antichrist die and are reborn as God. Actually, the Antichrist isn't really God. Satan possesses him and takes control over his mind and body. Both the Holy Spirit and the Beast give special power to those who believe in their respective Lords.

"With that structure of a negative trinity, Lucifer rules the world from his City of Peace. Another name for the city is New Baghdad. At some point, it will be referred to as the New and Improved Sin City. The Book of Revelation refers to it as Babylon.

"During the last seven years, Earth goes from peace and prosperity to being ruled by a hedonistic despot who claims to be God. Most of the entire world has become populated by those who rejected me. Many times I have destroyed them and began again as I did at the time of Noah. All during the history of the world, only a few believed in me. Throughout time, while most chose not to believe in me, there was always a remnant who did.

"The test is almost over, only eight years left. Because of the remnant of believers, Lucifer has been beaten. He will not accept defeat and attempts to destroy all mankind. Of course, I will not permit it. The final battle will result in the deaths of the unbelievers. The world will end, Lucifer and his demons will be punished forever. Those who believed in me will be reborn in immortal bodies and reside forever in a New Earth.

"That ends the summary of the rest of time on this Earth. You may share this vision with your acolytes and others who would benefit from knowing what is to come. Let me conclude with what will happen to you at the end of next year.

"When the last seven years begin, you will need more than the visions I've sent to you. On the first day of the last seven years, I will come to you as I did to Saul of Tarsus on the road to Damascus. I changed his name from his Hebrew name, Saul, to his Greek name, Paul, however, your name will not be changed. Before you ask, let me mention you will not go blind for a few days as Saul did.

"You will be in the chapel at the Angel of Mercy Assisted Living Complex with your two acolytes. No one else will be there when the presence of the Holy Spirit visits you. He will lay his hands upon you and give you all the abilities which were given to the twelve apostles.

"You will use those abilities whenever you believe they are appropriate. You will not hide your abilities from anyone. If you need to heal the sick or injured or resurrect the dead, do so in front of whoever may be watching, just as the other apostles did.

"In a moment you will sleep. When you arise you will remember every word I have said to you. You will share whatever you feel your acolytes need to know, but only them. While you remain a prophet, you will remain in the background, loosening the devil's grip on people you will be assigned to save. You will not be able to save them all, just do your best."

There was the briefest of pauses followed by, "Good-night, my good and faithful servant."

The End of **The Last Prophet**

I've been a fan of science fiction ever since I was in grade school (a very long time ago). In those days there were three outstanding science fiction authors: Isaac Asimov, Arthur C. Clark and Robert A. Heinlein.

My favorite author was Heinlein. He began writing his science fiction stories for young people. His first books were categorized as Boys Books. Today, they're called Young Adults. The stories Heinlein wrote were very believable to me and I couldn't wait to get to his latest book. As I matured, so did his books. I have read every book Heinlein published and still have most of them in my personal library. I think my all-time favorite Heinlein story is *Stranger in a Strange Land.*

My current favorite author is Orson Scott Card. Again, like Heinlein's stories, I find myself 'living' the story as it unfolds. *Enders Game* and *Prentice Alvin* are two of my favorite Card novels.

I've always had an interest in writing science fiction novels. I would read books by new authors and say to myself, "I could write a better story." However, when I tried, publishers didn't agree. When Covid-19 broke out, I had a lot of spare time on my hands and decided to give it another shot.

During the last four years, I have self-published eleven novels. The twelfth novel, *The Last Prophet,* will be published in September, 2023. The novel is set in the twenty second century and is a composite of several science fiction subgenres. Those that come to mind are Hard SciFi, Military SciFi, Action/Adventure SciFi as well as Christian SciFi. This novel has the potential for the beginning of a new series.